Shady Palms 2

FOWL PLAY

By FRANK CERABINO

Editor: Bill Greer
Illustrator: Pat Crowley
Designers: Michelle Mazzone and Dan Neal
Publishing liaison: Lynn Kalber

The Palm Beach Post

The Maple-Vail Book Manufacturing Group

The Maple-Vail Book Manufacturing Group
Willow Springs Lane
P.O. Box 2695
York, PA 17405

Printed in the United States of America

1st printing 2001

ISBN: 0-9705026-1-3

This book was printed by The Maple-Vail Book Manufacturing Group.

Originally published in *The Palm Beach Post*
from February 18-March 18, 2001.

$8.95 U.S.

Preface

When I finished writing the first Shady Palms novel, I expected it to be the only tale about the fictional condominium. I was content to let my characters remain frozen in time, stuck forever in the epilogue's final portrait.

But something happened I hadn't contemplated. As the serialized story ended, readers began asking me to continue.

"I didn't think it was ending so soon," Terry Knight, one of those readers, wrote. "What are we supposed to do?"

Those are heady words for a writer. More. More.

And scary too. Because there was no more. The wicked had been punished. Good had prevailed. The baby was born. C'mon. It was done. Over. The end.

But it wasn't. The world kept spinning. The real world. The one with Elian Gonzalez, citrus canker and the contested presidential election. These real stories and others conjured up a question in my head: How was this affecting life at Shady Palms?

Yes, life was marching forward in the fictional condo, too. I found myself telling people that Shady Palms led the nation in accidental Pat Buchanan voters.

What was I talking about? I hadn't even written this stuff down yet.

And so I did. *Shady Palms 2 — Fowl Play* picks up the action at the condo a year after the first story ended. The sequel was first published by the *The Palm Beach Post* in February and March of 2001. Now it's available in this paperback.

As for *Shady Palms 3*, yes, it's in the works. Life at Shady Palms, it seems, is harder to snuff out than I had once imagined.

1 The last hand

Bernie Hamstein tried to look disinterested as he watched the cards.

The three of spades came spinning his way, face up on Bernie's dining room table, making his blood quicken.

"And a t'ree for Bernie, no help," announced the dealer, Fred Fortunato, G Building's sunshine committee chairman.

No help? That's what he thinks.

The three was too good to be true. Maybe this was his hand, Bernie thought, his chance to pull himself out of that sinking spiral of bad luck. Finally.

"I'm out," announced Mickey Faraday, who was known around Shady Palms as Softer, due to the overwhelming consensus that he played the drums way too loud with The Swinging Palms, the condo's big band.

Faraday put his cards in a little pile and pushed away from the table.

"Got any more corned beef in the 'frigerator, Bernie?"

"Help yourself, Softer," Bernie said.

Archie Diamond, the shuffleboard captain who had folded two cards ago, was standing in the living room, flicking the remote control at the TV.

"This is the last hand, right fellas?" he asked, as he found the channel for the nightly Lotto drawing.

There was a moment of silence as all heads turned toward the TV, and then, when it was clear nobody there would be a millionaire that night, the poker hand continued.

Fred, who had the most showing with a pair of fives, tossed a red chip — the dollar one — on the pile in the center of the table and said, "Just to be sociable."

Bernie figured that Fred was thinking about staying in the game until the seventh card, with hopes that it would be another five.

But three-of-a-kind wouldn't be enough to win this hand. Bernie already had a straight. His four cards turned face up on the table were a six, a jack, a seven and a three, and his two down cards — the ones the other players couldn't see — were a four and a five.

"It's to you, Bernie," Fred said.

Bernie reached for a red chip, and then his hand went to a white one — the $5 chip — grazing it momentarily before scooping up one of the $10 blue chips.

"I bump a blue," Bernie said, tossing the red and blue chips on the pile.

Then the left cavity of his chest felt that familiar pain, the one that came clanging, gingerly at first, but then with more insistence.

He tried to ignore it and focus his attention on the other player still in the game, Johnny Fox, the flamboyant impresario of the Shady Palms Players, the condo's theater troupe.

Johnny, the big winner of the night, looked at Bernie with hooded eyes and a crooked smile.

"Mind if I smoke?" Johnny had said earlier that evening.

And before Bernie could say anything, he had lighted a hand-rolled cigarette, which he began smoking with long, deep drags. The strange smoke made the other men antsy.

"It's my medicine, Bernie," Johnny had said. "For my glaucoma. I have a prescription."

It's poker night at Bernie Hamstein's condo and on the last hand of the evening, Bernie makes a bold move to change his luck.

That was two joints and half a Key lime pie ago. Johnny's eyes were at half-mast now, and he was slurring his words.

"Hah!" Johnny said when he saw Bernie's $10 raise.

"I'll see your 10 and bump you 20 more," Johnny said.

Fred cut in.

"You can only bump 10, Johnny."

"No, that's OK, Fred. If he wants to bump 20, I'll see that 20," Bernie said, tossing two more blue chips on the table. "This is the last hand. We should be able to suspend the betting limits on the last hand."

C'mon, slow down, Bernie silently told his heart.

"You don't fool me, Hamstein," Johnny said.

Great, Bernie thought. He thinks I'm bluffing.

Fred folded.

"Game's too rich for me," he said. "You gentlemen ready for your last card? This one's down and dirty."

"Deal, schlemiel," Johnny said, laughing hysterically at his word play.

Archie looked over from the television and shook his head at Johnny.

Softer sat down at the table again, taking a bite of his sandwich, which squirted a glop of mustard on one of Rose Hamstein's newly upholstered chairs.

Under other circumstances, Bernie might have jumped up and tried to clean it. But he was too engrossed in the task at hand, which was to avoid having a heart attack while regaining much of the money he had lost to this loopy schlock theatrical producer/neighbor sitting to his left.

"Hey, Softer," Johnny said, "any more of that pie in the fridge?"

Bernie's heart gallops had begun two months ago. At first, Bernie thought it was a muscle spasm in his chest, maybe from taking the groceries in from the car. But one night, he sat bolt upright in bed, fearful that his 73-year-old heart was about to pound out of its moorings.

"What's wrong?" his wife, Rose, had asked, still groggy with sleep.

Bernie would have said, "I might be having a heart attack," except that he couldn't speak. Two minutes later, he felt better, laying his head down on the pillow, sweating despite the frigid air conditioning in their unit.

"Indigestion?" Rose had asked.

"Just thinking about condo business," Bernie had said.

No sense in telling Rose. Like most of the women at Shady Palms, she was of the belief that doctor visits were to be encouraged rather than avoided.

Bernie knew better. He went for his yearly PSA check, to keep tabs on what he called his "prostrate," but that was as far as he'd go.

"I'll tell you why health care in America is all screwed up," he told his wife one night. "It's because there are too many women who go to doctors as a form of recreation. With a $5 co-pay on insurance, getting an MRI is like going to the movies."

Rose was always after Bernie about his health. It was true, he was 20, maybe 25, pounds overweight. And he didn't get much exercise.

But he couldn't be like her and her friends, the Wonder Walkers. Prancing around the Boynton Beach Mall every morning like a bunch of fools. At their age.

"I don't need walking to get my blood moving," Bernie had told her. "Being building president does the job for me."

Bernie was in his last year as president of C Building at Shady Palms. At least, that's what he said. But he'd said "this is my last year" for the past three years now.

"Getting aggravated isn't exercise," Rose had said. "Running for office isn't the same as running."

She didn't approve of this either, the poker.

"You'd think you guys would have learned your lesson," she said.

It was nearly a year since the spectacular collapse of the football betting ring at Shady Palms. After that, the guys started playing low-stakes poker in the clubhouse. But nickel-dime-quarter betting quickly progressed to these higher-stakes games played behind closed doors.

Rose had no idea. She thought Bernie was still playing for loose change. She didn't realize he was down more than $300, most of it to Johnny Fox, who had given him handsome advances of cash from the ticket sales receipts of the Shady Palms Players.

The seventh card, dealt face down, was of little interest to Bernie. But he studied it, pretending to be counting on that card to make his hand. He wasn't sure if any of his deceptive behavior was being noticed by Johnny Fox, who seemed too far beyond the bend to notice such subtleties.

"The pie, Softer," Johnny was saying. "I thought you said there was pie."

The theater impresario had a pair of two's showing. So he got to bet first. He bet $10.

Bernie called the bet and bumped him $30 more, which got only a snort from Fox, who called the $30 and bumped $30 more.

"Jeez, Louise," Softer said with a mouth full of Bernie's corned beef.

Archie had lost interest in the television and stood over the table to watch.

"Gentlemen, gentlemen," Fred said. "I think you're both getting a little carried away."

Bernie's heart seemed to agree.

The flurry of bumps had wiped out his meager pile of chips. He could either ask Johnny for another loan or reach for his checkbook. Then he thought of something else, something crazy but appealing.

"I got an idea, Johnny. Why don't we make this simple. I owe you about $300. So why don't we just say double or nothing here? If I win, we're even. If you win, I give you double what I owe you already."

"You OK, Bernie?" Archie said. "You don't look so good."

Johnny Fox agreed so quickly to Bernie's proposal that Bernie almost felt guilty for taking advantage of a man in such an impaired state.

Fred shrugged his shoulders.

"Pot's right. What you got, Johnny?"

"Pot's right," Johnny repeated, then started laughing.

"In the future," Softer said, "I'm not sure it's a good idea that Johnny takes his medicine when we play cards."

Johnny rubbed his eyes and concentrated on his cards.

"OK, so I've got these deuces here," he said, pointing to the pair of two's in his hand. "But that's not all I got. Aha!"

He flipped over the first two down cards in his hand, and a pair of kings popped up.

"What'dya think of that, Bernie?"

Bernie tried not to betray his jubilation. The fool had just a measly two pair.

"Not bad, Johnny," Bernie said. "But unfortunately, I have a straight, seven high."

He flipped over his cards and arranged them to display his straight.

Softer patted Bernie on the back, and said, "Nice hand, Bern."

"Wait a second," Johnny said.

Bernie's hands froze, and he looked up in horror.

The words, and what they might mean, were scary enough to Bernie, but it was the tone of Johnny's voice that was most frightening. Johnny suddenly wasn't slurring his words, and his eyes were wide open now.

He didn't seem stoned at all.

"Did I say I was through showing my cards?" Johnny said, looking around the table. "I was merely showing you my first two down cards. Now, I admit, I was betting on those two pair, and I didn't think Bernie had a straight — I really thought you were bluffing, Bernie — but I guess this is my night."

With that, Johnny flipped over the last card dealt to him. Another king.

"Holy moley, a full house," Softer said.

"What happened to your voice, Johnny?" Archie said.

"Yeah, you seem to have sobered up, instantly," Fred piped in.

Bernie was too speechless, too much in the throes of general heart failure, to say anything at all.

"Gentlemen," Johnny said. "A man does not get to be a master thespian, as I am, without learning to play many roles. The discomfort from my glaucoma is sometimes alleviated by leafy medication. But my eyes feel pretty good tonight."

"So you've been putting us on?" Fred asked.

"I prefer to call it polishing up on my considerable acting abilities while enjoying a friendly poker game," Johnny said.

"And snookering all of us into thinking you were high as a kite," Archie said.

"But you sat here smoking those funny cigarettes," Softer said.

"Oregano," Johnny said, triumphantly.

"Unff," Bernie said, feeling the room get blurry.

"Oregano!" Softer repeated. "Boy, you really removed Bernie's trousers on that one! Isn't that right, Bernie?"

"Unff."

"Bernie?"

"I think I'm having a heart attack," Bernie whispered.

"Nice acting," Archie said. "But not as good as Johnny's performance. Good night, everybody, I got a wife waiting to nag me. Next week's at my place."

Softer got up to go.

"You OK, Bernie?" he asked, then looked at the others. "He really does look bad."

Their voices seemed to be coming from a distance now, and Bernie could feel his body beginning to slump.

Too bad Rose wasn't there. He always imagined she would be there when this time came. But she was out at her computer class, and he was home, done in by a schlock condo actor holding a full house, kings over twos.

"If he were really having a heart attack, his eyes would be rolling back in his head," Johnny said as he stood up to leave. "I'll show you how to fake it better next time, Bernie."

Bernie's mind went to the mustard stain on the chair. Rose would find it there when she came home. He needed to clean it before he died. The kitchen was a mess, nothing he could do about that, but maybe the mustard stain was something he could fix. And the dog. Somebody needed to let Lucky out of the bedroom. Rose would be upset that Bernie had banished the dog during his poker night. He couldn't let Rose find Lucky like that.

He tried moving his legs, and that's when his body went limp, and Bernie slid to the carpet.

Johnny stood up and clapped.

"Bravo, Bernie. Bra-vo!"

2 Breaking Bone

Brad Cohen ordered his second gin and tonic and looked at his diamond-studded Rolex one more time. Unbelievable. Forty minutes late.

The maitre d' had already threatened to give away his table reservation. Brad had to grease the guy $50 to hold it for another 15 minutes. This was Los Angeles, for crying out loud. Some Academy Award nominee might walk through that door at any second, and Brad's little table-for-two reservation would be as endangered as a polite freeway driver.

Didn't Brad say to be on time to the restaurant? Didn't he make that clear?

This was no way to treat a last chance. The sports agent pulled out his cell phone and checked one more time. Again, no messages.

He was tired of this, the baby-sitting, coddling and den-mothering of grown men. If the money in it wasn't so outrageously plentiful, he might try his hand at something else, something ... oh, there he was! Walking in the door, with that casual nonchalance of a guy with nowhere to go.

Even from his obstructed view at the crowded bar, Brad could spot the otherworldliness of the man's motions, just by the way he navigated a crowded restaurant.

Demetrius Bone sidestepped a gantlet of diners and wait-
ers in the bistro. The subtle moves reminded Brad of the first
time he saw Bone, a whirling figure in a grainy game film sent to
the agent by a football coach at a pathetic Division IV school in
East Texas.

Demetrius Bone was the real deal. He had the size of a
linebacker with the agility of a ballerina. He was faster than most
running backs a fraction of his size and stronger than players
who outweighed him by 50 pounds. He had the heart to run
unflinchingly in heavy traffic and the guile to make solo would-
be tacklers reach for empty air in the open field.

He was Barry Sanders and Earl Campbell rolled into one
body, a 23-year-old man who could, under the right conditions,
break all the records for halfback.

But right now, he was just breaking the heart of his agent,
Brad Cohen.

The National Football League once embraced people like
Demetrius Bone without question. But not any more. Too many
so-called "off-the-field problems." Teams have begun casting
wary eyes on potential players who seem to lack citizenship
skills.

This would explain why Demetrius Bone is currently not
employed by any of the 31 NFL teams, many of whom had
already written off Bone as a burden to anyone but criminal
defense lawyers.

Since high school, Bone has managed to spend more
games suspended from teams than suiting up with them.

He didn't go out for football until his junior year in high
school. He ran for more than 300 yards in each of his first two
games. But in the first quarter of the third game, he fumbled in
the end zone, a surprising and deeply embarrassing event for
young Demetrius.

As he hung his head and prepared to walk back to the sidelines, he heard laughter and looked up to find the opposing
team's mascot — a kid in a bear costume — making fun of the

Demetrius Bone knows he's good enough to be an NFL running back. The problem is that he has squandered his chances so far. Bone's agent has one last-ditch idea to salvage his career.

way he was walking.

Demetrius picked up the bear and tossed the mascot at the crossbar of the goal post. The kid in the bear suit got a broken nose. That wasn't the worst part. The kid was a girl. That wasn't the worst part, either. The worst part was that the girl with the broken nose was the school superintendent's daughter.

Demetrius was expelled for the rest of the year and banned from playing high school football there again. But his coach saw enough of Demetrius to get a small college to give him another chance.

He started at tailback in his freshman year and broke the school's season rushing record by his fourth game. In his sophomore season, he was well on his way to having an even better year when he had a run-in with another mascot during warm-ups before a game against a division rival.

While catching laterals from his quarterback, Demetrius was stunned when a kid in a pirate costume stepped in front of him, intercepted the lateral and pranced down the field as if he were about to score a touchdown.

The fans in the stands were cheering his comical jaunt toward the end zone. Demetrius didn't think there was anything funny about it.

The pirate never saw him coming. Demetrius planted his helmet in the middle of the kid's back and flattened him into the turf. The spectacular tackle was so severe that the boy had to be carried off on a stretcher. The opposing team's fans tried to pelt Demetrius with coins, fruit and whatever they could get their hands on. When Demetrius responded by standing on his team's bench and dropping his pants, a small group of booze-emboldened college kids spilled onto the field and ran toward him.

Others followed. Soon, there was a riot on the field, canceling the game and getting a brief mention in the national news. Demetrius ended up with three broken ribs, two loose teeth and a permanent expulsion from college football.

But those who had seen him play saw what Brad Cohen saw. And so he had hunted down Demetrius Bone, who had returned to his South-Central L.A. neighborhood and had taken up work as a bouncer at a bar Brad nearly didn't have the nerve to enter.

Brad got him a tryout as a free agent with the Oakland Raiders, a team that prided itself on its bad-boy image. Bone was well on his way to making the team. But during training camp, an unfortunate newspaper reporter who was far too enterprising for his own good decided to write a story about Demetrius Bone.

Demetrius had the distinct impression it would be about his impressive on-the-field progress in training camp. But it ended up being about his penchant for throttling mascots.

On the day the story ran, Bone felt betrayed. And his ears burned with the teases of the team's veterans.

He didn't get to carry the ball much during team scrimmages that day, either. After showering and getting dressed, he was about to walk out of the locker room when he heard a familiar voice.

"Hi, Demetrius. I got some nice reaction from my piece

about you today."

Bone picked up the reporter and stuffed him into his locker, where he was discovered later that night when a team trainer heard whimpering coming from the darkened room.

They had to use a bolt cutter to break the lock. The reporter wrote a story about his harrowing experience. The team made a formal apology. The police charged Bone with battery, and within a week, he was a bouncer again, frittering away the remains of what looked to be his last NFL paycheck.

That was a year ago. And it might have been the end of the story of Demetrius Bone's football forays. But Brad Cohen wasn't ready to give up yet.

He had an idea, one last chance to polish this diamond in the rough and cash in.

"You're late," Cohen said, as the waitress showed them to their table.

"Got me a contract yet?"

"I've got you something that could lead to a contract," Cohen said. "You staying in shape?"

Bone just grunted. Cohen could see that Bone had put on a little weight. And the agent watched in horror as Bone smeared nearly a half-a-stick of butter on a dinner roll.

"What team?" Bone asked, as he reached for another roll.

"The Dolphins."

"Who you talk to in Miami? Coach Wannstedt?"

Cohen took a long sip from his drink to steel himself for what he'd say next.

"Not exactly, Demetrius. We're not quite to the point of talking to anybody with the team yet."

"Then you're wasting my time!"

"No. Listen to me, Demetrius. We both know you can play football at the pro level. The thing we need to prove to the NFL is that you're a new man, a solid citizen in control of his emotions and capable of being a credit to his team, both on and off the field."

"Brad, I hope this isn't about sending me to another one of those head doctors. I'd rather sit down with a room full of team mascots."

"No more psychologists," Cohen said. "I promise. No, what I had in mind is something more radical. You need a change of scenery, a place where you can remove all the stress from your life. That bar where you work is no place to be. You don't need to be around drug users, gamblers and fast women."

Demetrius snorted.

"You planning to lock me up, Brad?"

"My mother's got a brother who lives in Florida. I spoke to him a couple weeks ago. Great guy. He was my favorite uncle growing up. He lives about an hour north of Miami. He's a big shot in his community. Anyway, I've arranged to have you rent a place there at his complex. I'm picking up all the expenses. That's how much I believe in you, Demetrius. Just give it six months."

"Whoa. Slow down, Brad. Where you sending me?"

"It's a condominium in a place called Boynton Beach," the agent said.

"No, no, no," Demetrius said, then laughed.

"It's called Shady Palms, and Uncle Bernie runs one of the buildings there. He said there's an opening in one of his units."

Brad Cohen got the idea to put Demetrius Bone in a Florida condo after reading the last psychologist's report. It said that Bone's current environment and job as a bouncer were likely to be too stressful and too full of bad influences to make personal development possible. The psychologist suggested that Bone needed a suitable role model and an environment devoid of stress and vice.

Brad Cohen had never set foot in a condo, but he had this idealized vision of wise old people living together in harmony to enjoy their sunset years.

"Brad, tell me I didn't come here tonight to find out your big plan is to put me in a raisin ranch with a bunch of your people."

"Demetrius, this is just what you need," Brad said. "No car, no girls, no distractions. You run every day in that hot Florida sun, focusing on getting yourself in shape. Meanwhile, you'll get to know your neighbors."

"Yeah, I'm going to fit right in. How many other 6-foot-3 young brothers they got there?"

"Uncle Bernie will take care of you," Brad said. "Don't you see the potential here? The Dolphins have been looking for a special running back for years. And now that Marino is retired, they're more eager than ever to find one. But they're a little squeamish about taking on another player with off-the-field issues. They've already had Tony Martin, Cecil Collins, Irving Spikes. But if I can go to the team and say that Demetrius Bone isn't only the greatest prospect at his position, he is also a solid citizen beloved by his elderly neighbors in this sleepy condominium just up the road from Miami, then I think we've got our foot in the door."

"What makes you think I'm going to be beloved?"

"It will be a great human-interest story. I'm sure I can persuade a local sportswriter to write a story about it."

"Yeah, let's hope it doesn't turn out like that last story you thought was going to be so great," Bone said.

"You'll be irresistible to the Dolphins," Cohen said.

"You're the one who needs the shrink, Brad."

"Demetrius, I just don't want to see you disappear into oblivion, which is what's going to happen if you stay where you are. Nobody wants the current Demetrius Bone. So let's go out and make a new one. What do you say?"

Bone didn't say anything. A good sign, Cohen thought. So he reached for his cell phone.

"I'm going to have you say hi to Uncle Bernie right now. You'll see what I mean. He's got a lot of heart."

Cohen had called Bernie earlier in the day, telling him to expect the call from the new renter.

"Just make him feel welcome, Uncle Bernie. That's all you have to do," Cohen had said.

Now, he dialed the number again and handed the phone to Bone.

Bernie didn't hear the phone ring because he was lying on the floor in the throes of a heart attack. Archie Diamond was giving him mouth-to-mouth, and Fred Fortunato was standing by the screened patio, looking for signs of an approaching ambulance.

"You still think he's faking?" he asked Johnny Fox, who was no longer clapping his hands and saying, "Bravo."

The Palm Beach County Fire-Rescue dispatcher had already called back once to verify information from the 911 call. So when the phone rang again, the men thought it was the dispatcher. Softer got to the phone first.

"Are you on the way or not!" he shouted.

Demetrius Bone looked across the table at his agent with a crooked smile. The man had really orchestrated the hard sell, that's for sure.

"Who is this?' Bone asked.

"Softer."

"Who is this?" Bone asked again, lowering his voice.

"Listen, I don't have time to go through a lot of crap with you. Just get your butt here before it's too late. Do you understand?"

"Hey, man. There's no reason to get nasty about it," Bone said.

Bone turned off the phone and handed it back to the agent.

"I thought you said your Uncle Bernie was a mellow dude."

3 A statue of liberty

On the night of Bernie Hamstein's heart attack, the shore-line of Palm Beach County was dark under a moonless sky and noisy from the sound of waves being whipped up by a northeast wind.

The 11-year-old girl sat up to get a better look, straining her eyes to make some sense of the huge shapes looming in the distance. But it was hard to focus because the small boat kept moving up and down.

Yolette concentrated, blocking out the nausea that had risen up in her during the bumpy voyage from the Bahamas.

"America," the girl said to Jezula, the middle-aged woman sitting next to her.

Yolette wished she could talk to someone other than Jezula, who spent more time crying and praying than the rest of the 12 refugees. But her mother had told the girl to beware of strangers. Jezula, a woman from their town in Haiti, could be trusted to make sure Yolette was safe on this journey. No one else could.

Yolette wished she could be seeing America with her mother.

"One day we will be together forever," her mother had told

her, hugging her on that final day in Port-au-Prince.

"Soon?" Yolette had asked.

"Soon enough."

Her mother had handed her a plastic bag with a photograph and a sealed letter inside. The photo was of a man, and the letter was for him to read — not her.

"Your father," Yolette's mother had said. "He will take care of you."

During the next five days, the time it took for Yolette to get from Haiti to the Bahamas and now to the coastline of Florida, she had studied the picture of that smiling face for hours.

"My father," she would repeat to herself, liking to hear that word, just as she had liked hearing the word "America."

Yolette knew more about America than about her father. One of the nuns at her school, the one who taught her English, told her about America. But her mother barely talked about her father, only that he had left Haiti before she was old enough to remember and that now he had a very big job in America and was ready to take care of her.

Haitian refugee Yolette Germond, 11, has come to America to find the father she never knew. But all she has to go on is an old photograph and the kindness of the strangest of strangers.

The boat became still for a moment, long enough for her eyes to see that the big shape in front of her was a house.

"Look," she said in Creole to Jezula, even though she knew Jezula was too nauseated to lift her head.

Yolette had never seen a house this big. It was big enough to be one of the biggest buildings in Port-au-Prince. This must be why people pay the $2,000 fortune to come to America, she thought, so they could live in houses as big as museums.

Then she heard a new sound in the wind, the sound of a helicopter. She heard it before she saw it, as it swooped toward them with a beam of white light sweeping the ocean like a blind man's cane.

The man they called Captain Bye-Bye then spoke an English word the nun at her school would not have approved of. The small boat's engine stopped, and the Bahamian mercenary stood up, looking first at the helicopter and then at them.

"Bye-Bye," he said, motioning to the ocean.

They were at least 100 yards offshore. Some of the people started screaming, "No! No!"

The boat captain looked at Yolette. He knew she was the only one who spoke English.

"Tell them it's shallow here," he yelled to the girl. "Tell them they can walk to shore from here."

Yolette hesitated, thinking of her mother's admonition about strangers. The others in the boat looked at her and asked what was going on. So she told them.

"Immigration!" Captain Bye-Bye said, pointing to the approaching helicopter.

That was a word that needed no explanation.

"Bye-Bye," he said again.

People started jumping off the boat. Yolette clutched the plastic bag holding the letter and the photo of her father, then grabbed Jezula's hand.

"No," the frightened woman said.

"Yes," Yolette said in Creole. "He said it is safe."

But it wasn't. The water was 12 feet deep there, and the surf was disturbed enough to be a challenge for even good swimmers.

Yolette and Jezula jumped together, holding hands. Their feet anticipated a bottom that didn't materialize. Instead, they both were swallowed up by the ocean, gulping sea water as their heads slipped below the chop.

The girl released the woman's hand and fought to get back to the surface. Yolette popped up, got a big breath of air, searching frantically for Jezula.

There were screams all around her. Some people were trying to swim back to the boat, but Captain Bye-Bye was beating
them away with a boat hook as he turned the empty boat
around, preparing to race back toward open water.

The helicopter was over them now, and the white light illu-
minated their thrashing.

Yolette felt a hand on her leg. She reached down and
pulled, and a moment later Jezula's head popped to the surface,
sputtering and coughing up sea water.

"Let us swim," Yolette said.

"No," the desperate woman said. "No swim."

And in a panic, she clutched onto the girl's shoulders, and
they both went under again. The frightened woman was hanging
onto Yolette even harder than her mother had hung onto her
during their farewell. The girl felt powerless to do anything but
sink with her.

But she could not die this way. Not with America so close.
Not while hugging a woman who was not her mother. Not with
her father's photo in her hand and a reunion so close. Not after
her mother had spent more than a life's savings to get her here.

Yolette slipped her head through the woman's stranglehold
and moved behind her, trying to pull both of them back to the
surface. Her lungs burned with a need for more air. She had to
fight the urge to let go of the plastic bag.

She made it to the surface, taking big gulps of air, and once
again found herself entangled in Jezula's petrified embrace.

"No," Yolette said, "you must relax."

But the woman was going down again and taking Yolette
with her. This time, Yolette knew she was too tired to fight her
way back to the surface with the both of them. So she did the
only thing she could think of to save her life. She bit the part of
the woman's arm that was pulling down on Yolette's shoulders,
then pushed herself away, feeling the sinking woman's fingers
desperately grasping for the material on Yolette's dress. She
hung on momentarily to the hem, pulling Yolette down with her.

But then the woman's hand went slack, and Yolette felt herself moving toward the surface.

She tried to block it all out. That final touch of Jezula's fingers. The agonizing fear and uncertainty. The shouts and screams around her. For now, she must survive. For her mother, and for the man in that photo, still there inside the bag that was now part of every stroke she made with her left arm.

She swam until the waves started crashing on top of her, pounding her body as they dragged her under and tumbled her toward shore. Yolette did not fight. She gave into the waves, holding her breath until they were through with her. Then she popped her head above the soupy white foam they left behind and began swimming again.

When she had finally reached the shore, she was exhausted. She staggered the last few steps and looked around her. She was surprised to see that the current had pulled her nearly a thousand meters north. The helicopter was still hovering off the beach. And there was another boat now with a blue flashing light, and many people on the beach, running with their flashlight beams bouncing in front of them.

Yolette saw that two men from her boat had made it to shore, and they were being handcuffed by the men with the flashlights.

"Freeze!" she heard from the dune behind her. "Palm Beach Police!"

The man was running toward her now, and she stood mesmerized by his flashlight beam for a few moments. But then her instincts told her to run, just like they had told her to fight off the death embrace of Jezula.

Yolette ran up the beach, away from the flashlight beams and into the darkness. She could hear the policeman yelling as he chased her. He wasn't dressed for a foot chase on the shore. And he didn't have as much to gain from catching Yolette as she had from getting away.

But then she saw another man with a flashlight descend

from the dune about a quarter-mile in front of her. The second officer began running toward her, cutting off her escape.

Yolette turned left and began running away from the surf. She could see a little sea wall ahead, and beyond the sea wall, one of those American museum houses. She pulled herself over the wall and stared out onto a lawn that was so big and so green that it took her breath away.

There was a swimming pool on one side, shimmering in the night, and a dimly lit patio on the other. And in the middle of the lawn was some kind of human-form statue. At first, Yolette thought it was a man. But as she ran, she noted that it did not move. It remained in one position, with one leg bent and dangling in midair and both arms extended from the body like a bird's wings.

She ran past the statue and hid in the shrubbery along the back side of the mansion. She made it just before both flashlight beams popped over the sea wall and the two officers walked on the lawn to look for her.

Then something happened that she could not believe. The statue on the lawn came to life, ending its frozen pose and walking toward the two officers.

She could hear conversation now between the statue and the two officers. The statue was pointing up the beach. And then the officers walked back toward the ocean and were gone.

Yolette held her breath as the statue went back to his place on the lawn and resumed his frozen position, but before he did, he spoke in her direction.

"You can come out now. They are gone."

Yolette walked uncertainly toward the talking statue, who remained frozen. As she got close, she noted that he was a little man, muscular and bronzed by the sun. He had an earring in one ear, and his gray hair was gathered in a ponytail. He wore only a skimpy pair of running shorts and the beatific expression of a man at peace with himself and the world.

Without looking at her, he said, "We all do things to survive. Ricardo does tai chi every night on his back lawn."

"Who is Ricardo?" she asked.

"Wait, Ricardo is almost finished," he said. "Then we will talk."

The statue/man moved to another frozen pose. Yolette suddenly felt exhausted. She lay down on the perfect American lawn and gazed at the stars. She stared at them, trying to block out the sound of the distant helicopter and the feel of Jezula's dying grasp on the hem of her dress.

She wondered how America could be so beautiful and so horrible at the same time.

She thought of her mother and imagined that she was looking at the same stars this very moment back in Haiti. Yolette lifted a hand as if to touch a star, and with it, the soft curve of her mother's cheek. The girl smiled as her eyes teared up, turning the stars into diamonds.

The statue/man shifted to another position, and Yolette felt herself submerging into slumber. She was in a restaurant now, a big beautiful restaurant in America, and her father was there, dressed in one of those American tuxedoes she had seen in a magazine. The American people smile at them, because this is her father's restaurant. He leads her arm-in-arm to a private table set for three. Her mother is standing behind her chair waiting for them.

Yolette had no idea how long she stayed on the lawn like this, dreaming while the little man/statue moved in slow motion above her.

And she was only vaguely aware of his strong, sweaty arms that lifted her off the lawn and carried her inside the mansion, putting her on a bed that felt as soft as a cloud.

Fatigue had caused her to let go of everything, everything except the plastic bag she clutched in her left hand.

4 A new chum

"He's got eyes for you, Rose."

Rose Hamstein pretended she didn't know what her friend, Lois, was talking about.

"Who?"

"Don't play possum with me, madam," Lois said. "You know who."

"Lois is right," Jacqui piped up from the back seat.

"The way he circled around you like that, Rose," Maddy added. "It was like a big old dog, marking his territory."

"You make it sound like he was staining the carpet, Maddy," Rose said.

The four women were in Lois' Chrysler, heading north on Interstate 95, back to the Boynton Beach Boulevard exit that would take them home to Shady Palms.

They called themselves the Wonder Walkers, because three years ago these C Building neighbors began meeting at the Boynton Beach Mall. Before the stores opened for the day, the women would exercise by walking up and down the long concourses of the mall and then end up in the food court, drinking coffee, eating sticky buns and talking.

Other women had come to join them, but over time, it was

these four — Jacqui Fisher, Madeleine Jones, Lois Rodgers and Rose Hamstein — who had remained the nucleus of the Wonder Walkers.

They were an odd grouping. The recently widowed Jacqui was the doting mother of her adopted gay son, Jake, an aspiring actor living in West Palm Beach. Maddy, the only black resident of the condo complex, had come to Shady Palms as a nurse to a homebound resident and ended up living there when the dying woman left Maddy the condo. Lois was the prettiest woman in Shady Palms but also the most difficult, due mostly to three failed marriages and a bout with breast cancer. And Rose, married for 47 years, was considered the most stable woman in the group. At least until now.

"What does Bernie think?" Lois asked Rose.

"Don't turn this into a soap opera, Lois."

This had been a bad idea, Rose thought, this nighttime outing of the Wonder Walkers.

They usually didn't go out at night together, and they had never gone to a hotel lounge before. Especially in a place like Boca Raton, which was too distant in both highway miles and attitude from their suburban Boynton Beach condo.

"I feel so weird," Jacqui had said as she sat at the piano bar earlier that evening. "I could be home watching the Lifetime channel."

Lois spent most of the night craning her neck to critique the cosmetic surgery she saw in the room.

"See that one in the red dress?" she had asked at one point. "Do you think it would be rude if I asked her who did her face?"

They had come to listen to Vince Campo, a man Rose had met several weeks earlier in her computer literacy class. Rose and Jacqui had begun going to adult education classes at a local high school. For Rose, it gave her something to do on Bernie's poker nights.

"I don't believe in those computers," Jacqui had said, opting to take a travel agent class instead.

So none of her friends had met the funny, charming man who transferred into Rose's computer class a couple of weeks after it started and ended up sitting at the terminal next to her.

"I'm lost again, Rose," he'd say, leaning over to her, and she'd show him where to move his mouse or what keyboard strokes to make.

Vince Campo had said he lived in Boca and was "in investments," whatever that meant. But what he really liked to do was sing.

"My father was a singer," Rose had told him.

"Really?" Vince said. "Tell me about him."

That's the way Vince Campo was. Always interested in being a listener. Rose felt comfortable with him right off the bat. And while he was a good 10 years younger than Rose and trimmer and more handsome than her Bernie, she never thought of Vince in the way her friends were making her feel now.

"Is this your first date?" Maddy had asked mischievously in the lounge.

"It's not a date," Rose said, perhaps too defensively. "If I wanted to date somebody, do you think I'd take you three cows along with me?"

Rose had never cheated on her husband during their long marriage, and as far as she knew, he had never cheated on her. There was that business last year, when Bernie got a notion to look up his old high school girlfriend. But that was nothing.

Rose Cangelosi, that wiry little Italian girl from Brooklyn, had fallen in forbidden love with the Jewish tailor's son, Bernie, and they'd lived too long and experienced too much together to dishonor that in any way, Rose thought.

But nevertheless, it was thrilling to talk with a man who — unlike her own husband — seemed to actually listen to her, look for excuses to talk to her and not know exactly what she was going to say before she said it.

"He's just a friend, that's all," Rose had explained to the Wonder Walkers over sticky buns at the mall that morning. "I just thought it would be fun to hear him sing. If you don't want to go, you ... "

"Oh, I want to go," Lois said. "I've got to meet this home wrecker. Is he married?"

"Divorced."

"And he lives in Boca but drives all the way to Lantana to take an adult education class at Santaluces High School?" Maddy said.

"Sounds fishy to me," Lois said.

"And he's a hunk, too," said Jacqui, who had seen him in passing at night school.

"You ladies have terrific imaginations," Rose said.

But she put up with their teases because she really wanted to hear Vince sing. Sometimes he'd sing at his computer terminal, and she could tell he had a great voice. He'd take requests from her as they tried to make sense of Windows 98.

"Hey, Rose," he'd said casually a week ago. "I won't be in class next week because I've got a friend who plays sometimes at a piano bar, and he's going to let me sing a set with him."

Rose decided it would be fun to surprise Vince and just show up. She could miss class for a week, too. But she didn't want to go all the way to Boca alone, and she didn't want to be there alone either and give Vince any wrong ideas.

"Tell me, Rose," Maddy said from the back seat. "Does Bernie know you went to a hotel bar in Boca tonight to listen to a crooner who has the hots for you?"

Bernie didn't know. The truth was that Rose wasn't sure how to explain it to him without making it sound as tawdry as her friends were trying to make her feel now. Bernie thought she was just going to her adult education class, as she did every poker night.

"No," Rose said, as they turned off the highway and began the final stretch home. "Not exactly."

"This is how it starts," Lois said.

Rose was too tired to argue and a little tipsy from the wine and the music.

Vince had been so pleased to see her there. He sat down with them and talked for a long time, and when he sang, he strolled around the lounge with a cordless microphone. He sang even better than she had imagined.

And then at one point, he whispered something to the piano player and announced, "This next song is dedicated to one of my school chums."

Then he started singing *I'll Be Seeing You*, Rose's favorite song. He remembered. It was just another thing he had asked her at some point during their classes together. She felt herself blushing, as he walked toward the Wonder Walkers' table and circled around the women.

"What did he call you?" Jacqui said as they drove west on Boynton Beach Boulevard. "His chum?"

"Yeah, she's the chum, and he's the shark," Lois said.

"Very funny," Rose said, eager to change the subject. "Speaking of guys, how's Ricardo these days?"

"We're in a cooling-off period," Lois said.

"Again?" Maddy said. "Lois is the only woman I know who could find fault with a Palm Beach millionaire who is great in bed."

"Sleeping with men is the easy part," Lois said. "It's living with them that's tough."

The courtship of Lois with the eccentric sugar baron Ricardo Vera had been a favorite spectator sport for her friends during the past year. After a string of bad men, Lois had thought she was through with romance. But despite her best efforts, Ricardo had charmed himself into her life. He was a little guy with a penchant for triathlon training and the nagging habit of referring to himself in the third person. Tired of being wooed by women who were attracted to his money, he found something endearing and challenging in winning over Lois, who had no idea of his wealth until she had fallen in love with him.

But this wasn't a perfect union.

"We're both crazy, which makes things difficult," Lois had said in announcing one of their many cooling-off periods. "And what makes it tougher is that we're crazy in different ways."

The most recent cooling-off period began when Ricardo suggested that he wear his heart-rate monitor during a romantic interlude. Lois had always been grossed out by the thick black strap around his chest. It has a wireless link to a wristwatch, which beeps heart rates and displays them in big digital numbers on the watch's face.

Ricardo was obsessed with observing the functioning of his heart. So she put up with the monitor. But she drew the line when he tried wearing it in bed.

"Just this once," he had said. "Ricardo wants to see if he reaches his aerobic threshold."

"I'm not some lab rat!" Lois exploded. "And for the millionth time, stop calling yourself 'Ricardo.' "

Her friends liked this story and pressed her for details Lois didn't want to give. So she flipped on the radio to fill the awkward silence.

The news station was broadcasting a bulletin: Nine Haitian refugees had drowned off Palm Beach earlier that night. Two of the refugees who managed to swim to shore were arrested on the beach; one eluded police and was still being sought.

"Those poor people," Jacqui said.

"I'm sick of Haitians," Lois said. "They should just stay in their pathetic little country."

"How can you say that, Lois?" Rose said. "They're no different from my parents and any other immigrants who've come to this country looking for a better life."

"Don't get me started on the Haitians," Lois said. "I used to like going to garage sales, but now — forget it. Full of Haitians. I think the first words they learn in English are 'fifty cent.' "

They had turned into Shady Palms now and were making their way down the main road that connected the 12 three-story buildings in the complex. They had to go a couple of speed bumps past the clubhouse to get to their building.

As they rounded the final curve, they saw the flashing lights of the Fire-Rescue ambulance in the C Building parking lot. There usually were ailing residents in each building. And Lois, in one of her more wicked moments, had once suggested that the condo's newspaper, *The Shady Palms Gazette*, should publish a list in each issue of all the residents who were near death. The list, Lois had said, could be published under the headline: Circling the drain.

When the women saw the ambulance in front of their building, all conversation stopped.

"Who we got circling the drain?" Lois asked.

"I don't know," Jacqui said.

"Nobody, as far as I know," Maddy said. "Phyllis Harper in 41C just had her gallbladder out, but I thought she was fine."

Then they could see a few men standing near the back of the ambulance.

Archie Diamond ... Johnny Fox ... Fred Fortunato ... Softer.

"Hey, aren't those the guys who play poker with ... Bernie?" Jacqui said.

"Where's Bernie?" Rose said, softly the first time.

She leaned forward in her seat, scanning the red-strobed light for her husband. "Where's Bernie? Where's Bernie?" she repeated, louder every time.

As the car got closer, she could see the looks on the other men's faces.

"Where's Bernie?" she shouted.

But she already knew.

5 Bernie, ducks, death

Bernie didn't die.

"You're lucky, Mr. Hamstein," said a man in a white coat who looked too young to be a doctor. "You've had a traumatic cardiac episode."

"Who are you?" Bernie asked.

"I'm your doctor."

"I don't have a doctor."

Then he heard a familiar voice pipe up from the other side of his bed: "I told you he would be a bad patient."

"Rose," Bernie said, turning his head and reaching out his hand for his wife. "You look awful."

She'd spent the night there at the hospital, paralyzed with dread that her husband wouldn't survive his heart attack. Now, it was noon on the next day, and while she may not have looked her best from all these hours at the hospital, she was feeling better than she had felt since seeing that ambulance parked outside C Building.

"You don't look so good yourself, Bernie," Rose said.

"Yeah," Bernie said. "I had an episode."

"The doctor says you'll have to make some lifestyle changes, Bernie."

"I've got to turn gay? At my age? What will you do, Rose?"

Rose looked up at the doctor for help.

"Mr. Hamstein, you're going to need to be on a low-fat diet and start getting regular, moderate exercise," the doctor said. "And of course, you need to eliminate stress whenever you can."

"We're going to eat vegetarian, Bernie," Rose said. "And we'll walk together. It's time you tell Herb Troutman to find somebody else from C Building to be on the board."

Bernie got a glimpse of his new life, and he waited for the doctor to tell Rose that there was no need to be so drastic. But the doctor just nodded his head.

"And one other thing," Rose said. "No poker."

Bernie made a whimpering sound, partly because he liked playing poker with his friends and partly because he just remembered the $600 he had lost the previous night.

"Let's get out of here, Rose," Bernie said, after the doctor had left the room. "This has got to be costing us a fortune."

"Not for a few more days, Bernie."

He settled his head back on the pillow. The television in the corner of the room was blasting something about Haitian refugees drowning off Palm Beach. Bernie nearly asked Rose if she knew what the winning Cash 3 number was, but he didn't want to chance having the Florida Lottery being put on his off-limits list.

"So how was your computer class last night?" he asked.

Rose pretended not to hear him.

"Terrible about those Haitians, isn't it?" she said.

Bernie got lots of visitors that day.

His youngest son, Sam, who lived in West Palm Beach, brought a T-shirt he had specially made. "Tofu — Real food for people with real bad hearts," it said.

"Thanks for reminding me," Bernie said. "So where's that grandson of mine?"

Little Bernie was 8 months old now.

"He's home with Margo," Sam said.

Margo, a detective with the Palm Beach County Sheriff's Office, first came into Bernie's life as a problem renter at Shady Palms. But her pregnancy, which drove the adults-only condo into a frenzy, turned into a blessing when Bernie's troubled young son met her, fell in love and married her, giving Bernie and Rose a new grandson — not biologically related, but a grandchild in all the ways that really mattered.

"Margo wanted to bring him," Sam said, "but I wasn't sure if you'd be up to it."

"Yeah, I'll have to check with my doctor to see if babies are on the list of things I can't be around anymore," Bernie said.

"Mom said you were already showing signs of not taking this seriously, Dad," Sam said. "Please, Dad, don't be foolish. We all want you around for a long, long time."

Sam reached out and touched his father's arm, which still felt strong and ropy like it did during the days when Bernie was a Big Top bread delivery driver on Long Island, and Sam was a little boy who would play-wrestle on the floor with him at night.

"Don't worry about me," he said. "I just had an episode."

That's what he told everyone who had visited him that day. Nothing but an episode. And it was quite a parade of people there in the hospital room and on the telephone.

Bernie even got a phone call from his nephew, Brad Cohen, the sports agent in California.

"Just an episode, Brad," Bernie said. "Everything's fine."

Bernie's sister, who was Brad's mother, was Bernie's favorite sibling. And when she was dying a few years ago, Bernie promised her that he would look after Brad — a symbolic gesture more than anything else, considering that the young sports agent was far better off financially than his Uncle Bernie.

So Bernie had felt honored when Brad called him on the

phone a few weeks ago, asking for a favor.

"Whatever it is, you got it," Bernie said.

Bernie couldn't figure out why his nephew wanted to put a football player at Shady Palms for six months. Technically, Bernie would have to present the renter to the board, and he would have to be approved.

But Bernie, eager to demonstrate his condo muscle to his nephew, said he would personally make it happen. And Brad was willing to wire all six month's rent and deposits in advance, which was something the unit's owner would snap up in a second.

"Just fly him out here," Bernie had said. "And I'll take care of the details."

Unit 26C, the one Margo had rented, was still vacant. The football player could just live there, Bernie figured.

"Is everything still set for Demetrius?" Brad asked his uncle.

"Who's Demetrius?" Bernie asked.

"The football prospect I was telling you about."

"Oh, yes. Right," Bernie said, completely forgetting about the promise he'd made to his nephew three weeks ago.

"I've got him set to fly out tomorrow," Brad said.

"No problem," Bernie said. "The unit's just sitting there."

"And Uncle Bernie, thanks for talking to him on the phone last night," Brad said. "Whatever you said really made him feel like you wanted him there. I appreciate it."

"Sure," Bernie said.

After he hung up, Bernie thought hard but still couldn't remember talking to a football prospect on the telephone. But Bernie didn't have much time to reflect. He was too busy with visitors.

Bernie's poker buddies. Rose's Wonder Walkers. Hector, the gate guard, stopped by on his way home. Even Herb

Troutman, the president of the Shady Palms governing board, made an appearance.

"Here to inspect the corpse?" Bernie asked Herb.

Bernie and Herb hadn't gotten along in years, ever since Rose accused Herb's wife, Gilda, of cheating at cards. And Herb was the last guy at Shady Palms anybody wanted to cross. Herb, the president of H Building, had been elected chairman of all the 12 building presidents at Shady Palms. It meant that he controlled the gavel and the agenda at the complex.

"I think maybe the board should appoint somebody to fill in for you as president of C Building," Troutman said.

So that was it. Troutman was here because he couldn't wait to push Bernie aside.

"No need to do that, Herb. I'll be back in the saddle in a couple of days."

"But I thought your wife said ... "

"Herb, I am still the president of C."

"I wouldn't want the stress ... "

"If I need to step aside, you'll be the first to know."

"You know, Bernie, this may not be the best time to mention it, but you have a significant Muscovy duck problem outside C."

"We have a man who feeds the ducks."

"I think it's a matter that needs to be addressed immediately," Troutman said.

"Haven't you ever fed ducks, Herb?"

"Bernie, I can tell by the tone of your voice that your duties as president may be too stressful for a man in your condition."

"Herb, if you try to overthrow me while I'm here in the hospital, you're going to need to worry about your own condition, not mine."

"Bernie, is that a threat?"

"G'bye, Herb. I need to take a nap now. And I want to make

sure you're out of here first, in case you get the urge to smother me with a pillow."

"Bernie, I was only ... "

"G'bye, Herb."

And then when Troutman tried to say something else, Bernie quacked like a duck at him until he walked out of the room.

Rose, who had gone to the hospital cafeteria, returned a few minutes later.

"Anybody here while I'm gone?" she asked.

"Herb Troutman," Bernie said. "We had a nice visit."

Bernie actually felt invigorated over his dust-up with Troutman. What do these doctors know? Maybe a little bit of stress is just what he needs.

The most stressful visitor of the day wasn't Herb. It was Johnny Fox, Shady Palms' theatrical impresario and medicinal marijuana card shark. Johnny waited for Rose to leave the room before speaking to Bernie about certain details of the previous night.

"I'm sorry about accusing you of faking your heart attack, Bernie."

"I don't even remember that, Johnny."

What Bernie remembered was owing Johnny $600.

"Now, about the money you owe me," Johnny began.

"Yes, about the money," Bernie said, relieved that Johnny had brought up the subject.

Bernie was desperately hoping that Johnny would say that in light of Bernie's heart attack and in light of the unscrupulous way Johnny had pretended to be high on his glaucoma medication, that the poker debt would be declared null and void.

Bernie was so glad that Johnny appeared to be willing to erase the debt without any coaxing.

Bernie had the conversation played out in his mind:

Johnny would say to forget the debt, and Bernie would make
some half-hearted attempt to pay, saying something like, "No
Johnny, a bet is a bet." And then Johnny would say, "No, Bernie.
I insist." And Bernie would say, "OK, if you feel that strongly
about it."

The actual conversation went like this:

"What is it, $600?" Johnny asked.

"Yeah, I think so."

"That's a lot of money."

"Sure is," Bernie said.

"And I duped you into betting that much."

"Yes, you did."

"So here's what I'm thinking, Bernie — and it's because I
feel so terrible about how things turned out."

"Yes?" Bernie said.

"You can take your time paying me back."

"What?"

"You don't have to pay me in one lump sum," Johnny said.
"You know, maybe $100 a week, something like that."

Bernie stewed over his poker debt for the rest of the day.
Somehow, he would have to figure out a way to repay Johnny
without letting Rose know about it. But how would he get his
hands on that much money behind Rose's back?

■ ■ ■

Day turned to night, and the hospital had grown eerily
quiet except for the sound of television sets in every room. It
was just the two of them in the room. Rose had turned down the
lights and pulled up a chair to his bed. They sat there, holding
hands and watching *Who Wants to Be a Millionaire.*

The phone rang. Rose frowned, looking at her watch.

"Don't people realize you need to rest?" she said, reaching
to pick up the phone.

"Hello?" she said.

"Rose?"

It was Vince Campo. She didn't know what to say.

"Rose ... I hope I didn't call at a bad time. I was trying to reach you all day, just to tell you what a thrill it was to see you last night. That was a great surprise to have you — and your friends, too — come to hear me sing."

Bernie was distracted by the television show.

"Tricky question," he was telling the television, then he turned to Rose. "What's the first day of the week, Rose? Sunday or Monday?"

"Sunday," she said.

"What?" Vince said on the other end of the phone.

Rose felt embarrassed and tongue-tied.

"Is Bernie OK?" he went on. "When I couldn't reach you, my mind started wondering if something happened to you on the way home. It was bothering me, so I remembered the name of one of your friends, Jacqui, and I looked up her number and called her, and she told me ... "

"Everything's fine here," Rose said, wondering why she felt so uneasy. He was just a friend. Just like other friends who had called. Right?

"I called at a bad time," Vince said. "I'm sorry."

Rose put the receiver back and tried not to act rattled.

"Who was that?" Bernie asked.

"Just a friend," she said.

"You know, Rose," Bernie said, "if I was on this show, I wouldn't want you to be in the studio audience."

"Why's that, Bernie?" she said, putting her head on his chest and closing her eyes.

"Because I'd want you to be my lifeline."

6 A foreign affair

Lois Rodgers was exhausted, and as she turned the key in the door of her condo, she thought about how nice it would be to get a long night's sleep in her own bed.

She'd spent nearly all of the previous night at the hospital with her friend Rose, snatching moments of neck-stiffening sleep in a waiting room chair. And then most of this day had been spent making trips back and forth to the hospital, ferrying items to her friend, and walking her dog.

After 24 hours of being a caregiver, Lois was ready to call it quits. It's not that she begrudged being supportive and helpful to Rose. It's just that being selfless for that many hours felt unnatural for Lois.

Oh, well, the Florence Nightingale routine was over, she told herself. Bernie was going to make it, and Rose was going to be able to handle things just fine. It was time for Lois to get back to her own universe of concerns, time to get a good night's sleep, then buy herself a nice present tomorrow. Maybe that gold bracelet she'd been eyeing for weeks at the mall. Or a new outfit. Better yet, the bracelet and the outfit, followed up with a manicure and pedicure.

Why not? She deserved to reward herself. And nothing

would get her centered again better than a day at the mall and the spa.

She walked into her condo and was surprised to hear the television. That's funny. She didn't remember leaving it on. But she could see the flickering shadow on the living room walls and hear Regis Philbin's voice from *Who Wants to Be a Millionaire*.

She flipped the light switch on, peeked in the living room and screamed.

Sitting on her couch, the couch she had recently spent a fortune to reupholster, was a black girl dressed in a man's T-shirt and eating Doritos — the ones she had just bought? — right out of the bag.

"Who are you, and what are you doing in my home?" Lois shrieked.

The girl's eyes grew big, but she did not say a word. Instead, she turned her head toward the kitchen, where Lois' on-again, off-again male friend, Ricardo Vera, walked toward the living room with a bowl of freshly popped microwave popcorn in one hand.

"Ah, Lois, my love," the little man said, "I see you have met Yolette."

Then he turned to the girl on the couch.

"Yolette, this is the lovely lady that Ricardo told you about."

Lois didn't even try to be nice. Instead, she took three steps toward Ricardo.

"How dare you bring some street urchin into my condo, not to mention yourself, without letting me know."

"Yolette is a wonderful girl who ... "

Lois cut him off.

"Give me the key," she said, holding out her hand. "I forgot you still had it."

"But Lois, I thought you ... "

"Give me the key. Now!"

During the blooming days of their romance, she had given Ricardo her key because he often rode his bicycle from his Palm Beach home all the way to her suburban Boynton Beach condo. And if she happened to be out when he arrived, she didn't want him to have to wait outside for her. But now that their romance was on shaky ground, she didn't see any point in letting him hang on to the key.

Ricardo put the key in Lois' hand.

"Now get out — both of you," she said.

"But Lois, do you not want to hear about Yolette?"

"Out!"

"She is from Haiti, and she just arrived to this great country last night under tragic circumstances."

"Out! ... What did you say?"

Lois looked at the girl closely, then at Ricardo.

"You brought a Haitian to my condo?"

"Her name is Yolette," Ricardo said.

"It's bad enough that you're here uninvited, but to bring a ... "

"Lois," Ricardo said. "Ricardo wants to speak to you in another room."

"Make it a room in another home, then," she said, "because I want you out of here right ... "

"Lois! Please!" he said.

In the months she had known him, she'd never heard him raise his voice to her. Until now.

"Just listen to me for five minutes, *querida*," he said, softer now.

He walked back into the kitchen, motioning for her to follow. She did.

Despite herself, despite all the times she told herself that she and Ricardo were not a good match, she'd find herself being drawn back toward him. Even now, as angry as she was at him, there was a part of her, a part she didn't want to acknowledge, that was happy that Ricardo had returned again after yet another fight that could have been a relationship-ending episode. But she wasn't about to let him know it.

"Five minutes," she said, setting the timer on the stove.

Ricardo told the story of finding Yolette on his back lawn and of hiding her from the border patrol agents, who had come back to his home three times to look for her.

He told Lois about how the searchers noted that her footprints led to his home and how they thought she was still nearby. That afternoon, Ricardo said, they returned with a dog that sniffed around his property. The dog went crazy at his back door, and the agents asked permission to search his house.

Ricardo would not give his permission, and they left with assurances that they would be back.

"Ricardo thinks they will come with a search warrant," he said. "And Ricardo cannot let them take Yolette. She has been through too much. So Ricardo started thinking where to hide her. Nobody I know in Palm Beach would be willing to take her, and it would not be safe there for her. So before the agents could return, Ricardo put her in the back seat of his car, covered her with a blanket and drove her here."

Lois cut in, "And you thought what? 'Hey, Lois would love to have a boat person at her condo?' 'Hey, Lois and I are currently fighting with each other, so I think I'll patch things up by unloading a Haitian on her doorstep?'"

Lois stepped back and looked at him.

"Ricardo," she said, "are you crazy?"

"The girl has a father here in Florida," Ricardo said. "We just have to get her to her father."

"Or get arrested first for alien smuggling," Lois said. "Didn't you see? This is all over the news about these Haitians. You need to take her back to Palm Beach, call up the police and say you just found her hiding in the bushes. Let the government track down her father."

"The government?" Ricardo said. "Now you are being crazy, Lois. The government will just ship her back to Haiti. Ricardo does not trust the government, not after what happened to poor Elian."

"Let's not get started on that subject," Lois said.

The Elian Gonzalez saga had led to one of the cooling-off periods between Lois and Ricardo. Right from the start, Lois had thought Miami's Cuban-American community was ridiculous in trying to keep the 6-year-old refugee from going back to his father in Cuba.

But Ricardo, whose family made a fortune in the sugar business in the United States after fleeing Fidel Castro's tyranny, thought Elian should stay with his relatives in Miami.

Ricardo donated $50,000 to the cause, a donation that got him an invitation to the house in Little Havana to meet the boy.

Ricardo had surprised Lois, saying he wanted to take her on a drive, and then — much to her dismay — driving his Bentley to the Elian house in Miami, which was surrounded by thousands of chanting supporters, television trucks and cops.

This was about a week before the now-famous government raid, and there was a feeling of power around that house and a sense that the boy could never be ripped from the midst of such a passionate throng.

"My people," Ricardo had said, standing on the fringes of the crowd.

"A bunch of nuts," Lois said.

Three men held an effigy of Castro over their heads so it could be pelted with coins and bayoneted by the tips of countless hand-held Cuban flags. A few steps away, a circle of people were kneeling on the hot pavement, their eyes closed as they prayed the rosary. Just beyond the prayer circle, men and women swayed and sweated to salsa music blaring from a radio station's brightly painted van. And everywhere, there were protest signs denouncing President Clinton and Attorney General Janet Reno as devils and proclaiming Elian Gonzalez as a pint-sized messiah for his people.

"Let us go meet him," Ricardo had said, pulling Lois along as he made his way toward the barricades.

"Armando Gutierrez said we could meet little Elian."

Lois didn't want to meet the boy, but she didn't want to be left alone standing in this rabble. So she followed.

Ricardo, due to his donation, got the red-carpet treatment. Two beefy men opened the gate for them in the yard and led them up the front steps and into the house, which was packed with people — all of them speaking Spanish.

Lois recognized Gloria Estefan, and she thought she got a glimpse of Andy Garcia, who seemed to be always in the center of a circle of people. The mayor of Miami was filling up his plate at the makeshift buffet set up on the kitchen table, and the one they called The Fisherman was asleep on the sofa.

"Let's get out of here," Lois whispered to Ricardo, who chatted politely with a few people.

"Not yet," Ricardo said.

They found the boy in the back yard, going up and down a yellow slide.

"This is a tragedy," Lois said, but Ricardo was already moving away from her to bend down and talk to the boy.

Ricardo and Elian talked briefly in Spanish, while Lois counted the news helicopters that were making lazy circles over the house. Then Ricardo stepped away, summoned by a guy who appeared to be shaking down the sugar baron for another donation to the cause.

Unexpectedly, Lois found herself standing alone with Elian. He looked up at her and said something in Spanish.

"Your father is the one who really loves you," she said. "These people here don't really care about you. They just care about getting Castro or getting rich and famous. And that cousin of yours, take it from me, I know crazy when I see it!"

The 6-year-old boy looked at her, trying to decipher the strange language from this American woman.

"Get me out of this zoo," she said to Ricardo when he came back.

They made their way to Ricardo's parked Bentley, and she was horrified to watch him attach a Cuban flag to the car's antenna. They argued all the way back to Palm Beach County, and Ricardo nearly drove off the road when she told him what she had said to Elian.

"Ricardo should not have taken you," he said.

"Ricardo," she said, "will not take me anywhere if he doesn't remove that obnoxious flag from his car."

They didn't see each other for three weeks after that, and the only communication they had was on the morning of the government raid.

"Good!" Lois said into the telephone, hanging up before Ricardo, who had been woken from a dead sleep, had any idea what she was talking about.

Lois thought she and Ricardo were finished, a casualty of Elian politics. But in time, Ricardo pedaled his bike to her condo, and in time, she let him stay for dinner ... and beyond.

Until their next spat. And now, here he was again, back in her condo with this Haitian girl, trying to work his way back into her life.

"Forget it, Ricardo," she said.

"But Lois, you said Elian belonged with his father," Ricardo said. "That is what Ricardo is doing, trying to get this girl to be with her father. The mother of Yolette put her on that boat so she could get a better life here in America. Ricardo cannot turn his back on this child, and Ricardo cannot rely on the government, which has already shown the contempt it has for the children who risk their lives for freedom."

The girl fixed her eyes on the television, acting as if she didn't hear a word of their arguing.

"Ricardo," Lois said, "I'm tired of needing a foreign policy with you. Most couples that have problems go see a counselor. But we ... we need Henry Kissinger."

The timer on the stove buzzed.

7 A father on every corner

Yolette's eyes were on the television in the living room, but her mind was in the kitchen where Ricardo was arguing with the pretty American woman.

Ricardo had told her that the pretty American woman would like her. But Yolette could tell that Ricardo was wrong.

"She has a big heart," he had told her.

But so far, the only thing big from this lady was her temper.

Yolette wished she were still back in Ricardo's house, that big American mansion on the ocean. But Ricardo had told her that if she wanted to see her father, it was important they find him before immigration found her.

So she had run to his car and hid under a blanket while he drove her to this place, Shady Palms, where they waited for this Lois to arrive.

"Just one or two days," Ricardo was telling Lois in the kitchen. "I cannot take her back to Palm Beach now. It is too dangerous."

"And what am I supposed to do?" Lois asked.

"Just be your charming self, my dear. And meanwhile, Ricardo will find her father."

"I'm busy tomorrow," Lois said.

"Doing what?"

"Shopping."

"Perfect," Ricardo said. "Take her to the mall with you. She needs clothes. Ricardo will give you some money to ... "

"I'm not taking a boat person to Macy's," Lois said.

"She is a little girl, Lois, who has just left her mother and needs to be with her father."

"She is an illegal alien."

"Look at her, Lois," Ricardo said. "How can you turn your back on a child in need?"

Yolette kept staring at the television and this strange show, in which Americans win enough money to feed a village for years just by answering silly questions.

America must have so much money that people need to constantly give it away, Yolette thought. She wondered if this television person named Regis, who always seemed happy when contestants were getting more of his money, had ever given her father money.

Maybe her father had enough money to bring Yolette's mother to America, too. Maybe he would even have enough money to allow her mother to fly to America. Yolette made a mental note to insist that her mother not have to ride a little boat and swim to America.

"Does she speak English?" Lois said. "I haven't heard her say a word."

"She speaks better than Ricardo," he said.

"That's not saying much."

"Yolette," Ricardo said, "say something to Lois."

Yolette turned her head and looked at the American woman. Her mind raced, trying to think of something pleasant to say, but here is what came out:

"Jezula grabbed me, but I pushed her away."

"Who is Jezula?" Ricardo asked.

"The woman from the village," Yolette said. "She was going to take me to my father."

"You need to take this girl to Jezubel, or whatever her name is, and not to me," Lois told Ricardo.

"Jezula would not swim," Yolette said. "I told her to swim, but she just hung on my neck."

"Oh," Lois said.

"I pushed Jezula away," Yolette said, "because she was making me drink the water. It was too salty."

Ricardo sat down next to Yolette and put his arms around her.

"You did the right thing, my dear," he said.

Yolette put her head against the little man's chest. And for the first time since landing in America, she cried. For Jezula. For her mother in Haiti. For all the people on the boat with her.

Through her sobs, she could hear the American woman speaking again, but her voice was different this time.

"OK, Ricardo," Lois said. "You win. One night, and one night only. That's it. She can sleep out here on the hideaway."

"Maybe I should be nearby," Ricardo said. "Perhaps in your bed, my love."

"Perhaps in your dreams, Ricardo. I'd suggest you get out of this condo as quickly as possible before I change my mind."

"I was just leaving," Ricardo said.

Yolette looked up at him in alarm.

"Do not worry, Yolette. She will be nice to you. Believe Ricardo on this. Ricardo knows all about this crazy American woman. She is like the lychee fruit. Prickly and hard on the outside but sweet in the middle."

Ricardo kissed Yolette on the top of her head, and then tried to get a peck at Lois' cheek, but she was too fast for him.

"Don't let me have to set the oven timer again," she told

him.

"Ricardo is going," he said. "Ricardo has a busy day tomorrow. While you entertain the lovely Yolette, Ricardo will be finding her father."

"Wait a minute," Lois said. "I didn't say anything about entertaining Yolette. I just said she could spend the night here."

Yolette looked at Ricardo.

"You will bring me to my father tomorrow?"

"Ricardo will find him, yes," he said. "Just tell me everything you know about him."

Yolette showed him the photo of her father.

"His name is Jean Claude Germond," she said. "Jezula was going to take me to him."

"Do you know what city he lives in?" Lois asked.

"No."

"Do you have a telephone number? A street name?"

"No."

"Do you have anything?" Lois asked.

"He is in the restaurant business."

"And do you know the name of this restaurant?" Lois asked.

"Jezula told me on the boat."

"Great!" Ricardo said. "He is as good as found."

"What's the name of the restaurant?"

"It starts with the letter D," Yolette said.

Lois shook her head.

"Young lady, you will have to think hard to remember the name," Ricardo said.

Lois stood up and walked toward the kitchen.

"I'm going to make myself a very strong drink," she announced.

Yolette wondered why she was disappointing them. Could there be that many restaurants that begin with a D?

"At least Ricardo has the name," Ricardo said. "He can work with that."

It wasn't until an hour later, after Ricardo had left the condo and Lois had made Yolette a bed out of the couch, that the girl knew the name of the restaurant where her father worked.

"That is it!" she shouted, running toward Lois' bedroom. "I know it. I know the name of the restaurant," the girl said as she stood next to Lois' bed in the dark room.

Lois, who had just fallen asleep, was startled by the girl's intrusion into her bedroom.

"Out of this room!" she said, sitting up, and turning on the light on the small table next to the bed. "This is my bedroom. You can't come in here."

"The restaurant," the girl was saying.

"Stand out in the hallway there," Lois said.

Yolette walked to the threshold of her bedroom and craned her neck around the opened door to look at Lois.

"That's better," Lois said. "Now, what is it that is so important as to wake me up from a sleep I so desperately need?"

"I know the name of the restaurant now," Yolette said, and when she saw no reaction on Lois' face, the girl added, "the restaurant where my father works."

"It just came to you now?"

"I just saw it on television," the girl said.

Lois reached for the phone and called Ricardo's home.

"We have a name for the restaurant where the girl's father works," she said.

Then to Yolette she said, "What's the name?"

"Denny's," the girl said.

Yolette was beaming, and she could not figure out why Lois suddenly looked so disappointed.

"Is that a hard restaurant to find?" Yolette asked.

"No," Lois said. "I think there's one on every corner."

■ ■ ■

Ricardo woke up before dawn the next morning, as he usually did, and consulted the workout calendar he kept on his dresser.

Today was the day he would reunite the Haitian girl with her father, he remembered. But that didn't stop him from making time for his primary obsession.

At 69 years old, Ricardo was one of the premier triathlon athletes in his age group, an achievement he attained by a wealth that allowed him unlimited leisure time and the willpower to stick to a grueling training schedule of swimming, cycling and running.

His calendar told him that today was a day he was scheduled to bike for 20 miles, then do a 5-mile run.

Ricardo got on his bike just as the sun was coming up, and he pedaled through the silent streets of Palm Beach and down A1A. As he breezed around the traffic circle at Southern Boulevard and under the canopy of trees that led back to the glorious sight of a flat ocean, Ricardo felt completely at peace.

He monitored his gauges. His heart rate was 150. His speed was 23.5 miles per hour, and his cadence — the revolutions per minute he was pedaling — was 90. Perfect, he thought, as he leaned lower on his aero bars, extending his body even farther along the main axis of his titanium frame bicycle.

By the time his southward trek along A1A took him past Sloan's Curve, his mind had wandered back to little Yolette and Lois. What a combination.

Ricardo had suspected that Lois would be angry when she found him the previous night in her condo with the Haitian girl. But Lois needed prodding from time to time, he figured.

Ricardo got a thrill out of dueling with Lois, much like the thrill he got out of pedaling against a strong headwind or running up inclines. On the other hand, Palm Beach women were far too compliant for him. Oh, they were sticklers about their creature comforts, but they did not have the kind of stubborn self-reliance and survival instincts that Lois had.

He would have to call her condo as soon as he got back from his ride.

He looked at his speedometer. He was up to 25 miles an hour, courtesy of a northerly breeze that was pushing him through South Palm Beach. He wound his way down the condo canyon, listening only to the sound of his breathing, the gentle whirring of his chain and the wind grazing off his helmet.

Then he heard the car. In front of him, off to his right. The car's driver was pulling out of a condo driveway just 50 feet up the road from Ricardo. And the driver did not even hesitate. He must not have seen Ricardo and his bicycle hugging the white line on the side of the road.

Ricardo whistled and popped up from his aero bars, scrambling to reach his brakes. But he knew he did not have enough distance. The best hope he had would be if the driver suddenly saw Ricardo and stopped his turn, allowing Ricardo to move to the left and pass in front of his hood.

But the driver continued his turn, and Ricardo's wheel hit the Buick square on its front fender. The next few seconds were like a slow-motion movie. He felt his body launch over the handlebars and his shoes getting ripped out of his pedals. He was going so fast on the bike that his body never even touched the hood of the car. Instead, he sailed over the car like Superman, heading straight for a PalmTran bus sign on the other side of the driveway. Ricardo remembered thinking he ought to do everything in his power to keep his head away from the rapidly approaching bus sign.

And that is the last thing Ricardo remembered.

8 Dislocated Bone

Demetrius Bone couldn't believe he was actually here. The regret had begun seeping in during the three-hour layover at O'Hare. And now, as the plane made a big swoop over the Florida Everglades, Demetrius felt the full measure of his folly.

He looked out of the window, craning his neck for signs of a big city but saw only swamps.

"Dag!" he said aloud, startling the old white woman sitting in the window seat next to him.

Demetrius didn't enjoy packing his 6-foot-3 frame into the middle seat in coach, and he didn't enjoy this old woman who kept shrinking away from him, unable to conceal her fear of a large young black man.

All during the flight, she had been hanging on to that big purse of hers hard enough to make her knuckles whiten.

"Don't worry, I don't plan to mug anybody until I get off the plane," Demetrius said at the beginning of the flight, hoping to lighten the mood.

But instead, it made the woman more fearful. And it made Demetrius more depressed.

He could have been back in Los Angeles now, chilling and thrilling, hanging out in the hood. Sure, he wanted to play in the NFL, but he had never imagined this would be the way back to the big league.

When his agent, Brad Cohen, had spelled out his plan in
the restaurant the other night, it didn't sound as crazy as it did
right now to Demetrius.

The agent's pitch came at a low point for Demetrius. His
rent was three months overdue, and he'd been ripping up evic-
tion notices for the past few weeks, expecting to come home one
day and find his stuff on the sidewalk. The new owners of the
bar where he worked didn't appreciate him as much as they
should.

And the women, well, they were much more enthusiastic
when he was in NFL training camp.

So he had gone along with Cohen, allowing himself to be
hustled out of town in a hurry and put on this plane.

And now, Demetrius knew why. Cohen didn't want him to
think about it. Given time, Demetrius would have shaken off the
effects of his agent's sales pitch and reconsidered Cohen's bril-
liant plan for what it was: a far-fetched idea to save a career that
probably wasn't salvageable.

The three drinks Demetrius had on the plane did nothing
to deaden his dread. Instead, they made him more morose,
more certain of what must be the true desperation of his future
as an NFL player.

The plane landed at Palm Beach International Airport, and
as Demetrius walked from the jetway, he looked at the row of
people holding out signs that spelled out which passengers they
were trying to meet.

Nobody was there for him. Cohen had told him to take a
cab from the airport, but Demetrius figured the agent just wanted the waiting limo to be a surprise. So, he scanned the line of
placard holders, fully expecting to see a card with his name on it.

"Dag!" he said again.

It would be an exclamation he'd repeat several times that
afternoon. The next time was when he emerged from the frosty
air-conditioned terminal and got his first dose of South Florida

humidity.

"Dag!" he told the cab driver, as he sat in the back seat. "Is it always this sticky?"

"This is nothing," the cabbie said, "wait until August. As-Salaam-Alaikum."

"Back at you, bro."

Demetrius had grudging respect for those Nation of Islam dudes. He liked their independent attitude, but he didn't care for their abstinence from too many of the pleasures of life.

"My name is Akbar."

"Demetrius."

"Where to, my friend?"

Demetrius pulled the piece of paper out of his jeans.

"Shady Palms."

"The big condominium in Boynton Beach?"

"Yes," he said, "in Boynton Beach."

Boynton Beach. It sounded exotic. Tropical. Demetrius envisioned palm trees swaying over a shoreline of sugar sand bordering a tranquil emerald sea.

So he wasn't ready to see the cab turn off Interstate 95 and begin heading west on a road lined with strip shopping centers that appeared to be anything but tranquil.

"This is Boynton Beach?"

"Yes, my friend."

"But where's the beach?"

"You're new here, aren't you?"

"From L.A."

"Lower Alabama?"

"No. Los Angeles."

"Ah, California," the cabbie said. "I'd like to be there."

"Me, too, I'm beginning to think."

"Are you taking a landscaping job?"

"Say again."

"At Shady Palms," the cabbie said. "You working on a land-scaping crew?"

"No, man," Demetrius said. "I'm going to live there."

The cab driver looked in the rearview mirror to see if the big man in the back seat was joking. He seemed about to say something but then stopped.

"What?" Demetrius said. "What were you going to say?"

"Nothing."

"Are there any brothers at Shady Palms?"

"Sure," Akbar said. "But they all have leaf blowers strapped to their backs."

"Dag!"

The cab pulled off the road, and there was Shady Palms, a sprawling complex of three-story concrete block buildings. Akbar slowed his cab as they approached the guard house and the orange-and-white striped gate. On the side of the entrance was a wooden sign. It had the word "No" in large letters followed by several lines of smaller words that spelled out all that was forbidden inside the gates — everything from skateboarding to pickup trucks to loud radio playing.

A line of cars were steadily making their way through the entrance under the watchful eye of a barrel-chested gate guard, who wore a gray uniform that appeared to be spray painted on him.

Hector was waving the cars through and tipping his cap at the Shady Palms residents who were driving them. But as the cab approached, the gate went down and Hector stepped outside, adjusting his mirrored sunglasses.

Akbar rolled down the window of the cab, and Hector peeked his head inside, looking at the passenger in the back seat.

"The management office is closed for the day," the guard said.

"Management office?" Demetrius said.

"I can give you an employment application and you can ... "

"Whoa, hang on, Pedro," Bone said, leaning forward from the back seat. "I'm not here looking for a job. I live here."

Nobody patrols a guard gate with more vigor than Hector Hernandez, who keeps a close eye on the comings and goings at the condo.

Hector stiffened. His name plate clearly identified to all that his name wasn't Pedro.

"I know everyone who lives here," Hector said. "And you don't live here, Rufus."

"Dag!" Demetrius said.

"Calm down, my brothers," Akbar said. "We people of color must band together in our struggle for what is rightly ours."

"Pedro isn't my brother," Demetrius said.

"My name is Hector," the guard said.

"And mine is Demetrius, and I am coming here to live."

Hector glanced dubiously at his clipboard. Demetrius reached into his pocket and pulled out a piece of paper, reading the name on it.

"It's all been arranged by a guy named Bernie Hamstein," he said. "Just call up Bernie and he'll tell you."

"That's not possible," the guard said. "Mr. Hamstein is in the hospital."

"But I just spoke to him the other night and he told me to ... "

"Heart attack."

"Dag!"

The car behind the cab tooted its horn.

"I know Mr. Hamstein, and he never said anything about a new renter in C Building. He would have told me."

"Yeah, well, maybe he was going to tell you, Pedro, but he had a heart attack."

The car behind the cab tooted its horn again.

Demetrius stepped out from the back of the cab and glared at the driver, who visibly cowered behind the wheel when he saw the young man.

"Please get back in the car, sir," Hector said.

"I think I'm going to walk around here and take a look at my new neighborhood," Demetrius said, stretching.

"That would be trespassing, sir."

"But I live here."

"I am going to count to 10, and then I am dialing 911."

"Tell me, Pedro. I didn't read that sign so closely back there. But under the word, 'No,' do they list black folks?"

"Nine. Eight. Seven."

Demetrius walked back to the car behind the cab. He could hear the automatic door locks click as he approached.

"Any brothers here?" he shouted into the glass, as all four people stared straight ahead with wide-eyed stares, as if he weren't there.

"Six. Five. Four."

Akbar called out to Demetrius.

"Come, my friend," the cabbie said. "Seek not the comfort of white men, who have a long history of turning their backs on our people."

"Three. Two. One."

"Save your breath, Pedro. I'm leaving. You can keep this place."

Hector walked back inside the guard house and dialed 911.

"Friendly here, aren't they?" Demetrius told Akbar, who drove the cab over the grassy median and headed back out toward the street.

"Now what, my friend?"

Demetrius looked in his wallet, which was stuffed with cash. Cohen had given him $3,000, for what he called an advance on future earnings.

"Akbar, how far is it to Miami Beach, where all those wild discos are, and the super models?"

"My friend, there is nothing but sin and debauchery there. Nothing but the evil temptations of a wicked life."

"Perfect."

"But I could not be responsible for delivering a strong, young brother like yourself into that den of iniquity."

Demetrius peeled off two crisp $100 bills and put them on the seat next to the cabbie. Akbar glanced in the rearview mirror and smiled.

"I can have you there in a little more than an hour."

9 Lois bags a lucky break

Lois was furious.

The longer the day dragged on, the more she stewed, dreaming up new ways to tell off Ricardo when he showed up.

He had ruined her day, absolutely ruined it.

She had imagined herself spending a leisurely day shopping. But instead, here she was minding some boat person, a Haitian girl who stared at the television as if her lost father was about to jump out of the screen at any moment.

"When is Ricardo coming?" the girl had asked.

"Soon," Lois had said.

That was about 9 o'clock, when it became clear that Lois would have to feed Yolette breakfast. She had held off feeding the girl as long as possible, thinking Ricardo would walk in the door at any moment.

After all, that's what he'd said. He'd be by in the morning to pick up Yolette and then go find her father.

But soon it was noon, and then 1 p.m., and Lois was reluctantly feeding Yolette lunch. Of course, she had tried calling Ricardo's Palm Beach home. The butler, Manuel, said Ricardo's cars were still there, but his bicycle was gone.

This was bad news, Lois knew, because it wasn't uncommon for Ricardo to ride 80 miles some days.

"I know what he's up to, and I don't like it," Lois told the butler, before slamming the phone down.

This was typical Ricardo. He was forcing the Haitian girl on Lois, thinking that if they spent time together, Lois would come to like the girl and be more willing to let her spend night after night in her condo.

Well, nothing could be further from the truth. Yes, she had managed to work up some sympathy for the girl during the previous night. The way the girl had cried seemed real, and Ricardo's compassion — as loony as it seemed to Lois right now — managed to briefly short-circuit Lois' considerably self-centered perspective on life.

But that was temporary insanity, Lois now believed. She wondered, much to her own horror, if she had agreed to let the girl stay because she secretly had wanted a way to allow Ricardo to creep back into her life.

And that only made her more angry. At Ricardo. At herself. At this silent little castaway who seemed to take Lois' obvious disdain in stride.

Ricardo was crazy to think Lois would embrace this girl's troubles and make them her own. And she was crazy last night to allow Ricardo to walk out of the condo without the girl.

By today, Lois had her wits back. Ricardo might think they'd be spending this time bonding, but in reality, Lois was just counting the minutes until the girl would be out of her life.

Meanwhile, she thought about how she could keep the girl from contaminating her little condo with her presence. The girl's sheets would have to be washed in a separate load in hot, hot water. And Lois made a special pile of the plates, forks and spoons used by the girl and debated whether to wash them or simply throw them out as if they were paper.

She resented the girl's intrusion into her orderly life too

much to even make small talk to her.

Lois had missed Wonder Walkers at the mall that morning because she didn't trust leaving Yolette alone in her condo. The same thing went for shopping.

"Manuel," she said, calling the Palm Beach butler again on the phone. "I want you to go out and find Ricardo. Right now. Just drive up and down A1A until you ... "

"But, *señora*," Manuel started to say. "*Señor* Vera does not like to be interrupted when ... "

"I don't care what *Señor* Vera likes," Lois said. "It's what I don't like that matters right now. And I don't like being forced to harbor an illegal alien. So if you don't find your boss very quickly, I will do whatever I have to do to be a responsible American citizen."

After Lois hung up, she saw that Yolette was looking at her now from the couch.

"What are you staring at?" Lois demanded.

Yolette went back to staring at the television.

"I'm taking the dog for a walk," Lois told her. "You just sit there."

That was another thing. The dog. Since Bernie Hamstein's heart attack, his wife, Rose, had spent nearly all day at the hospital with him.

This meant their pampered little mutt, Lucky, the stray Bernie and Rose found last year outside the 7-Eleven, was left alone in their condo. So Rose had asked Lois to look after the dog and take him on frequent walks, to make Lucky feel less neglected.

Apparently, Lucky wasn't taking the separation from Bernie and Rose in stride. During the first day, he had managed to soil the Hamsteins' carpets with a variety of excretions.

"He's just angry at being abandoned," Rose had told Lois. "I feel so bad."

"Worry about your husband," Lois had said. "I'll worry about the stupid dog."

"Lucky's not a stupid dog," Rose said. "He's just lonely."

Lois had gotten stuck with Lucky because Rose's other Wonder Walker friends, Maddy and Jacqui, had frequently articulated how revolting they thought pets were in a condo. Lois wished now that she had been more vocal.

"I'm not taking your dog in my condo," Lois had told Rose. "But I will take him on a few walks each day."

"OK," Rose had said. "Whatever you can do is appreciated."

Lois didn't want to do anything, especially now with this human stray to keep an eye on. Before fishing the key out of her purse and heading over

With Bernie in the hospital and Rose by his side, Lucky has to rely on Lois Rodgers, a woman not accustomed to dog sitting.

to Rose's condo, Lois went into her bedroom, closed the door and opened her jewelry drawer.

No sense in tempting the Haitian girl with all this expensive jewelry so close at hand. Lois filled a green cloth bag with her pearls, diamond earrings and a variety of gold necklaces and bracelets.

"You just sit there," she told the girl again, before heading out the door with the small jewelry bag in her hand.

Lucky was more excited to see her than she was to see him, especially after Lois spotted a small pool of discolored carpet near the front door of the Hamstein condo. While Lucky did circles around her and tried to lick her hands, Lois got a handful of paper towels and the squirt bottle of Resolve stain remover. Maddy and Jacqui were right about dogs in condos, she thought.

After cleaning the carpet, Lois put Lucky on his leash and

walked him in the small rectangle of grass outside C Building. It was miserably hot, causing Lois to feel sorry for herself, yet again.

She was ready to go in, when she noticed a shiny new Cadillac make its way to one of the visitor spots outside C Building. She lingered long enough to spy on the visitor, because visitor spying is considered a compulsory activity for condo ownership at Shady Palms.

The Cadillac's door opened, and much to her surprise, Vince Campo stepped out, looking marvelous in black slacks and a cobalt blue shirt left unbuttoned to reveal a thatch of chest hair and a necklace that sported a crooked gold horn. He had one of those man bags in his hand, a sort of purse that men who wear tight pants carry rather than have anything in their pockets.

Lois watched in fascination, as he walked around to the passenger side of his gleaming black car and picked up what looked like a casserole from the red leather seat. He spotted her as he started to walk toward the building's entrance.

"Lois?"

She wished she had at least brushed her hair or reapplied her makeup. She felt frumpy, standing there smelling of Resolve and squinting without her sunglasses while waiting expectantly for a mutt to do his business in the hot Florida sun.

"Vince?"

He walked over to her smiling, and Lois couldn't help wondering what a guy like this saw in her friend, Rose. Sure, Rose was funny and warm, but men go out of their way for one thing, and it isn't personality, Lois knew. Subconsciously, she ran her hands through her hair and wiped her tongue across the upper front row of her teeth.

"What brings you here, Vince?"

"I heard about Rose's husband, and I just thought that the

last thing she's going to have on her mind is cooking, so I made a lasagna here and ... "

"Oh, how thoughtful," Lois said.

Lucky began jumping on Vince's pants legs and wagging his tail excitedly.

"Stupid dog," Lois said, jerking his collar.

"That's all right," Vince said, bending down to pet Lucky, who immediately rolled on his back to give Vince access to his belly. "He just smells my girls, Barbra and Judy."

"What's his name?"

"Lucky. But you can just call him Rock, which is short for Rock Around My Neck."

"Oh," Vince said, putting on one of those silly voices people use when talking to dogs. "You are a such a lover boy, aren't you?"

Lucky sighed and stretched his body in the hot grass.

"Hector, the guard at the gate, told me that I could drop this casserole off with either you, Maddy or Jacqui, and that you'd make sure Rose got it," Vince said.

"C'mon," Lois said. "This is her dog here, I'm just walking him for her. Follow me. I'm heading up there now."

Lois wasn't sure if Rose would want her to show Vince her condo, but on the other hand, she wasn't about to try to carry the lasagna while walking Lucky back into the building.

Once they were inside Rose's condo, Vince stood in the living room, petting the dog, while Lois walked into the kitchen with the casserole, rewrapped it in tin foil and found a way to wedge it in an already crowded refrigerator.

"When will Bernie be coming home?" Vince asked.

"Couple of days, maybe. Can I get you a drink of something?"

"No thanks," he said. "But can I use the restroom real quick? I don't think I can make it back to Boca."

Well, at least Ricardo had better bladder control than most men his age, Lois thought.

When Vince emerged from the bathroom, he asked, "Is there anything I can do to help?"

"No," Lois said. "Unless you want to drop this dog in the middle of the Everglades on your way home. See that wet spot by where you're standing? That's the one I just cleaned before you arrived."

Lucky was sitting next to Vince's legs, sniffing his pants again.

"I can baby-sit Lucky," Vince said. "I don't mind it, and my two poodles will love it. He's probably just lonely here all alone."

Vince was petting the dog and putting on that silly dog voice again.

"Wouldn't you like to meet Barbra and Judy? Yes, you would. Yes, you would."

Lois was conflicted. She desperately wanted to get rid of her dog responsibilities, yet she wasn't sure she should facilitate getting her friend, Rose, in deeper with a guy who was obviously smitten by her. If Rose was going to wreck her marriage, Lois didn't want to be part of it.

But in the end, the smell of Resolve on her fingers and the thought of cleaning up future messes on her friend's carpet tipped the balance.

"Are you sure?" Lois asked.

"Positive," Vince said. "I'd love to."

Lucky's ears perked up. Somehow, he had an idea that his life was about to improve. Maybe he wasn't such a dumb dog after all, Lois thought.

Lois felt so relieved seeing Lucky drive away that she completely forgot about her bag of jewelry, which wasn't in her hand as she stepped back in her condo to the sound of a ringing phone.

10 Ricardo in, Bernie out

The phone stopped ringing as soon as Lois put her hand on the receiver.

"Why didn't you answer it?" she told the girl, who had been sitting on the sofa looking at the ringing phone.

"You told me not to move," Yolette said.

"That was probably Ricardo calling," Lois said.

The girl smiled.

"Ricardo?"

"Yes," she said. "That must have been him telling me he was on his way to pick you up and take you to your father."

"Oh," the girl said. "Thank the Lord."

"The Lord?" Lois said, then laughed. "Don't tell me that after all you've been through, you think there's some kind God presiding over this."

"Yes," Yolette said. "The Lord watches all of us. I have been praying to the Lord while you were gone."

"Whatever you say," Lois said.

"No, Ms. Lois, it is true."

Lois didn't want to debate theology with an 11-year-old, but she couldn't help herself. She and Ricardo had debated the subject, and naturally, he had infuriated her with his simplistic belief in a benevolent and attentive God who pulled the strings.

"You and Ricardo can have a nice pray together when he comes and picks you up," Lois said. "Maybe God will tell you why he let all those people on your little boat drown."

The words seemed to take the wind from the girl, who moved her lips but did not say anything.

"I'm sorry," Lois said. "That wasn't very nice of me to say."

Yolette looked at Lois, and her eyes widened.

"But God did not let me be killed," she said. "He has a plan for me."

"I don't know if he does," Lois said, "but I do."

She dialed Ricardo's Palm Beach home, deciding to tell him he had exactly 30 minutes to collect his castaway or she was going to call immigration. She could still squeeze in a manicure today if Ricardo hurried up.

Manuel, the butler, answered the phone.

"Manuel, this is Lois. Did Ricardo just call?"

"*Señora* Rodgers, I am so glad to hear your voice. Where are you?"

"Home," Lois said. "Let's skip the small talk, Manuel. Put your boss on the phone."

"But I called you and ... "

"I just walked in the door. Listen, Manuel. I'd love to chat, but right now, I just want to hear Ricardo tell me that he's on his way here."

"I am afraid, that is not possible, *señora*."

"What?"

Manuel told her. About how after the last call, he heeded her advice and drove up and down A1A looking for Ricardo and his bicycle. Manuel got to the accident scene in South Palm Beach too late to see Ricardo but still in time to see his crumpled bicycle on the side of the road. A police officer filling out an accident report gave Manuel the particulars: Alive, but in bad shape.

"He is at the emergency room at Good Samaritan, *señora*."

Lois hung up the phone.

"Has Ricardo found my father?" Yolette said.

Lois shook her head.

"What is wrong, Ms. Lois?"

"Your God is working in mysterious ways, again," Lois said. "Ricardo's been in an accident. I'm going to see him."

"May I ... "

"You may stay here," Lois said, "unless you want to end up in that prison they have in Miami for Haitians who come here without invitations."

The girl sat back on the couch.

"I will pray," the girl said.

"Terrific," Lois said, as she made a mental note to put her bag of jewelry in her purse.

And that's when she remembered she no longer had the green cloth bag, and she had managed, somehow, to return from Rose's condo without it.

She walked back there now, trying to recall what she had done with the bag. She probably put it down somewhere in the condo because she had to clean up the dog's mess on the carpet.

And then what? She didn't remember holding the bag when she walked the dog outside. So it should still be in Rose's condo.

But after searching every surface of the condo and not finding the jewelry bag, something else popped into Lois' mind. Vince Campo. He had followed her up to the condo to drop off that casserole. And he was in Rose's living room while Lois spent a few minutes putting new foil on the lasagna and finding a way to fit it in the refrigerator. It was certainly enough time for him to spot the cloth bag on the dining room table and slip it in that little leather purse he was carrying. And then he went to the

**The ducks outside C Building
have everybody squawking.**

bathroom, perhaps to get a better look at what was in the bag.

Lois' face grew flush.

Could it be? Was Vince Campo a thief?

She walked to her car in a daze. Her life, which had been so orderly only 24 hours ago, was in complete disarray.

What else could go wrong?

When she got to her Chrysler, it was spotted with droppings, and a large Muscovy duck was walking across her hood. She swung her purse at the duck's behind, sending it squawking to the pavement.

"Schweinehund!" a voice shouted from across the parking lot.

It was that hunchbacked man in 46C, the guy Bernie liked to call Herman the German. Herman Schmidlapp kept his distance from the humans of C Building but never met a duck he didn't like. He was solely responsible for the gaggle of those big, ugly Muscovy ducks, which made a nuisance of themselves outside the building while waiting for Herman's daily feedings.

Lois got into her car, started the engine and flicked her windshield wipers, which did nothing but smear the duck yuck into a creamy paste across her field of vision.

After backing up the car, she saw that her path out of the lot was blocked by the ducks, which were clustered around

Herman Schmidlapp and his bag of bread.

Lois beeped her horn.

Schmidlapp didn't move. Instead, he looked up at her and said, "Haf reeshpect for zee animals!"

Lois thrust her arm out the car window, extending a finger. Rather than relieving her tension, the defiant gesture only made her angrier. That's because it dawned on her that the finger she was extending, until this afternoon, used to have a beautiful ring with an amethyst stone. It was a ring she would wear for dressy occasions, a ring, she figured, that would soon be pawned by a silver-throated con man named Vince Campo.

It was all too much for Lois. She gunned the engine, pressing her foot on the accelerator so hard that the big Chrysler left rubber on the pavement as it zoomed across the lot in the general direction of the flock of poultry.

Schmidlapp was able to back up a few steps in time, but the ducks weren't as adept at processing information. And the presence of a free meal had clouded their survival instincts, making a quick getaway impossible.

Most of the ducks avoided the Chrysler, but it was clear from the squawks and the brief shower of feathers that Lois would have to go to a car wash that afternoon to rinse away more than droppings.

"Murderer!" Schmidlapp shouted, waving his fist at her as the Chrysler headed toward the condo gate.

■ ■ ■

That afternoon, Bernie Hamstein was released from the hospital. It was exhilarating to drive away, to reenter the stream of everyday life as a survivor. And it was strange to be sitting in the passenger seat of his car while his wife, Rose, drove and lectured him on how their lives would have to change.

"From now on, Bernie, we're eating vegetarian," Rose said.

"Don't follow that truck so closely, Rose."

"Are you paying attention, Bernie?"

"These trucks kick up stones, Rose."

"Nothing but whole foods. Lots of vegetables," she said, still tailgating the truck. "And plenty of exercise."

"Do me a favor, Rose. Exercise a little more caution when you drive."

After they had pulled off the highway, he tried to get her to stop at 7-Eleven for Lotto tickets, but she kept going.

"A new life, Bernie," she said.

"Rose, there's no cholesterol in the Lotto."

"Stress, Bernie. You need to eliminate stress."

"I don't get stress from playing numbers. I get stress from having conversations like this."

They drove in silence until Rose pulled into their reserved parking space in front of C Building at Shady Palms.

"Home sweet home," Bernie said. "I'd get out and kiss the ground, if it wasn't for all the duck poop."

When Rose opened the door to their condo, she was surprised Lucky didn't come bounding up to them.

"Maybe Lois took Lucky to her condo," Rose said to Bernie. "I'm going to walk over there and get him. I'll be right back."

Bernie sat down at the dining room table. He didn't want to say anything, but he wasn't feeling so hot. The little walk from the car to their condo had taken the starch out of him. He debated whether to take one of his pills, the ones the doctor told him to take if the pain got bad.

But then the phone rang. It was Herman Schmidlapp, complaining about some atrocity perpetrated on his beloved Muscovy ducks.

Bernie listened with a smile on his face. He had been home less than five minutes, and already he was being asked to deal with condo business. Yes, he was alive. He was back.

"Herman, slow down," Bernie said. "Take a deep breath, and begin at the top again. In English this time. OK, you were feeding the ducks and ... "

Bernie, standing in the kitchen with the phone, absently wandered over to the refrigerator and peeked inside. He was a little hungry, and even though it was nearly time for dinner, a little snack wouldn't hurt.

As Herman the German carried on, Bernie spotted the tray of lasagna, pulled it out and got himself a little plate. There was a note on top of the lasagna. Bernie read it, then put it on the counter. While trying to soothe Herman the German, Bernie cut himself a wedge, zapped it in the microwave and ate while it was still too hot, unable to wait any longer.

He was marveling at how good real food tasted after eating hospital food for two days, when Rose walked back in the door.

"Herman," Bernie said, "don't go to Herb Troutman. Please. Let me see what I can do? OK? Gotta go. Yes. I'll get back to you."

Rose was frowning as Bernie hung up the phone.

"I thought we discussed this," she said. "Condo business is too stressful for a man in your condition."

"I think you did all the talking during that discussion," Bernie said.

"And what's this you're eating?" she said, picking through the lasagna, exposing bits of chopped meat and Italian sausage.

"It was in the fridge," Bernie said. "A friend of yours left it. The note's on the counter."

Rose walked over to read the note. She stood frozen there with her back to Bernie.

"So," Bernie said. "Who's this Vince Campo fella?"

11 Ricardo draws a crowd

Lois breezed through the emergency room at Good Samaritan Medical Center until she found Ricardo, who appeared to have most of his upper body wrapped in bandages.

"Ricardo," Lois said, "are you all right?"

"Mmmm," he said.

Lois then heard a man's voice behind her and turned around to see a doctor who appeared to be barely out of high school.

"We had to wire his jaw shut," he told her.

"Thank you," she said. "It's been on my list of things to do for months now."

"Are you his wife?" the doctor said.

"Mmmm," Ricardo said.

"Heavens no," Lois said. "We're just ... friends."

"Mmmm."

"Please, Mr. Vera, try not to talk," the doctor said.

Then he explained to Lois that Ricardo had managed to break his clavicle, dislocate his jaw and crack several ribs. But thanks to his helmet, his brain appeared to be fine.

"That's what you think," Lois said. "How long will he have to be here?"

"A few days, maybe," the doctor said.

After he left the room, Lois looked at Ricardo and patted his chest.

"Mmmm!" Ricardo said.

"Oh, sorry. I forgot about the ribs."

She sat down heavily in the chair and told Ricardo what a lousy day this had turned out to be for her. Sitting there all day with that Haitian girl, waiting for him to call. Unloading Rose's dog, only to have her jewelry stolen by that Vince Campo guy. And then, Herman the German and his ducks.

"You picked a horrible day to have a bicycle accident, Ricardo."

"Mmmm," he said, waving his right arm at her in the direction of a small table next to the bed.

"And now I've got to play charades with you," she said.

"Mmmm," Ricardo said again.

"OK, I see it," Lois said, handing him a pen and a pad of paper that was on top of the little table.

She watched as he placed the pen inside the folds of his bandaged hand

Because of a wired jaw, Ricardo asks about Yolette by drawing her.

and slowly drew a stick figure of a girl and a question mark.

"She's at the condo, probably rifling through my closets by now."

"Mmmm," he said, clutching her hand with a surprisingly strong grip.

"I hope that's not supposed to mean that I need to keep taking care of her," Lois said. "Enough is enough."

Ricardo ripped off a sheet of paper and began drawing again with the pen.

This time he drew a girl with huge tears popping out of her

eyes. Then he framed the figure with a rectangle and added vertical stripes.

"Ricardo, if they lock her up, it's not my fault. She's here illegally. You can't expect me to ... "

He grabbed her arm and pulled her down on him. She could see his eyes go wide with pain, but he did not let go.

"Mmmm!" he said, shaking her. "Mmmm! Mmmm!"

Lois tried to pull herself free.

"Don't you raise your voice at me, Ricardo Vera! And let go of me, before I call security."

"Mmmm!"

"No, I will not put myself on the line any more for that girl. You are being ridiculous."

"Mmmm."

He held her tighter, and Lois found him, even in his current state, too strong for her.

"I believe your behavior right now falls under the category of sexual harassment," she said.

Which only gave Ricardo the idea to try to grope her with one of his mummified hands.

"You're disgusting," Lois said, but instead of pulling away, she found she was boosting herself onto the edge of his bed as his clubbed hand improvised behind her back.

"Mmmm," he said, this time in a low throaty voice.

"Don't try to sweet talk me, Ricardo."

"Mmmm."

He tried to ease his bandaged face up to hers, but he was incapable of carrying out the smooth motion. So instead of a gentle ascent, his head jerked up, conking her in the forehead with the kind of motion soccer players use while heading a ball into a goal from 20 yards away.

"Ooow," Lois said, rearing back and steadying herself for balance by inadvertently pressing the "nurse call" button on the bed. "You hurt me."

"Mmmm."

The nurse came in to find them both in bed and Lois about to slap Ricardo in his broken jaw, which was making another pass at her face.

"Mmmm!" Ricardo said, after Lois batted him in the side of the face.

"What's going on here?" the nurse shouted.

Soon, their little room was filled with five people in white coats. The slap on Ricardo's bandaged face had ended his amorous overtures. He lay back on his pillow staring at the ceiling and moaning.

Lois was still in his bed and now was faced with the embarrassing task of getting out of it without losing too much of her dignity. As five sets of disapproving eyes watched, she pushed her dress back down, untangled herself from the mummy and stepped back on the floor.

"There," she said, turning around to face the doctors and nurses. "No need to worry. I'm fine."

But they seemed to be only concerned about Ricardo. They rushed past her, staring daggers at her while examining Ricardo, who was making reassuring "Mmmm" sounds.

At least, that's the way it sounded to Lois.

"See, he's fine," she said.

One of the nurses turned to her and said, "Leave now, before we charge you with battery."

"Battery?" Lois said, incredulously. "That man was mauling me. I'm the one who should ... "

"Mmmm," Ricardo said, reaching past the ring of people around her, trying to get at the pad of paper and pen again.

"Please, just rest, Mr. Vera," one of the nurses said.

But he waved them away. They handed him the pad and watched as he began drawing again. It occurred to Lois then that

Ricardo might not be literate in English. Had she ever seen him reading anything during their time together? No, come to think of it, she hadn't.

He drew another figure of a little girl, and this time drew her with a woman. Both figures were smiling. Everybody watched him as he continued to write on the pad.

Ricardo motioned his white-coated attendants aside and handed the pad to Lois.

Under the figures were the letters, "PLS."

The others in the room looked at Lois for an explanation. But she was looking at Ricardo now, whose eyes tried to convey everything he could not say or draw.

When she realized the others were staring at her, she was flustered.

"Oh," she said. "Yes, well. I guess I have to get home and see about our granddaughter."

"Mmmm," Ricardo said, nodding his head.

"That's her initials, PLS — Penelope Lois Smith," Lois said. "Her middle name was named after me."

But she knew Ricardo had struggled to write the word "please."

"I thought you said you weren't his wife," the doctor said.

"I'm not," Lois said. "We split up. But if there's a way you can keep that jaw of his closed, I might reconsider."

She patted Ricardo on the leg.

"Mmmm."

And she walked out of the room without giving anybody there another moment of her time.

As Lois drove back to Shady Palms, she realized it was nearly dinner time, and she was starving. She stopped off at Publix and considered going to the deli counter and picking up some of the hot meatloaf or fried chicken.

But this wasn't one of the nights she could have a normal

dinner. She needed a special meal tonight, a meal that never failed to elevate her spirits when life's events seemed to conspire against her.

So she headed for another part of the store and made her purchase. While walking back to her car, she nearly screamed when she saw the grille of her Chrysler, which had clumps of feathers and duck gristle protruding from her radiator. Now, she was really glad she didn't get chicken for dinner.

She'd have to go to a car wash to get her car cleaned up. But not now. She needed to get home with dinner before it spoiled.

When she got to her condo, she could hear the television was still on and Yolette was sitting in the dark on the couch in the same spot she had been when Lois left.

"You could have put on a light," Lois said. "You didn't have to sit in the dark."

"Oh," Yolette said, switching on the lamp next to her. "How is Ricardo?"

"Better than ever," Lois said.

"Is he looking for my father?"

"Not yet," Lois said, putting the plastic bag from Publix on the dining room table.

"Ms. Lois?"

"Yes."

"May I go to the bathroom?"

Lois pointed the way, realizing that the girl must have sat there for hours, afraid to even use the bathroom, sitting there in the dark watching silly shows on television.

When Yolette came back from the bathroom, she sat down on the couch in the same indentation she had made from the afternoon.

"Someone knocked on the door, Ms. Lois," she said. "But I did not say anything. I just sat here quietly."

"Good," Lois said.

"The person kept banging on the door," Yolette said. "She said her name was Rose."

"Oh, Rose," Lois said. "Don't remind me."

Lois was going to dread talking to Rose and telling her about letting Vince Campo take her dog. And then she would have to call the police to report the stolen jewelry and persuade them to raid Vince Campo's house. She didn't want to think about it. Not until after dinner.

She was glad she got her special meal.

"Yolette," she said. "Today has been a tough day. Come here and sit at the table with me."

The girl stood up obediently and walked to the dining room table and sat opposite Lois.

She pushed a spoon across the table to the girl.

"You hungry?"

"Yes," the girl said.

"Good. One of these is yours, and the other is mine."

She reached in the bag and slid a pint of Ben & Jerry's Chocolate Fudge Brownie ice cream across the table. Then she took the other pint and began eating from it.

"I hope you like chocolate," Lois said. "I think of it as medicine."

She watched as the girl popped the lid of her container and looked inside.

"Ever have ice cream before?"

The girl shook her head, no. She took a bite and smiled.

"Welcome to America."

12 The busted spoke

"They're lentils, Bernie."

"I know what they are, Rose."

"Then why aren't you eating them?"

Bernie pushed the disc-shaped beans around his plate.

"They can use a little sausage or something," he said. "And what's wrong with white rice?"

"Brown rice is healthier."

"Brown rice is like spackle. At least let me put some butter in it."

"Bernie Hamstein, do you want to live or not?"

"I am not being allowed to live!"

Driving his car. Eating meat. Playing poker. Handling condo business. Plunking down his daily lottery bets.

All these activities were suddenly off-limits, all discouraged by a watchful wife who showed her love by saying "No" to nearly everything he wanted to do or eat.

About the only thing Rose wanted Bernie to do was walk. She'd presented him with a new pair of what she called "excellent cross-training shoes" when he got home from the hospital.

"They'll make you want to walk," she said.

"A Reuben sandwich at the finish line will make me want to walk," he said.

She ignored him.

"For starters, you should come with me in the mornings to the mall," she said.

"With the Wonder Walkers? Rose, are you kidding?"

"OK, if you don't want to be seen with your wife in public, then you should start going to the clubhouse and use the treadmill."

■ ■ ■

To humor her, he tried it. He set the treadmill on its slowest speed and programmed it for 10 minutes. But after three minutes, he stopped it and got off.

"Now I know how a hamster feels," he told the woman who was huffing on the treadmill next to his.

Bernie wandered through the clubhouse, trying to waste some time before walking back to his condo. And that's when he bumped into Mort Granger, the publisher of *The Shady Palms Gazette*, the condo newspaper that routinely found ways to throw fresh gasoline on dying fires.

"Bernie, just the guy I was looking for," Mort said.

Normally, Bernie would cringe when Mort said something like this. But Bernie was starved for action, even if it came from a troublemaker like Mort.

"I got an item in the next issue about your heart attack," he said.

"If you print that I've died, I'll demand a retraction."

"But that's not what I want to talk to you about," Mort said. "My big story will be about the ducks outside C Building."

"Did Herman Schmidlapp call you?"

"Bernie," Mort said. "Murder at Shady Palms! This is a great story."

"Mort, don't make it worse than it already is," Bernie said.

Mort's condo newspaper had the motto: "All the news that's fit to print — and a whole lot more." And to Bernie, Mort spent more time making sure the "whole lot more" part got in, at the expense of the "fit to print" part.

Herman Schmidlapp does more than feed the ducks outside C Building. He talks to them and considers them his closest friends at the condo.

"What are you going to say, Mort?"

"This is the kind of issue that defines a community. Cleanliness vs. Compassion. Life vs. Death. Man vs. Nature. Where do you stand, Bernie? I hear you're pro-duck?"

"I'm anti-tofu, Mort. That's where I stand. Herman the German called me the other night and told me what happened. Then he called Herb Troutman, who called me. Then my wife took the phone out of my hands and told Troutman to leave me alone. And then I choked down the rest of my Tofutti dessert."

Mort chewed on his cigar stub and put his hand on Bernie's shoulder.

"Are you relinquishing your building's presidency, Bernie?"

"No, Mort, I'm not. I'm just catching my breath."

"Meanwhile, C Building is in an uproar. In a scientific poll I took of 20 households in the building, 18 of them said they wanted the ducks removed — killed if necessary — and they supported that Lois Rodgers woman who brutally killed two of them in a drive-by."

"A drive-by? You make it sound like C Building's a crack house. What happened the other day was an accident. I don't believe Lois intended to run down any ducks."

"That's not what Schmidlapp says," Mort said.

"Yeah, and Schmidlapp also says that the ducks tell him what Nasdaq stocks look good."

"When I talked to the respondents of my poll, they said you are the main problem. You've been pro-duck and unwilling to deal with Schmidlapp."

"What's next? Squirrels? Is somebody going to say they don't like the way the squirrels knock bark off trees or chase each other, and then we're going to start rounding up the squirrels, too?"

"Ah, so then you are pro-duck! Interesting!"

Why is it, Bernie thought, that no matter how bad he felt, Mort Granger could always make him feel a little bit worse.

"When's your paper coming out?"

"Tomorrow," Mort said.

"Thanks for the warning," Bernie said. "I'll disconnect my phone."

Speaking of Bernie's phone, he'd been getting frantic phone calls the past couple of days from his nephew in California, Brad Cohen, who had been getting increasingly worried that Bernie hadn't heard from his football prospect, Demetrius Bone.

"I know he got on the plane, Uncle Bernie," the younger man said. "I drove him to the airport myself."

"Well, he never got here," Bernie said. "I got the apartment sitting empty for him, but he never showed."

The mystery of the missing football player didn't concern Bernie as much as a mystery that was developing right under his nose. He'd been married to Rose long enough to know that she was keeping something from him.

It began with that lasagna he found in the refrigerator after getting home from the hospital.

"Who's this Vince Campo fella?" he had asked Rose.

"Just a friend," she had said.

"What building does he live in?"

"He's not from Shady Palms," she said. "He's just some-body in my computer class."

Rose was trying too hard to sound casual, Bernie thought.

"Nice friend," Bernie said. "He must be pretty close to leave you a beautiful lasagna like this. Even your Wonder Walkers friends didn't bring you food."

"No, he's just a friend."

And then Bernie wondered where Lucky, their dog, was. And Rose said, again trying to be casual, that this Vince Campo character was watching the dog.

"Is he married, this guy?" Bernie asked.

"He was," Rose said.

" 'Was' doesn't count," Bernie said. "What's he look like?"

"Bernie!" Rose said. "Are you insinuating that Vince and I are anything but just casual friends?"

"Now, it's 'Vince and I.' Since when do you have male friends? Male friends who make you food and take care of your dog?"

"For your information, Bernie, he made the food for the both of us."

"If it's for the both of us, why can't I have any?"

"Because it has meat in it," she said.

"So then it's not for me," Bernie said.

"He didn't realize ... "

"Or maybe he was just trying to kill me."

"Bernie! Stop it! And I did not ask him to watch Lucky. That was all Lois' doing."

Lois, now there was another mystery under Bernie's nose. Since returning from the hospital, he could tell something was up with Lois, the way she and Rose had been having all these conversations that suddenly stopped the moment Bernie walked into the room.

And then Rose, trying to sound casual again, asked Bernie the other night whether he had seen a green cloth bag lying around the condo.

"No," he had said. "What's in it?"

"Oh, nothing," Rose had said, finding some excuse to suddenly dash off to another room.

And there was something else that bothered Bernie. Yesterday morning, Herman the German called him again to demand that he do something about Lois. It was his usual diatribe about murder, defenseless ducks and how the animals are much nicer than the people at Shady Palms.

"I know zis Rodgers vooman is friend of your vifes," Schmidlapp said. "But she is evil schweinehund."

And that's when Herman said something that surprised him.

"I been keeping eye on her," Schmidlapp said.

"Herman, I thought we already discussed about how the residents in F Building have complained about you and that telescope of yours."

"Not with teleshcope, Hamshtein. Vith own eyes. I see leettle block girl in that vooman's condo. Shtanding on porch."

"I think you must be seeing things, Herman."

"Do you know this vooman keeps block girl?"

Herman was going off the deep end, Bernie thought.

But when he had casually mentioned to Rose what Schmidlapp had said to him, she reacted differently than Bernie had imagined she would.

Sure, she said it was preposterous. But not at first. At first, she recoiled slightly, as if being stung — as if she knew it was true and was shocked to hear that somebody else knew. It was just another one of those things that didn't add up to Bernie.

So, as he walked back from the clubhouse after his brief encounter with Mort and the treadmill, he found himself glancing up at Lois' unit. Nobody was on her porch now, and her car was gone from its assigned parking space.

When he got inside the building, he decided that instead of going straight to his unit, he would walk to Lois' door and listen.

He could hear that the television was on. Well, maybe she left it on when she was out. Some people did that as a safety measure. But then he thought he heard another sound. A cough maybe.

He knocked on the door.

"Lois?"

Nobody answered. He knocked again.

"Lois?"

Something was going on here.

Bernie, who had gotten used to being the hub in C Building's wheel, felt like some busted spoke now, useless and on the outside. It seemed he was privy to nothing any more.

When he walked into his condo, Rose could see the cloud over his face.

"What's the matter, Bernie?"

"Herman the German may be right about somebody in Lois' apartment," he said.

"You don't actually believe that crazy old fool, do you?" she said, but she was looking away.

OK, if that's the way she wanted to play the game, he would play too.

"No, I guess you're right," he said.

He said he was sleepy and was going to take a nap. He went to their room and stretched out on the bed, waiting for her to leave for the supermarket.

When he heard her start up the car from the parking lot below, he got out of bed and began rummaging through Rose's side of the dresser. He knew what he was looking for.

Lois had given her condo key to Rose six months ago. It was right after that woman in G Building slipped in the bathtub and spent two days there before the fireman broke down her door.

He found the loose key in Rose's jewelry box and put it in his pocket. A few minutes later, he was outside Lois' door. He put the key quietly in the lock, opened the door and stepped inside.

13 Miami beached

Demetrius Bone opened his wallet and looked inside, trying to adjust his eyes. Even the poor lighting in the club was sufficient to tell him that what was once an impressive wad of greenbacks had shrunk to a stack small enough to make him no longer want to count.

Surely, it couldn't be enough for another $350 night in that Art Deco hotel up the street on Ocean Drive. Oh, well, this wasn't the time for accounting. Not just yet. Demetrius had been at it for two days now, bouncing around Miami Beach with an explorer's zeal, drinking, dancing and drugging himself into a haze of constant self-gratification.

So far, he had nothing to show for it except a splitting headache, perpetual cotton mouth and the surprise of finding out that the most beautiful woman he had ever met turned out to be a guy.

That was last night. Tonight would be better, Demetrius thought, ordering his third shooter to take the edge off the anxiety building inside him. It had begun earlier in the evening when he tried to put the moves on a waitress at one of those sidewalk restaurants.

"So what do you do?" she had asked.

"NFL football player," he said, trying to sound nonchalant.

"Do you play for the Dolphins?"

"Um, not yet."

"Who do you play for?"

"Um, actually, I'm kind of between teams right now."

He saw her skepticism growing. She had asked him for his name, and he watched as she quietly conferred with another employee at the restaurant, a guy who glanced over at Demetrius and shook his head. Demetrius imagined the conversation, how the guy was telling the waitress that Demetrius Bone wasn't an NFL running back he had ever heard of.

When the waitress returned to his table, she was polite but no longer putting out vibes that he had a chance with her.

"You don't believe me, do you?" he said.

"Do you want potatoes or rice with your entree?"

"I'm not jiving you. You'll see. One day, you're going to be telling people that you met Demetrius Bone, the NFL's leading rusher."

"And one day you're going to say that you were served mahi mahi by a supermodel," she said without smiling.

He choked down his food and left quickly. The exchange had soured him, made him begin to feel like a loser. He needed a pep talk from his agent, who could always be counted on to say what a special player Demetrius was and how success in the NFL was just around the corner.

But, of course, talking to Brad Cohen was out of the question. Cohen wanted him to be in that raisin ranch in Boynton Beach. That was Brad's idea of clawing his way back to the NFL. Brad would be furious with him now, especially the way Demetrius was spending his money.

No time to worry about that now. He would face the future when the money ran out, maybe wait tables on South Beach or do something to make ends meet and come up with his own

NFL plan.

The tequila burned all the way down. He glanced around the bar.

It was nearly midnight, still early by South Beach standards, and the club was just starting to fill with the people who would still be at it when the sun came up. There was something called a foam party, he had heard, a place where people dance in waist-high soap suds. He would have to check that out. Later.

For now, he was content just to sit there at the bar and let the tequila numb his senses.

It was after his fourth tequila that he saw the two big guys walk in the club. They had that walk, that unmistakable swagger of athletes, and about five pounds of gold jewelry on their necks, wrists and fingers. The women they were with were gorgeous and, Demetrius figured, real women.

"Dag!" Demetrius said to the bartender, who was also watching their arrival.

"The NFL is here," he told Demetrius.

"No lie?"

"We get a bunch of the Dolphins here."

Demetrius was drunk enough to think they'd welcome him to their table with open arms. He stood up unsteadily and walked over to their little table to introduce himself.

But before he spoke, one of the guys looked up at Demetrius and waved him off.

"No autographs."

"I don't want your autograph," Demetrius said, pulling up a seat, without sensing how unwelcome he was. "I'm just here to rap, player-to-player."

They looked at him closely now, and Demetrius wished he had been running more regularly like Brad Cohen told him he should. He was getting a little flabby around the waist. And this was the second night on his shirt, which he just realized was probably beginning to stink in South Florida's humidity.

The men quickly sized him up to be an imposter.

"We're here with our ladies," one of them said. "We're not here to talk football with the fans."

"The fans?" Demetrius said. "You think I'm just ... "

"Who do you play with?" the foxy woman sitting next to him asked.

Demetrius could see that the woman's question irritated her guy, who didn't want Demetrius to be around for another second.

"Actually, I'm between teams right now, and ... "

The guys laughed at him, which began to make Demetrius angry.

"You dudes think you're all that!" Demetrius said. "But one day, you're going to be sitting on the sidelines sucking on your oxygen masks while you watch Demetrius Bone tearing it up on the field."

"Demetrius Bone," one of them said, as if to make fun of his name.

The other said, "Tearing it up on the field. The brother here lays sod. He's a groundskeeper."

They high-fived each other, and one of the women giggled so hard she spilled a little bit of her cocktail from the edges of her collagen-enhanced lips.

One of the men looked up and glanced at the door, and a few seconds later, Demetrius felt the unmistakable talon-like grip of the club's bouncer on his right shoulder.

He knew the technique. As a bouncer, he had done it many times before. Exhibit a little display of strength on the unruly drunk customer. A subtle show of force to persuade him it would be in his best interest to leave quietly, rather than make a scene.

Well, it wasn't going to work. Demetrius wasn't going to lose face this badly. Not in front of these guys and their fine women. Not when they had bruised his already fragile ego so cavalierly.

As the bouncer's paw dug into his shoulder, separating muscle from bone, Demetrius willed himself not to scream. Instead, he batted the hand away and faced the bouncer, who turned out to be an enormous bald man with a gold earring in one ear.

"Listen, Mr. Clean," Demetrius said. "Me and my brothers here are having a little talk, so if you don't mind ... "

He did mind, apparently. Because this time, he deftly grabbed Demetrius and had one of his arms twisted behind his back before Demetrius knew what was happening.

"Owww!" Demetrius said, unable to resist shouting from the pain shooting from his twisted arm.

The arm lock had spun him around so that he now had his back to the bouncer and was facing the table with the football players.

As the tears of pain and humiliation swelled in his eyes, he saw them laughing at the spectacle of what was shaping up to be a very ignominious exit.

No way. Demetrius wasn't going to let their encounter end like this. So in the moment before he was about to be dragged backwards out of the club, he picked his right foot off the floor, put the toe of his shoe at the edge of the round table and kicked it over. The toppling table sent a shower of alcohol and broken glass on the players and their dates, who no longer were laughing.

The crash also startled Mr. Clean sufficiently to allow Demetrius to slip out of his grasp and move a few steps away toward the dance floor. Other men might have panicked at this point. But not Demetrius.

He had gotten used to the sight of very large men trying to tackle him. To him, this was no longer a bar fight — it was just football. He put his head down and ran right between the two soggy players, surprising them at the last moment with a side-stepping motion worthy of a highlight film. Even with four tequilas under his belt, Demetrius still had enough legs to spare for these guys, who reached for him but grabbed air, bumping into each other.

Mr. Clean was strong, but he didn't have the agility necessary to catch Demetrius, who hurdled a chair, sidestepped patrons and made it out to the street, untouched.

While in pursuit, the bouncer bounced off people, knocking them aside like bowling pins and slowing himself down each time it happened. But now it was the bouncer and the two football players who had their pride at stake and their evenings ruined. So the three of them didn't hesitate to run out of the club and begin chasing Demetrius up Ocean Drive.

The street was crowded with people, so Demetrius had to weave his way up the sidewalk. He could hear his pursuers coming after him, but he knew they weren't fast enough to catch him.

He wondered if that waitress at that sidewalk restaurant saw him as he darted by, gracefully vaulting a table that was in his way. NFL, baby. Pure NFL material here.

And then trouble. A police officer walking from a side street rounded the corner just in front of Demetrius, who didn't have time to react.

Demetrius put out his hands and tried to stop, but he ended up bumping into the cop.

"Excuse me, officer," he said, taking his hands off the policeman's shoulders and trying to move away.

But the cop grabbed Demetrius by the arm.

"Not so fast," he said. "What's the hurry?"

"Um," Demetrius said. "Just in a rush, that's all. Excuse me."

But the cop didn't let go of his arm.

"Wait a minute, pal."

Demetrius didn't have a minute. Mr. Clean and the two football players were panting their way up the street and yelling for the officer to hold him there.

Demetrius pushed the cop's arm away and started to run but not fast enough this time. One of the football players, he never knew which one, tackled him from behind. Must have been a linebacker, because it was an excellent tackle.

It caught Demetrius in the small of his back, knocking him to the sidewalk like a felled antelope and cutting open his lip. After that, it was all a daze. He remembered getting quite a pummeling, and he remembered all that tequila bubbling back up.

He remembered feeling the handcuffs on him and watching as the men pulled the wallet out of his pocket and took every last dollar.

"Hey, that's my money!" he said.

But the cop just smiled at the others and said, "I don't see any money."

But what he most remembered, as he was being hauled into the back of a squad car and led off to the Miami-Dade County Jail, was that a small group of people had gathered around the players, who had begun signing autographs.

"You should be getting my autograph!" Demetrius shouted from the back seat of the squad car. "I'm the real football player here! Those clowns weren't quick enough to lay a hand on me!"

But nobody was listening to him.

14 A meating of the minds

Lois Rodgers didn't expect to see Bernie Hamstein sitting on her couch and watching *Oprah!* with the Haitian girl.

"Bernie, what are you doing here?"

"Yolette and I were just getting acquainted," he said.

Lois had shopping bags in her hands and daggers in her eyes.

"She didn't call me," Bernie said. "I let myself in. I used your key, the one you gave Rose."

"Since when do you think you can just waltz in here and ..."

"Herman the German told me he had seen the girl here, and ... "

"Great! How many other people know?"

"Besides Rose?"

"She told you?"

"No. But I've been wondering what you two had been whispering about behind my back these past couple of days," Bernie said. "Since my heart attack, I've been left out of a lot of secrets around here."

Lois put her shopping bags down and walked into the kitchen to pour herself a glass of wine.

"I take it Rose doesn't know you're here right now," she said.

"She thinks I'm taking a nap. I waited for her to go shopping."

Yolette just sat there, attentive but silent.

"I can't believe I got myself in this situation," Lois said. "It was Ricardo's fault. I should have just said 'no' from the very beginning."

"How is Ricardo?"

"His jaw is wired shut — that's the good news. They say he might be out of the hospital tomorrow. Then he's going to have to deal with the girl. I've done more than my share."

Bernie patted the girl on her knee.

"We've got to help Yolette find her father," Bernie said.

Lois rolled her eyes.

"At this point, I just want her out of here before the INS finds me," Lois said. "If Herman Schmidlapp knows, it won't take long for somebody to come breaking the door down here."

"Nobody's going to come breaking down your door, Lois," Bernie said. "But you do have to worry about Herman the German over those ducks. He went to Mort Granger, and it's going to be all over *The Gazette*."

Lois took a big gulp of her wine and shook her head.

"I didn't kill those ducks on purpose," Lois said. "I was aiming for Herman."

"I'll tell him that," Bernie said. "I'm sure it will make him feel better."

Lois rummaged through her bags until she found the one from Limited Too. After visiting Ricardo in the hospital, she made a therapeutic trip to the Saks Fifth Avenue in The Gardens mall. But she soon found herself in the Limited Too, a store devoted to fashions for pre-pubescent girls.

Lois had been to malls thousands of times and had never

ventured into that store. But there she was, going through the racks, imagining what size Yolette would wear, and picking out an armful of outfits.

"Here," she said to the girl, handing her the bulging bag of brightly colored clothes. "Go in the bathroom and try these on and see it they fit."

She could see Yolette's guarded demeanor melt when she saw the clothes. She pulled them out of the bag and stroked them as if they were a beloved pet. Her eyes widened, and the corners of her mouth poked up in the beginnings of a smile.

"Go ahead," Lois said. "Try them on."

The girl took the bag into the bathroom and shut the door.

"You're doing a great thing, Lois," Bernie said.

"I'm just tired of looking at her in the same clothes day after day," she said.

But she did get a thrill out of shopping for the girl, although she wasn't about to admit that to Bernie Hamstein.

"Now, give me that key," she said to him, holding out her hand. "I don't want you to make a habit of breaking into my condo."

He handed it to her.

"As long as I'm going to be in trouble with Rose, do you have a piece of meat you can feed me — a roast beef sandwich, maybe?" he said.

"Bernie, I refuse to be an instrument of your death."

"One little sandwich isn't going to hurt," he said. "Do you know what it's like eating bean curd every day? That's what will kill me."

"Will you take the girl off my hands?"

"Take the girl? Why can't she just stay here until we find her father?"

"Because I don't want to go to jail, Bernie. You know the way information spreads around here."

Yolette walked out of the bathroom, wearing an orange and yellow polka-dotted top with matching yellow shorts. She looked adorable, Lois thought. The girl smiled as she stood before them.

"OK, that fits," Lois said. "Try on the next outfit."

Bernie waited until Yolette was back in the bathroom before he spoke.

"See?" he said. "There's a mother in you, after all. This is doing you good."

"When Mort Granger writes, 'Shady Palms Woman Harbors Illegal Alien,' that won't do me much good," she said.

"I think you're letting your imagination run away with you, Lois," Bernie said.

The phone rang. Lois walked over to pick it up.

"Hello? ... Yes ... No ... No! ... Listen, before you make accusations like that, I think you need to get your facts straight and stop believing the delusional rantings of a crazy old man! ... I have a cleaning lady who comes once a week. That's probably who he saw."

She slammed the phone down and stood before Bernie, shaking.

"My imagination, Bernie? That was Herb Troutman. Apparently, our friend Herman has already gone to the chairman of the board."

Yolette was back with a powder blue dress. She twirled around in front of them with her arms stretched wide, as if she were a fashion model.

"It is beautiful," she told the adults.

But neither of them was smiling now.

"It fits," Yolette said, fearful that they did not like it and would not let her keep it. "It fits just fine, do you not think so, Ms. Lois?"

Lois nodded.

"Yes," she said. "You've got one more outfit to try on."

When Yolette was back in the bathroom, Bernie told Lois his plan.

There was an empty condo down the hall, 26C. Bernie was holding it for a renter who never showed up. They could set the girl up in there. Bring her food. Give her a television to watch. Magazines. Whatever it would take to keep her comfortable and quiet.

"We'll find her father, and she'll be out of there before anybody knows what happened," Bernie said.

"I don't know," Lois said. "It's still harboring an alien."

"You want to call the INS on her now?"

Lois had to admit she didn't. Yolette was a rock around her neck, but she wasn't a difficult child. She was polite and obedient, and although she had suffered quite a bit in her young life, she had a sense of dignity that Lois admired. She had treated the girl like a subhuman guest, and the girl had still managed to be grateful for it.

Buying the clothes for her, Lois now realized, was actually as much for Lois as it was for the girl. Somehow, it was a way for Lois to acknowledge to herself that she needed to be a better person to this child, who had asked for so little and received even less.

"No," Lois told Bernie. "I don't think I could just hand her over."

Yolette was back with a lime green outfit that highlighted her flawless eggplant-hued skin.

"Which outfit would you like to keep?" Lois said.

If Yolette was disappointed in being told she could not have all three outfits, she did not show it. She furrowed her brow and thought about it. There was no trace of disappointment in finding out that life had, once again, offered her less than she had imagined.

"I'm only teasing," Lois said, suddenly sad to witness the girl's acquiescence. "You can have all three outfits."

"Do you mean it, Ms. Lois?" the girl asked.

"They all look so good, it would be hard to choose just one," Lois said. "So you might as well keep them all."

The girl rushed forward and hugged Lois. It was the first time they had touched in the three days they had lived together. The girl hugged her tightly, and Yolette did not seem to mind that Lois' body was frozen and that the older woman did not wrap her arms around the girl's back.

"Well," Lois said, waiting for the girl to release her grip.

When she did, stepping back and smiling at Lois, she thanked her again. Lois waved the girl away but still felt the sensation of her embrace on her.

Yolette went back to the bathroom to get her new clothes.

"OK," she said to Bernie. "We set her up in that empty condo."

Bernie smiled. "Perfect. Now, how about that sandwich?"

"The roast beef is on the second shelf of the refrigerator," Lois said. "But I'm not making it for you, Bernie. You're going to have to kill yourself."

He scampered to the kitchen and began making himself an enormous sandwich.

"Tell me about this Vince Campo guy," he said as he returned to the living room with mayonnaise dripping between his fingers. "What's he want with my wife?"

"Ask Rose, don't ask me," Lois said.

"That's just it," Bernie said. "Every time I try to talk about him, Rose shuts me down. And yet, the guy's got our dog, he's dropping off casseroles at the condo ... "

"He stole my jewelry, Bernie."

"No!"

"Yes," she said. "I had a lot of my jewelry in a green cloth bag. I left it on a table when I was talking to him, and now the bag is gone."

"Son of a ... "

"Watch out for him, Bernie."

"And Rose? Why is she so protective of him?"

"Bernie, I don't want to get in the middle of your marriage."

"What are you saying, Lois?"

"I'm saying, watch out for this guy. Have you ever met him?"

"No."

"Well, he's smooth, good-looking and extremely charming."

"More charming than me?"

Lois didn't say anything.

"Lois, you don't think Rose ... I mean, we been married 47 years and she ... I mean, you don't think she's actually, you know, thinking about, you know."

"I just know that you need to watch out for him, that's all."

Yolette was back in the room, all smiles. Lois told her the plan to move her to 26C.

"Don't worry," Bernie said. "We'll be looking out for you."

The little girl seemed happy.

"So, Mr. Bernie, you will help me find my father, too?"

"Yes," Bernie said.

But the guy he was thinking about now was Vince Campo.

"Thanks for the heads-up," he told Lois before heading back to his condo. "And thanks for the roast beef."

Lois winked at him.

"What roast beef?"

15 Bad boys

Demetrius Bone was released the next morning from the Miami-Dade County Jail with an empty wallet, a puke-stained shirt and the unbearable stench of defeat.

As he walked the streets near the jail, a tangle of highway underpasses strewn with litter and neglected grassy medians, he had a sinking feeling that Miami Beach was far away. It took him most of the day to walk there. It rained on him one moment, and a few minutes later, the sun would beat down so fiercely that he wished for the downpour he had recently cursed.

The police eyed him suspiciously. Respectable people inside their air-conditioned cars locked their doors when he crossed in front of them. And the homeless looked on him as one of their own.

By the time he walked across the MacArthur Causeway and into Miami Beach, his feet were blistered, his head pounded and his stomach groaned for food. He was no longer able to blend into the scenery of Ocean Drive. Even though its sidewalks were crowded, he could swing his arms in any direction and not manage to touch anyone.

He tried to get into the hotel where he had been staying. But he was stopped in the lobby.

"I'm a guest here," he explained. "Demetrius Bone, room 215."

"Mr. Bone, your bill, which we placed under your door yesterday, explained that unless we received $853 from you, you would not be able to stay here any longer," the man at the desk said.

"I'm going to give you the money," Bone said. "But I need to get my clothes first."

Bone didn't have any money in his suitcase. But that was a problem he'd deal with after getting a hot shower, a shave and fresh change of clothes.

"Your clothes have been locked up by the concierge. You'll get them after you pay your bill."

"You can't keep my clothes! Give them back to me now."

"Sir, if you give us a credit card we can ... "

"I don't have a credit card," he said. "I have a future, and if you don't help me out right now, you'll regret it. When I'm the toast of the town, I'm going to remember this flea-bag place. You think you're so hot with all this Art Deco crap. Well, I've got news for you. Art Deco is just old. That's all it is. Just old junk."

He was raising his voice. Other people in the lobby now didn't try to hide the fact that they were listening. Newspapers were lowered into laps. Elevators came and went without anybody getting on. A second man behind the desk quietly dialed 911.

Demetrius saw it and heard the man's soft voice imploring the police to arrive.

"The next time, I'm staying at one of those modern hotels. A new one, that doesn't have people who think they're better than everybody else, just because they are in an Art Deco building. Just because some wrecking ball was stopped from doing what it should have done."

No sense waiting for the police to arrive. He didn't feel like spending another night in jail, so he walked out of the hotel. And as soon as he hit the street, he started running, looking for back alleys whenever possible.

He found a pay phone a few blocks away from the beach and dialed the number of his agent, Brad Cohen.

He hated to do this, but there was no other way.

"Brad."

"Demetrius, where the hell are you?"

"Miami Beach."

"I've been sick worrying about you, calling my Uncle Bernie for the past two days, wondering what happened to you. What are you doing in Miami Beach?"

"Chilling."

"Chilling, my eye. You're supposed to be in Boynton Beach, working out, living a sensible life, being a good citizen."

"Yeah, well I thought I'd be a good citizen in Miami Beach for a while."

"Don't lie to me Demetrius. I know you're not there to visit the Holocaust memorial. You're boozing and womanizing again. I didn't send you cross country to do what you were already doing in L.A."

"Brad, I'm just checking out my future fans here in Miami."

"And so why did you call? Let me guess, you're in jail."

"You've got a wild imagination, Brad," Demetrius said. "No, I was just wondering if you could advance me some money. Maybe wire it through Western Union. They got one here at ... "

"Hold on a second, Demetrius. Correct me if I'm wrong, but didn't I give you $3,000 in cash just three days ago? Don't tell me you ... "

"Just another couple grand will get me through ... "

"You did! I don't believe it! You already blew $3,000!"

"Brad, it's not what you think. You see, there were these

couple of dudes in this club and ... "

"I don't want to hear it, Demetrius."

" ... and this crooked cop, he ... "

"Demetrius, I don't want to hear it. Save your breath."

"C'mon, this is the last time I'll ask for you for an advance."

"Didn't you even go to Boynton Beach?"

"I went there. They said your man, Bernie, was in the hospital. The gate guard wouldn't even let me in. He treated me like I was some landscaper coming to apply for a job."

"And so you go to Miami Beach?"

"C'mon Brad. That Shady Palms place looked worse than Miami's jail."

"So, you have been to jail already."

"Just passed through," Demetrius said. "No big deal."

"I'm not giving you any more money, Demetrius."

"Brad, what am I supposed to do?"

"You're supposed to be living in Shady Palms."

"That's unreasonable. There are just old white people there."

"You didn't give it a chance."

"I gave it as much of a chance as it's getting."

"Then we have nothing to talk about, Demetrius."

"You flew me out here, Brad. The least you can do is get me back."

"Goodbye, Demetrius."

"What do you mean, 'Goodbye, Demetrius'?"

"I mean that you'll have to find yourself another agent, because I'm through with you."

"C'mon, Brad. Last chance?"

"No. Not unless you're willing to give Shady Palms a try."

"No way, Brad. There's just no way I can ... "

And then he heard the dial tone. The agent had hung up on him.

Demetrius banged the phone down on its cradle and started to walk away. Then he saw the police cruiser heading slowly up the block. He ducked into an alley and waited for it to pass.

When the coast looked clear, he went back to the phone booth and dialed up the agent's number again.

"I changed my mind," he said to Brad Cohen.

"You sure?"

"Yes, Brad. Just send me a couple of grand, and that will give me enough money to pay off my hotel bill here, get my clothes back and rent a car."

"No, Demetrius. That's not the way it's going to be. You're not getting another dime from me."

"But I thought you said ... "

"Give me the phone number where you are. I'll call you back in a few minutes."

■ ■ ■

Three hours later, as previously arranged, Demetrius was standing in front of the Fontainebleau hotel, when he heard the toot of a car horn. The Toyota Camry's automatic window on the passenger side went down.

"Demetrius?"

"Bernie?"

He got in next to the old man, grateful to be out of the South Florida humidity and conscious of how smelly he was.

"Sorry about my current condition."

"That's all right," the old man said. "My nephew said to expect the worst."

And he smiled at the younger man. So, this was Uncle Bernie. Demetrius could see from his forearms that he once had been physically strong. And he didn't seem to act with the typical kind of fearful alarm that Demetrius had come to expect from people the old man's age and color.

"I'm sorry to be putting you out," Demetrius said.

"No, it's a pleasure," Bernie said. "First time I got to drive since the heart attack. Doctor says I shouldn't, and the wife, Rose — wait till you meet Rose, what a pistol — anyway Rose has been chauffeuring me around like an invalid."

"So how did you spring yourself?"

"She's out at her computer class. Fortunately, it was one of her friend's turn to drive. So the car was just sitting there. I was thinking of coming up with some reason to make a jail break, and then Brad called up, and bingo, here I am."

Bernie navigated his way out of Miami Beach.

"What about my suitcases at the hotel?" Demetrius asked.

"They're in the trunk," Bernie said. "Brad wired the money to the hotel. I picked up your bags before I got you."

The men talked amiably as Bernie drove north on Interstate 95, and Demetrius expounded on his first impression of Shady Palms.

"You think it's bad now?" Bernie said. "Wait until you get to know the people there. Your impression will get worse."

Demetrius looked at Bernie to see if he was smiling. But the old man appeared to be serious, until he looked across at Demetrius and winked.

"Bernie, you're a trip!"

"The key to being happy in a condo is learning which neighbors to avoid like the plague," Bernie said. "Unfortunately, it's usually more than half the population."

This time Bernie didn't wink.

"Dag!" Demetrius said.

Bernie expounded on his condo philosophy, which to Demetrius, sounded very similar to the advice he once got on how to survive in prison.

"But we'll have some fun," Bernie said.

Demetrius wasn't sure any more, and a part of him had begun regretting that he didn't try to tough it out in Miami

Beach for at least another day.

"There's something else I've got to tell you," Bernie said, "and it's got to be kept quiet. I didn't know you would show up, today, so I have a girl living in your unit right now."

"Dag!" Demetrius said. "You stashin' a little honey right under your wife's nose, Bernie! You the man!"

Demetrius imagined what Bernie considered "a girl" — probably some wrinkly old white woman in her 60s, instead of her 70s.

"Rose knows about her," Bernie said.

"Dag!"

"Demetrius, when I say a girl, I mean a girl — I'm talking about 11 years old."

He told Demetrius the story of Yolette.

"I haven't figured out how we're going to work it out," he told Demetrius. "Meanwhile, are you hungry?"

"Starving. I haven't had anything to eat since that sorry excuse for a breakfast in jail."

Bernie pulled off the highway in Boynton Beach and into a Checkers burger joint. He ordered two double-cheeseburgers with bacon, handing one to Demetrius and taking the other one himself.

They sat in the parking lot and ate.

"Don't tell Rose about this," Bernie said, raising the burger mound in his hand. "I'm supposed to be on a meatless diet."

The double-cheeseburger improved Demetrius' spirits. He looked over at Bernie, who was eating with his eyes closed.

"Bernie, I believe we're just a couple of bad boys."

16 A mission to Margo

Rose Hamstein walked into her adult education computer class with a sense of fear and expectation. She didn't know what to think of Vince Campo, who was sitting there beaming at her as she took her seat at the next terminal.

"How you doin', kiddo?" he said.

Rose nearly blurted out, "Where's Lois' jewelry?" but instead, she turned red and stammered, "Bernie seems to be improving."

"That's great," he said.

She looked for a trace of insincerity in his face but couldn't see any. She had gotten tired of defending him during the past couple of days. Ever since meeting him, her friends had warned her to be careful, that he was a home wrecker.

And now, Lois was accusing him of being a jewel thief, too.

But Rose had a better opinion of him than her friends. She saw something different in Vince Campo, something she couldn't define but trusted was there.

"How's Lucky?"

"He gets along great with Judy and Barbra. You should see the three of them, running in circles around the furniture, chasing each other."

"I appreciate you taking care of Lucky while Bernie was in the hospital," Rose said. "But now that he's home, I ought to take Lucky back."

The last thing Rose wanted was to have Vince Campo knock on her door. She didn't want him anywhere near Bernie, who, like her friends, had grown suspicious. Just this morning, Bernie began another rant about Vince.

"I mean, we don't know anything about this guy," Bernie was saying. "He could be a serial killer. Or a thief."

One of her friends must have told Bernie about the jewelry. Why else would he use the word "thief" with Vince Campo? Rose would have to bring up the subject at tomorrow morning's Wonder Walkers session in the mall. But for now, she just needed to arrange a way to get her dog back.

"I can drive up from Boca and return Lucky to you," Vince said. "I'd like to meet Bernie, too."

"Well, that's nice of you, Vince, but ... but, I don't think Bernie should have much company right now. He pretty much sleeps all day."

"Oh, right. I'm sorry," Vince said. "Then, maybe you can come down to my place sometime."

"I don't want to trouble you, maybe we could just meet halfway and ... "

"I've got an idea," Vince said. "Tomorrow. Come by for lunch. I've wanted to show you my home, anyway. This will be perfect. We can eat outside. I just bought this new umbrella table for the patio, and I've been looking for an excuse to use it."

"Well, I don't know if ... I mean, Bernie may need me."

"Do you have to watch him sleep?" Vince asked, then smiled, placing a hand on her knee.

Rose nearly jumped when he did that. He had never placed his hand on her before. Not in such a familiar way like that. She was turning red again.

"Maybe I'll bring Bernie," she said.

"Sure," he said. "Bring Bernie."

Once again, Rose couldn't see a trace of insincerity in his voice. Maybe she was just imagining things, getting worked up over nothing, all because of her overprotective friends. Vince Campo wasn't being a wolf. He was just being a friend. He didn't mean anything by that hand on her knee, she told herself.

"On second thought," she said, "maybe I'll leave him home. He just gets cranky when I drag him out with me, because he's not supposed to drive yet. He's the worst back-seat driver, always telling me I'm going too fast or too slow or I'm in the wrong lane."

So it was set. Rose would be there for lunch the next day. Now, she would just have to figure out a way to make sure Bernie didn't come with her.

The rest of the class passed without incident. She and Vince laughed and joked like they always did, and he constantly asked her how to do simple functions on the computer, ones he never seemed to remember from previous classes.

"You ought to pay better attention," she told him once.

"I just don't have a head for this stuff, Rose," he said. "Song lyrics, I never forget. But this stuff? In one ear and out the other."

On the way home from class, Rose's friend, Jacqui, pumped her for information, and like the rest of her friends, gave her plenty of unsolicited advice.

"So, a lunch date?"

"It's not a lunch date, Jacqui," Rose said. "I'm going there to pick up my dog."

"And the two of you will be having lunch together?"

"Yes."

"I call that a lunch date," Jacqui said.

"I call that picking up the dog."

"And so, did you do what Lois asked you to do?"

Lois had insisted that Rose confront Vince about the missing jewelry bag, even going so far as to suggest that she knew Vince had the bag. But Rose refused to be that confrontational, especially since she didn't believe Vince was a thief.

"I asked him if he had seen a green bag while he was in my condo," Rose said. "And he said, 'What sort of green bag?'"

Rose tried to persuade her friend that Vince Campo seemed honest when denying any knowledge of the jewelry bag.

"What did you expect he'd say?" Jacqui asked. "He's not going to say, 'Oh, yeah, the jewelry bag I stole! Now, I remember.'"

"I don't think he stole anything," Rose said.

But a part of her wasn't sure.

When she got back to Shady Palms, she was surprised to see that her car was missing from its parking space.

"I'm going to kill that husband of mine before his heart does," she told Jacqui. "He knows he's not supposed to be driving."

There was no note in the condo, either. Rose began rehearsing the lecture she would give Bernie when he walked in the door. But she was distracted, having to also think about how her husband would react to her having lunch with Vince the next day.

He'd probably say something like, "Well, don't wear any jewelry."

Rose wished there were some way she could put that jewel thief talk to rest. Lois was so flighty, she probably lost or misplaced her jewelry on her own and was now blaming it on Vince. Then Rose got an idea.

She dialed the West Palm Beach telephone number.

"Hello?"

"Margo, I hope I'm not calling too late."

Rose Hamstein wants to trust her new friend, Vince Campo, but she can't resist making a call to her daughter-in-law, Margo, to check up on Vince.

"No, no. Sam is putting your grandson to sleep, and I was just watching TV. How's Bernie? Everything all right?"

"I guess. After spending days praying that he wouldn't die, I'm back to saying that I ought to kill him."

"That's a good sign," Margo said.

"Yeah. He's out driving the car tonight, the moron. Probably buying Lotto tickets. Anyway, I didn't call to talk about Bernie. I need to ask you for a favor."

"Sure, Rose."

"I remember you said that with these computers at the Sheriff's Office you can find out all sorts of things about people. Like whether they were convicted of a crime or spent any time in prison. Things like that."

"Yes."

"There's somebody I'd like you to check out."

"You've got a suspicious character there at Shady Palms?" Margo said. "If you'd like, maybe I can ask one of the guys in the patrol division to swing by tomorrow."

"No, Margo. It's not somebody here, and it's really just an

informal thing. If you can keep it unofficial, I'd appreciate it."

"OK, fine. I can check this person out myself. During my lunch break tomorrow. How's that?"

"Perfect. The name is Vince Campo. C-A-M-P-O."

"Do you have his date of birth?"

Rose was surprised to realize she did. Vince had once mentioned to her that he was born on the Fourth of July. And he said he was coming up on Social Security age next year. So that made him 64.

"I'll run the name and the D.O.B. and see what I come up with," Margo said. "So, what's the deal with this Vince Campo character?"

"Oh, nothing," Rose said, trying to sound casual.

"Is he the new renter in my old unit there?" Margo asked.

"No, that's a whole other story," Rose said. "It's best you know nothing about that."

"Ah, Shady Palms," Margo said. "The land of ten thousand secrets."

"And please, don't mention any of this Vince Campo business to Bernie, either."

"Make that ten thousand and one secrets," Margo said.

Rose heard the key in the door. Bernie was back.

"Gotta go," Rose said, "Bye."

She hung up the phone as Bernie walked inside the condo. He looked at her.

"On the phone with Vince Campo?"

"Don't change the subject, Bernie."

"I didn't know there was a subject."

"The subject is you driving the car. At night, too. I hope you didn't go any farther than the clubhouse."

"I went to Miami Beach."

"Very funny."

"So how was Vince Campo?"

Rose moved over to her husband.

"Don't be silly."

She put her arms around him and put her head on his chest, conscious of hearing his heart beating under his shirt.

"I could never be with anybody but you," she said.

"When is he going to give us back our dog?"

"I'm going to get Lucky tomorrow," Rose said. "We're going ... I'm going to meet him halfway between here and Boca, and he's going to hand me the dog."

"You should invite him up here and let me meet him."

"Bernie, stop being impossible. Believe me, the only thing you've got to worry about is your heart."

"I'm not worried about my heart," he said. "You're worried about my heart."

"It's because I want you around for many more years," she said. "I want to grow old together."

"Rose, we're already old together."

"Speak for yourself," she said, snuggling closer to him.

Then she looked up and kissed him. It was one of those kisses that had, over the past 47 years, signaled more than just a casual sign of affection. Bernie's brain sent a messenger to his heart, which began dispatching troops to the south.

But a moment later, Rose pulled away. Repulsed. Disappointed. And suddenly in a mood that was significantly less than romantic.

She glared at her husband and ran her tongue over her lips, before uttering the single word of condemnation.

"Bacon!"

17 A sight for sore eyes

The girl was watching television in 26C when Bernie walked in with Demetrius.

"Yolette, I'd like you to meet your temporary roommate," Bernie said. "Mr. Bone here is going to help you find your father, too."

Bernie didn't say anything about that to Demetrius, who looked at the old man now and wondered what sort of other arrangements had been decided before his arrival.

"When Brad gave me some money to furnish this place for you, I got a hide-a-bed for the living room," Bernie said, pointing to the couch where the girl was sitting. "You can fight it out who gets the bedroom and who gets the hide-a-bed."

Yolette looked at Demetrius and smiled.

"I do not mind," she said.

"Good," Demetrius said. "I'll take the bedroom then."

He carried his suitcases to the bedroom and plopped down on the mattress, grateful to be somewhere he would get a decent night of sleep.

"I'm going to leave you two to get acquainted," Bernie said. "I've got to get back to my place and face the music with Rose. I'll see you in the morning."

Haitian castaway Yolette shows Demetrius Bone the photo of the father she is hoping to find in America.

Demetrius, in no mood to nurture the girl's hopes, is more interested in getting a good night's sleep.

Demetrius waved Bernie away, without getting up from the bed. He was suddenly exhausted. He would get a long, hot soapy shower and then sleep for about 12 hours, he thought.

He opened one of his suitcases until he found some clean clothes and his shaving kit and then headed off to the room down the hall.

Fifteen minutes later, he emerged from the bathroom with a freshly shaved face and a handful of dirty clothes that were going straight to the trash.

The little girl, he noticed, had stopped watching television. She was standing outside his door with a photo in her hand.

"What's that?" he asked.

She showed him the photo of the man, who looked about Demetrius' age.

"That is my father," she said.

"Nice," he said, handing the picture back to her. "Well, I'll be going to sleep now."

But she stayed there at the entrance to his door.

"You will help me find my father, Mr. Bone?"

"Listen Yolanda ... "

"Yolette."

" ... I'm here to get in shape to play football."

"Mr. Bernie said that you ... "

"Yeah, Mr. Bernie, he says a lot of things. But I don't work for Mr. Bernie."

"Oh," she said, tucking the photo away in a plastic bag that held a business-sized envelope.

"You got money in that envelope?"

"No. That is a letter for my father."

"What does it say?"

"I do not know. It is just for my father to read."

"If you can find him," he said.

"We will ... I will find him," she said.

"Yeah, well, I wouldn't get your hopes up. Fathers aren't all they're cracked up to be. I'd just stick close to your momma if I was you."

He could see the girl's eyes well up.

"My mother, she sent me here to be with my father."

"You and me, Yolette. People are just sending us off without asking whether we want to go. Doesn't seem right, does it?"

"No," she said.

He got in bed and was ready to turn out the light when he realized the little girl still hadn't moved from the doorway.

"Goodnight."

"Are you the father to anyone?" she asked.

"Hell, no."

"You do not wish to be a father?"

"I'm too young," he said. "I've got a big career in front of me. Kids just hold you back."

"Oh," she said.

"Goodnight."

But she did not move.

"Do you think I held back my father?"

"Damn, Yolette. I don't know," he said. Then seeing that she still was troubled by the thought, he added, "Obviously not, or else he wouldn't have left you and your momma."

But that just made her frown more. Why couldn't this little girl just leave him alone? If this kept up, he would have to ask Bernie for a private apartment.

"Goodnight," he said, again. "I've had a long day and need to get some sleep."

"Where is your father?" she asked.

"Yolette, we can talk in the morning."

"Did you hold him back, too?"

"I got an idea," he said, getting out of bed. "How about I walk you back out to the living room and help you get in that hide-a-bed."

She smiled at that. So he followed her out and tucked her in. She looked up at him expectantly, as if he was supposed to do or say something as he hovered over her. But Demetrius had no idea what that might be.

He was the next superstar running back in the NFL, not a nanny for some Haitian girl. Eddie George didn't have to baby-sit. Jamal Anderson didn't have to play house in order to get a good night's sleep. The only females he should be tucking in were some of those models he saw from afar on Miami Beach. This was embarrassing.

"Go to sleep," he told her.

He went back to the bedroom, closing the door for emphasis, and in five minutes was sound asleep.

But not for long. He was startled awake shortly afterward by the girl standing next to his bed and shaking his shoulders.

"Someone is at the door!" the girl whispered.

He could hear the gentle knocking on the front door of the condo.

"Well, answer it," he said.

"No," Yolette said. "Remember? I have to hide."

"Dag!" Demetrius said, rubbing his eyes and throwing off the sheets. He was in no mood for this. Whoever it was had better have a good reason to be there, he thought.

"What the hell do you want?" he said, throwing open the door.

■ ■ ■

Lois Rodgers had spent a frustrating evening with Ricardo, who was released from the hospital that afternoon and had returned to his Palm Beach home. She used to think that his speaking pattern was annoying, the way he always referred to himself as "Ricardo."

But Ricardo with his jaw wired shut turned out to be equally annoying. Being with him was like constantly being on a game show, always trying to make sense of the picture puzzle he was drawing.

His lack of literacy in the English language made communication difficult between them. Ricardo didn't seem to mind. He sat there like a sketch artist, doodling away on a little pad of paper he carried around with him.

She could get the simple stuff. For example, the letter "U" followed by a drawing of a bottle was his way of asking her if she wanted something to drink. Simple enough. But communicating that tomorrow he wanted to begin looking for Yolette's father turned into a game of charades that lasted for 15 minutes.

By the time she left him and began driving back to Shady Palms, it was nearly 10 o'clock. As she pulled into her parking space, she thought of how nice it was going to be to walk into her condo and not find the television on and that little castaway staring at her from the couch. Maybe now she could get her life back and some of the freedom she had lost while keeping Yolette. No meals to fix her. No idle conversation to make. No questions to answer.

Just peace and quiet.

But as Lois walked into C Building, she found herself wondering how Yolette was doing in 26C. Lois couldn't imagine what it would be like to be alone in a foreign country the way Yolette was.

Was she crying herself to sleep tonight in that empty apartment? Was she hungry? Frightened? Afraid to do anything but stay in one place, like she had been in Lois' condo?

Lois had begun to feel guilty about her behavior. If she had been more generous to the girl, she wouldn't have assumed that she was a thief, an assumption that led to the real thief — Vince Campo — stealing her jewels, Lois thought. She could have been kinder to the girl, even though she was an imposition on her life, Lois thought.

Buying her those outfits from Limited Too was a start but not enough to completely assuage Lois' conscience.

So, as she held her key ring in her hand, selecting the key to the front door of her condo, she walked instead to 26C. She wasn't going to invite the girl to stay with her, that's for sure. But what harm could there be in just checking in to say goodnight?

She knocked on the door and waited. She knocked again. And again.

When the door flew open, she was shocked to see a young, muscular black man fill the other side of the doorway. He said something in a loud and hostile voice, and Lois' hand immediately reached for the little Mace canister she kept on her key ring.

Lois had kept Mace on her keys since she was mugged in a West Palm Beach parking garage last year. And she had managed to use it a few times already, squirting a UPS driver and a Jehovah's Witness (both in accidental panic), and a man who fought with her for the last unblemished nectarine at Publix (with intentional zeal). It's a good thing her friends hadn't suggested she get a gun.

The large shirtless man filling the doorway seemed like a good enough reason for Lois to reach for the Mace again. She squirted the man with a quick blast to the eyes. He recoiled, rubbing his eyes and howling. And as he crumbled back into the apartment, Yolette rushed toward Lois with her arms out.

"Oh, Ms. Lois, what have you done to Demetrius?"

"Who's Demetrius?" she asked unnecessarily, as the big man cursed her passionately while making his way to the bathroom.

"There's no need to be crude," Lois shouted to him, then softly to Yolette, "Is that man bothering you?"

"No," Yolette said. "Mr. Bernie, he brought him here to stay."

"With you?"

"Yes," she said.

"Who is he?"

Just then Demetrius returned from the bathroom, and while he was able to wash the Mace off his face, he wasn't able to wash away his anger.

"Who are you?" he shouted as he walked toward her.

"Don't come any closer!" Lois said.

"You're a crazy woman, spraying me with that stuff."

"I said, don't come any closer," Lois said.

But Demetrius was too angry to obey Lois' simple request, and having never met Lois before, he had no idea of how capable she could be of ruining a person's day.

"I ought to sue you, that's what I ought to do," he said. "If there's any damage to my eyes, and I have trouble catching the football, I'm going to take you to court for all you're worth, you silly old ... "

He didn't get the rest of his sentence out.

Psssshhh.

Lois gave him another blast in the face.

"I told you not to come any closer," she said matter-of-factly, then she turned her attention back to Yolette. "As you were saying, deary?"

18 Adjusting with Bernie

Bernie Hamstein noticed that his wife looked too dressed up for someone who was just going to pick up a dog.

"Is there a new dress code for I-95?" he said, watching Rose apply makeup in front of their bathroom mirror.

Bernie thought his wife was retrieving their dog, Lucky, in a roadside swap. But Rose was actually getting dressed up because she was going to Vince Campo's house in Boca Raton to get the dog. It was a misapprehension on Bernie's part that Rose had no intention to correct. She quickly sidetracked him by going on the offensive.

"I hope you'll just rest while I'm gone," she said. "Don't worry about the little Haitian girl."

But Rose knew that was too much to ask. For even though Bernie had a bad heart, he had a good one, too. So she didn't press him on that, not like she did about food.

"If you're hungry, make yourself a Not Dog."

"Just because somebody shapes tofu in the shape of a hot dog doesn't mean you should treat it like a hot dog," he said.

She looked at him, shook her head and walked by him to get her purse. Bernie was glad she'd be out of his way for a little while. He needed the time to straighten out some condo business, the kind of business Rose was insisting he give up.

As soon as she was gone, he dialed Herb Troutman's condo. Troutman had called earlier that morning. But Rose, who picked up the phone, wouldn't let Bernie talk, telling the Shady Palms board of directors chairman that Bernie was "resting and couldn't be disturbed."

"What's up, Herb?"

"Bernie, that you?"

"Yeah."

"I hope you're through resting, because you got some problems that need addressing in C Building."

"What the matter, Herb?"

"For starters, 26C is the matter. Are you trying to pull a fast one on us, Bernie? Sneaking somebody in there and thinking nobody will notice?"

Bernie's heart sank. Troutman must have found Yolette.

"Listen, Herb. I can explain. I hope you didn't call the ... "

"I saw him this morning," Troutman said, cutting Bernie off.

Him. Troutman was talking about Demetrius, not Yolette. Bernie was relieved.

"Oh, him," Bernie said.

"He went out jogging early this morning in nothing but a pair of gym shorts and sneakers. Scared half the tennis ladies to death. And he had these bloodshot eyes. I think he was already drinking. Three people called the police claiming a burglar was on the loose at Shady Palms."

Bernie went on the offensive.

"Thanks for telling me, Herb. I'll go talk to Demetrius this morning and apologize for the racist behavior of some of our neighbors."

"Bernie! Don't play games with me. This has nothing to do with racism. This is just another example of you using bad judgment."

"Wait a minute, Herb. Is there something in the condo documents that says African-Americans can't live here?"

"Look around you, for cryin' out loud, Bernie. Other than that one lady in your building, there are no black residents here."

"Now there's Demetrius."

"I thought he was Greek. Didn't you tell me he was Greek?"

"I think when I handed you the application, I said Demetrius was a Greek name. I might have said that. But I never said that Demetrius was Greek."

"Once again, Hamstein, you're disrupting the social order here at Shady Palms. The last person you allowed to rent in 26C was a pregnant undercover detective ... "

"Hey, watch what you say about my daughter-in-law, Herb."

" ... and now you got some big black guy who is scaring half the population here."

"I've got an idea. Maybe we can get Mort to run a story in *The Shady Palms Gazette* that informs all the residents here that blacks are full-fledged citizens who can live where they please, vote in elections and be productive members of society."

"Very funny, Bernie."

"Not if your neighbors treat you like a criminal just because of the color of your skin."

"Listen to me, Dr. Martin Luther Hamstein. I didn't call for a lecture. I called to tell you that the first time this prized tenant of yours screws up, he's out of here. I'd suggest you get him to keep a low profile."

"What do you want, Herb? To get him to wear a landscaper's uniform when he steps outside?"

Troutman just ignored him and moved on to his next subject.

"There's something else you need to worry about too, Bernie. Did you see the newspaper this morning?"

"No, I was resting."

"Well, your friend Mort has done it again. By making a big deal over those stupid ducks outside your building, he's managed to alert the local media. There was a small item in *The Post* today, and already I've gotten calls from two television stations who want permission to videotape the birds outside C Building."

"And?"

"Of course, I told them 'No.' But I don't think we've heard the end of this. Not unless you can calm down Herman Schmidlapp. If not, we may be in for it. There was some animal-rights woman who was quoted in the paper this morning — one of those women with a hyphenated last name."

"Oh, oh," Bernie said. "First big Negroes, now ballsy women. What's next? Locusts?"

"Hamstein, are you making fun of me?"

"Anything else, Herb? I got some tofu in the oven I need to tend."

Bernie never failed to be exhilarated after a chat with Herb Troutman. He hung up the phone and began searching for that article in the newspaper, when his post-Herb euphoria was quickly extinguished by a knock on the door.

"I hope I'm not coming at a bad time," Johnny Fox said, as he sat down on the couch. "It's just that I saw your wife leaving, and I thought this would be a good time to talk."

"To talk?" Bernie said.

"Yeah, you know, about the money."

"The money?"

"The $600 you owe me. From poker."

"Oh, that money," Bernie said. "How could I forget."

"Like I said Bernie, I don't need all of it right away. But I would like maybe a couple hundred ASAP."

"And how soon is ASAP?"

"Before tonight's game."

"You're playing cards tonight?"

"Yeah, tonight's the night. We're over at Archie's condo tonight."

"Just the four of you."

"No, we got a fifth. Howie from G Building."

"You've already replaced me?" Bernie said.

"You can always come back, Bernie, you know, when your wife eases off, and ... you know, when you get some money again."

"Johnny, you're breaking my heart."

"So what do you think?"

"About what?"

"About the money."

"I think I'm broke, Johnny. I just got out of the hospital."

"So you can't give me even just a ... "

" ... I can't give you squat, Johnny."

"This is bad," Johnny Fox said.

"Are you running out of ticket-sale money from the Shady Palms Players?"

"Bernie, if that gets around I'll be ... "

"Don't worry, Johnny. I'm not a snitch. And I wish I had the money to pay you. But the truth is, I'm flat-out broke. You can check the coffee can in my trunk. It's empty."

Bernie thought of the money his nephew Brad had given him for Demetrius. Maybe he could use that money to ... no, that would be too foolish. Johnny Fox would just have to wait to get paid.

Johnny pulled out one of his hand-rolled joints, put it in his mouth and lit it. Bernie was too cowed by Johnny's financial hold on him to object to his glaucoma medication being smoked in his condo.

"I need it to relax me, Bernie," Johnny said, taking a long pull on the joint. "You don't mind, do you?"

Bernie just shrugged.

"Maybe I'll get a job at Publix as a bag boy," he told Johnny. "Maybe I can save up enough to pay you from that."

"Your heart, Bernie," Johnny said, in a pinched whispery voice. "Not a good idea to be schlepping groceries in the hot sun."

"Yeah," Bernie said.

Johnny took another drag off the joint, then started laughing.

"Hey I got an idea," he said, after his giggles subsided. "Maybe you can work off the money with me."

"What do you mean, Johnny?"

"Acting. I can never get enough men to be in the shows. No shortage of women, but for some reason, I've got to break arms to get men."

"I'm no actor, Johnny."

"You're a building president, that's close enough," he said. "I'm doing Shakespeare next. Sort of a musical revue set to Shakespeare snippets. Shakespeare is very hot these days."

Bernie thought he'd rather schlep groceries, heat or no heat, than be in one of Johnny's productions. But further discussion was abruptly ended with an angry rap on the door, followed by the doorway-filling appearance of Demetrius Bone.

"Demetrius, what happened to your eyes?"

"I'm through with this place, Bernie," Demetrius said. "You got to get me out of here. I've been here less than 12 hours, and already I've been Maced, I had the cops sicced on me, and that little girl is driving me crazy."

"What little girl?" Johnny asked.

"Ah, never mind, Johnny," Bernie said. "This is Demetrius Bone, he's the new renter in 26C."

Demetrius paced around the condo, ranting about Lois, whom he referred to as simply a certain body part, and Troutman, whom he referred to as another body part — a male one, this time.

"And then, during my run, I hear this noise, and the biggest, ugliest duck I've ever seen is chasing me down the road," Demetrius said. "Even the ducks are after me!"

"Ah, so you've met the Muscovies," Bernie said. "If you think they're bad, wait till you see the old kraut who feeds them."

The phone rang. It was Brad Cohen calling from

California. Not wanting Cohen to talk to Demetrius while he was in such an agitated state, Bernie took the phone in the other room.

"He's doing great, Brad," Bernie said. "Yes, I picked him up yesterday and got him set up in his condo here."

"Uncle Bernie, I don't know how I can ever repay you for what you've done," the nephew said. "I just know that once Demetrius settles in there, he'll be getting the kind of positive influences on his life that he desperately needs."

"Yeah, well. I hope so," Bernie said.

"How's he adjusting?"

"Oh, you know," Bernie said. "It's not easy getting adjusted to condo life, even if you don't happen to be a 6-foot-3 young black guy in a world of shrinking old white people. I think it's going to be a little rocky at first for him."

Bernie glanced into the living room, where he saw Demetrius, who had apparently stopped ranting long enough to pick up the unusual scent in the air. He was now sitting next to Johnny, who was lighting a second joint and sharing it with the younger man.

"But you think he'll adjust OK, Uncle Bernie?" the sports agent said.

Bernie watched Demetrius close his eyes and take a long drag on Johnny's medication.

"He's already showing signs of adjusting."

19 Lunch with Vince

Rose Hamstein followed the directions to Vince Campo's house, which turned out to be a two-story home on a canal in Boca Raton. A Roman fountain gurgled out front, and an archway of bougainvillea led to a set of double doors accented with a ring of inlaid cherubs frolicking around the frame.

"Some nice house you have here, Vince," Rose said, after ringing the doorbell and walking into an entryway with a cathedral ceiling and an enormous chandelier.

A moment later, she could hear the scampering of dogs' feet on tile floor coming from a distant part of the house. And before long, Rose found herself surrounded by her little black mutt, Lucky, and two of the whitest, most meticulously groomed, miniature poodles she had ever seen.

"Barbra's the one with the pink rhinestone collar," Vince said. "Judy's wearing ruby red."

Rose bent down and petted her dog, who was trying to lick every part of Rose at the same time.

"Oh, Lucky, I missed you, too," she said, stroking his flanks and noticing that his fur had been beautifully cut and shampooed to a luster Rose never thought was possible.

"Vince, if Lucky was smarter, he'd be hiding under the bed

until I was gone."

"I hope you don't mind that I took him to the groomer," Vince said. "My girls happened to have an appointment yesterday, so I just brought Lucky along."

"You didn't have to go through such trouble, Vince."

"No trouble," he said, guiding her through the house, which was full of large oil paintings, statuary of naked human forms and an L-shaped leather couch big enough to seat the Shady Palms bridge club.

From somewhere near the ceiling, Rose could hear the piped-in music of Frank Sinatra singing *The Summer Wind* at a volume barely above a whisper.

"What a house, Vince!" she said. "Such a big place, and you live here all by yourself?"

"Just me and the girls," he said, as the two poodles yapped and circled around them.

When they walked out back, she saw the table where they would be eating. It was already set with two places, a bottle of wine chilling in a bucket and crystal glasses glinting in the sun. Beyond the table was the canal, with a private dock and a boat named Plea Bargain tied to it.

"Do you fish, Vince?" Rose asked.

"No, I just putter around in the Intracoastal once in a while," he said.

■ ■ ■

Lunch was delicious. Vince had obviously fussed. As Rose cut into her veal chop, she thought of Bernie and how much he'd love to be eating a piece of meat like this. Vince must have read her mind.

"So how is Bernie?" he asked.

"He's doing his best to act like a man who has never had a heart attack," Rose said.

"It's too bad you didn't bring him today," Vince said.

"Yes, well ... he's resting."

"Not that I'm disappointed that it's just you here," Vince said, reaching across the table and patting her hand. "Even though we've only known each other a short time, I feel like I've known you forever, Rose."

Rose took a long sip from her wine and steered the conversation in another direction. But it was hard to get Vince to give much detail about his own life.

She learned that he had made the money to afford a house like this through his work as an investment counselor.

"Do you have an office?" Rose asked.

"Not per se," he said.

Then he quickly moved on to something else.

Over lunch, Rose was able to learn that his marriage lasted less than a year, he had no children and he was an only child.

"People hear an Italian last name, and they assume you have 30 relatives over for dinner every Sunday," he said.

"I had one of those big families," Rose said.

"Tell me about it."

"Eight kids," she said. "I was number six. It was always a zoo at the house. And then my dad left."

"What happened to him?"

"The usual," Rose said. "He met somebody else and moved out. I heard he lived only a few blocks away. But he never came back. One day in the beginning, I was walking home from school, and I saw him. He was following me, looking at me from across the street. I was maybe 10 years old. So I ran across the street toward him, yelling, 'Daddy, Daddy.' But instead of coming toward me, he started backing up. It made me stop. I was just a few feet away from him, and I said, 'Daddy, why won't you come home?' And he said nothing. He held out his arms to me. But I just stood there. I was mad at him for not wanting to come home. I sometimes think, even now, that if I ran into his arms,

**Vince Campo seems like a real computer novice in computer
class, yet when Rose visits his house, she finds he has
a room full of sophisticated computer equipment there.**

maybe I could have dragged him back home with me. Maybe
everything would have been different, then. But that's ... that's
the last time I saw him."

Rose realized she was getting teary-eyed, and as she
looked over at Vince Campo, she could see him sniffling, too. He
reached out his hand to her and patted it again, this time leaving
his hand on top of hers.

"Oh, listen to me," Rose said. "It must be the wine."

She pulled her hand away and glanced toward the dock.

"I need to get back to Shady Palms," Rose said. "There's no
telling what mischief Bernie will be up to without adult supervi-
sion."

Vince gave Rose directions to a bathroom on the first floor.
She walked there while he cleaned the table outside, and in her
journey, Rose managed to take a left where she should have

taken a right.

Instead of the bathroom, she found herself in a room with two computer terminals and a table full of spreadsheets and software programming manuals. Vince, who carried on as if a cut-and-paste procedure in their computer class was akin to understanding quantum physics, was apparently more adept at computers than he led Rose to believe.

She quickly left the room and found the bathroom.

Before driving back to Shady Palms with Lucky, Rose nearly asked Vince why he would take a beginner's computer class when it was clear from his computer room that he didn't need it. But she didn't want to seem like a snoop, and he had been so nice to her.

"For your condo," he said, handing her a potted plant and giving her a parting hug in his driveway before nuzzling Lucky and putting him in the front seat beside Rose.

"Oh, Vince, you're so thoughtful."

■ ■ ■

Rose's thoughts of Vince Campo evaporated when she walked into her condo and noticed a strange smell that Bernie had been trying to mask with air freshener.

"What's that smell?"

"Oh, I was just cleaning up in here and I sprayed some of that ... "

"Not the air freshener, Bernie. The other smell."

He tried changing the subject.

"I've got big news, Rose. Remember when you ... "

But her mind was still on the smell, which had sent Lucky on a room-to-room search.

"You know what it reminds me of?" she said, putting the plant Vince had given her on the dining room table. "When Sam got us tickets to that concert at the Coral Sky Amphitheater, and we sat out on the lawn. And as soon as the music started, we began smelling this unusual kind of ... ”

“Rose, forget about the smell. I’m trying to tell you about ...”

“Marijuana! That’s what it is. Remember, we asked Sam, and he said it was just people smoking marijuana.”

“ ... what I found when you were gone.”

“My God, Bernie! Don’t tell me you’re smoking dope!”

“Rose, for cryin’ out loud. Forget about the smell. It’s just Johnny Fox’s medicine.”

“Johnny Fox was here?”

“Yes, that’s what I’ve been trying to tell you.”

“You weren’t playing poker, were you, Bernie?”

“No, Rose. He was just paying me a visit, and anyway, I ended up feeding him lunch, and he knocked over a glass of chocolate milk on the carpet.”

“Oh, Bernie. I’ve told you a million times not to eat in the ...”

“So, I clean up the spill, and decide to squirt a little Resolve on the stain. And when I go to the cleaning supplies cabinet, guess what’s sitting behind the bottle of Resolve?”

“Is it so hard to sit at the dining room table to eat? Is that asking too much? Why is it that as soon as I leave ... ”

“Rose, you’re not listening. The Resolve. Guess what I found behind the Resolve?”

“ ... you start acting like an irresponsible child who needs ... ”

Words alone were not going to derail Rose, so Bernie reached for the green cloth bag and tossed it at her.

“Catch,” he said.

Lucky assumed the begging position, assuming a treat was coming his way.

“Bernie, what’s this?” she said, opening the bag and discovering it full of Lois’ jewelry.

"That's the jewelry bag that Lois said was stolen," Bernie said. "It was behind the Resolve, in the cleaning cabinet."

Bernie now had Rose's full attention.

"It was never stolen," Bernie said. "Your ditzy friend, Lois, just put it down and forgot where she put it."

Rose pieced it together now. How Lois must have put the jewelry bag down when she picked up the Resolve to clean up a mess made by Lucky. And then she put the cleaner back in the cabinet while forgetting to pick up her jewelry bag again. Then later, when she couldn't find the bag, she assumed Vince Campo had stolen it because he was in the condo unit with her.

"I knew it!" Rose said. "I just knew Vince wouldn't have done something like that."

She seemed elated, which made Bernie's good mood evaporate.

"Yeah, your boyfriend's in the clear," he said.

"Bernie Hamstein, don't you start on your jealous routine. Just because somebody ... "

The phone rang, and Rose picked it up as she continued to talk to her husband.

" ... is nice to me, doesn't mean that ... Hello?"

"Rose."

"Oh, hi, Margo."

Rose could hear the sheriff's office radio traffic in the background, so she knew her daughter-in-law was calling from work.

"Remember that guy you asked me to check out? Vince Campo?"

"Oh, Margo. I wish now I never bothered you. You know, after I told you, I started thinking to myself that maybe I would get you in trouble for checking out personal... "

"Rose, I checked him out this morning, and ... "

"I'm sorry to have wasted your time, Margo. It was all just

a bunch of hysteria on Lois' part ... "

"Rose, be careful."

"Yeah, the next time Lois tells me something, I'm going to take it with a grain of salt. It's not right to accuse people of things just because you ... "

"Rose," Margo interrupted. "I'm not telling you to be careful about Lois. I'm telling you to be careful about this Vince Campo guy."

"What?"

"He's a crook, Rose. A major con man. White-collar stuff. He started out with securities fraud. Then he ran a boiler-room operation. His latest venture was a Ponzi scheme with orchids."

"But I was just at his house. He's got a beautiful place in Boca."

"So does just about every other white-collar crook in America," Margo said.

Bernie was out of earshot in the next room, looking at the potted plant Rose had left on the table.

When Rose hung up the phone and walked back toward him, Bernie wasn't paying enough attention to realize that his wife had gone pale.

"Rose," he said, "what do you want me to do with these orchids?"

20 Yolette and the helicopters

The next day was a chaotic one at Shady Palms, dominated by two major events that everybody noticed and one that only a few residents of C Building would learn about.

By noon, a sheriff's helicopter and two TV news helicopters were circling overhead, and a cluster of sheriff's office cruisers were gathering in the parking lot of C Building.

Yolette, peeking through the blinds, wished she was not alone. Her roommate, Demetrius Bone, left that morning, saying he was going running, and he never came back. She was counting on Demetrius to help her look for her father. But so far, he had been no help. He was not like Ricardo. Ricardo wanted to help her, but Demetrius, he did not seem to care about anyone but himself.

Yolette wished Demetrius had his jaw wired shut instead of Ricardo. Ricardo had come by yesterday, and she was so happy to see him. But all he could do was draw pictures and say "Mmm" to everything Yolette asked him.

Demetrius, he only wanted to talk about "getting more medicine" from some man named Johnny. Yolette did not know why Demetrius wanted medicine. He did not look sick.

Yolette peeked through the blinds and, with each hour,

grew more anxious. She wanted to run outside her door and find Ms. Lois or Mr. Bernie. But she had no idea where other people lived here. When she had moved from Ms. Lois' place, she remembered walking out in the corridor and seeing all these doors, one looking exactly like another, and behind each one, a different person, a different home.

She was sure if she ran out in the hall now, she would be as lost as she could be and end up banging on the wrong door. So she stayed put, waiting and watching and hoping that somebody would tell her if she was in danger now.

She sat down on the couch and flicked on the television. Yolette tried to pay attention to the TV show, but it was hard. She was watching a station that had a white man with a big smiling face who talked about Jesus most of the time and about money the rest of the time. The smiley man closed his eyes and said he felt that miracles were happening. Then he would pick up a telephone, and someone on the other end of the line would thank him for getting Jesus to answer her prayers.

Yolette knew the telephone on the table next to her was one of those things she should not touch. But what harm could there be in getting the smiley man to ask Jesus to help find her father? Especially now. Yolette had a sense that she was running out of time and that all the activity outside the condo was somehow related to her. She expected that at any moment, a bunch of people would burst through the door and take her away — not to her father, but to some prison.

So she carefully dialed the long phone number on the bottom of the television screen and listened to the rings, until she heard the reassuring voice of a woman.

"Praise Jesus," the voice said.

"Praise Jesus," Yolette said, feeling the tension begin to drain from her.

"How can we help you?"

Yolette did not know where to begin.

"I need Jesus," was all she could think of as a way to begin.

"Would you like to be hooked up for an on-air prayer with ... "

"Yes, yes," Yolette said. "Hurry, please."

"And what card will you be using?"

"Card?" Yolette said.

And then it hit her. She had heard talk of these cards before. These cards determined who got to stay in America and who had to leave. On the boat they talked about them. Green cards. There was another word, too. Then she remembered it.

"You mean, visa?"

"Yes, a VISA card will be fine," the woman's voice said. "Please give me the number, the exact name on the card and the expiration date."

Yolette hung up the phone. Crushed. The smiley man and Jesus were only teaming up to answer prayers for people who were in America legally. She did not know that Jesus worked so closely with the Immigration and Naturalization Service.

She turned off the television and went back to the window, looking through the blinds again. If she had watched a television station that had a noon news program, she would have been reassured about the growing tension outside the walls of C Building.

The day's first outbreak of commotion came when a group of animal-rights activists gathered outside the front gate to protest what they called the "wanton killing of defenseless ducks" in the condo complex. The leader of the group was Lori Kirkland-Smythe, a bird lover who nevertheless managed to dis- place dozens of her beloved woodpeckers with the construction of one of her three country homes. Kirkland-Smythe said she and her group were there to speak for the Muscovy ducks that were being senselessly butchered outside C Building.

A couple of the more zealous members of her pro-bird commando group, CHIRP — Citizens Hoping to Irritate Ruthless People — had managed to get past Hector, the gate guard. Their mission was to splatter plastic baggies of simulated blood on the windshields of cars in the C Building parking lot.

Lou Margolick loves his orange tree. So much that he is willing to risk his life to protect it from citrus canker eradication.

But when the pro-testers got inside the gates, they noticed the C Building parking lot was already full of sheriff's cars. They assumed the cops were there to pre-vent a forced rescue of the ducks.

But it actually had nothing to do with the ducks. It had to do with Lou Margolick, the only man in Shady Palms to have both a Purple Heart and an artificial one. Margolick's battle these days was over the citrus tree in front of his unit on the bottom floor of D Building.

Theoretically, the tree is part of the condo's common area. But Margolick had always considered it his tree and had taken it upon himself to both fertilize it and parcel out its fruit as he saw fit.

Everybody humored Lou Margolick until a state agriculture inspector came by last month and determined that his beloved orange tree had citrus canker and needed to be chopped down. The inspector marked the tree for destruction by spraying the trunk with a garish shade of paint.

At first, Margolick wept. But then he felt the fight boil inside him, the same fight that had sustained him through Iwo Jima and had become buried under 50-plus years of suburban living, but alas, was not dead yet.

On this morning, when he heard the wood chipper truck drive into the D Building lot, he knew what he had to do. He calmly walked outside his building in his old Army uniform and lashed himself to the trunk of the orange tree. He wore his Purple Heart medal on his shirt and his dog tags around his neck. But what the tree trimmers noticed first were the five grenades hanging from his clothing and a semiautomatic rifle cradled under his left arm.

"Nobody's getting a piece of this tree without getting a piece of me," he announced to the tree trimmers, who assured him they were just subcontractors who'd rather hang out at the 7-Eleven drinking Big Gulps until everything could be worked out peacefully. But when they radioed their supervisor, they were told to hang tight. And before long, a S.W.A.T. negotiator was there, and Margolick looked to be having the fight he'd been itching to have for a half-century.

The sheriff's hostage team gathered in the nearby C Building lot so as not to make Margolick do something foolish at the sight of all their vehicles and firepower. So when the CHIRP protesters made their way to C Building, they saw cops dressed in military-style helmets and bulletproof vests. It seemed like an excessive amount of force to protect a few vehicles from having simulated blood splattered on their windshields.

Meanwhile, Hector the gate guard had initiated a gate-crasher alarm that sent three of the condo's security vehicles out to hunt for the protesters.

The whole scene was being observed by the three helicopters that circled overhead, and it was their rotor sounds that made Yolette more uneasy than anything else. The sounds of those helicopters reminded her of that night off Palm Beach, the night when the helicopter circled overhead as people from her boat drowned or were arrested on the beach.

The helicopter sounds were clear evidence they had found her and were coming to get her, Yolette thought. Someone, maybe Demetrius, must have alerted immigration that she was hiding out. Maybe that is why Demetrius was gone this morning.

And now they had come. Men with rifles like soldiers. Helicopters. Even policemen with dogs. All for her.

America was a strange country, she thought. But a strong one. Americans had even managed to get Jesus to go along with their immigration rules. She nearly cried, thinking of the futility of her situation. To have come so far, only to have failed. Her mother would be disappointed in her. Her father, wherever he is, would be heartbroken to learn she had come so close to him, only to be sent back across the ocean — maybe after being left for months to wait in that big prison they have for Haitians in Miami.

She looked to the door of the condo, and she would not have been surprised if at any moment, it shattered into a million pieces and men ran in and grabbed her. The helicopters seemed to be getting closer, then they would fade away. Then they would come closer again.

Why were they torturing her like this?

She peeked through the closed blinds again and saw two men crouching behind a parked car with bags of blood in their hands. They had even sent Voodoo priests to get her! Imagine that.

Yolette suddenly had the urge to run. She could not stand waiting any longer. Maybe she could escape. She had done it on the beach, she could do it again. She wished there was a way she could take all her Limited Too outfits with her. But she knew there was only one thing she would have to carry, the plastic bag with the photograph of her father and the sealed envelope inside. She picked it up and stepped outside her door, not knowing what to expect.

Much to her surprise, the hallway was silent and empty. A big sign with an arrow said "Exit." She followed it, down the stairs and around a corner.

She could not go out the front door. They would get her there. She heard voices, someone ready to walk out one of the doors. She quickly looked around for a place to hide. She saw an open door at the end of the hallway and ran for it. The room was a big one full of washing machines and clothes dryers. And at the end of it was a window, and beyond the window was a fence and a road. And beyond the road were some woods, a place where she could hide.

Yolette ran to the window. She pushed a chair in front of it and opened the window far enough to get her body through. She jumped, tumbling on the grass. She stood up and looked around, realizing she was now on the back end of the building. One of the helicopters seemed to be coming closer, so she crouched in the bushes for a minute.

Then she sprinted for the chain-link fence, climbing it easily. It was not until she was on the other side of the fence that she saw the canal. It was narrow and mucky, and Yolette did not want to ruin her outfit. So she took off her shoes and rolled up the edges of her shorts, hoping the water was not too deep.

But after her first step from the bank, she felt her body sliding into the mud and the water, which was over her head. She did everything in her power to hang on to that plastic bag and her shoes, flailing in the water as she splashed her way to the other side.

She did not have far to go. She clawed her way up the other bank and looked back on the three-story buildings of Shady Palms. Then she heard a helicopter sound getting louder. No time to waste.

She put on her wet shoes and ran across a two-lane road and into the woods. She ran deeper and deeper into the woods, scratching her legs on the branches but not pausing until she could barely hear the rotors of the helicopters.

She sat down under the protective canopy of trees, clutching the plastic bag, feeling the mud drip down her legs and listening to the insistence of her runaway heart.

21 Duck!

It was Lois' turn to drive the Wonder Walkers that morning, and as she and her friends returned from the Boynton Beach Mall, they had no idea of the scene that awaited them at Shady Palms.

The four women were still too engrossed in their conversation, which had lasted over two rounds of post-walk sticky buns at the mall's food court, to notice the helicopters circling over their home.

"The point is, the man is a con artist," Lois was saying. "Even if he didn't steal my jewelry, he's obviously up to no good."

Rose had broken the news to her friends that Vince Campo apparently had a career as a white-collar crook.

"I wouldn't go back to that computer class," her friend Maddy said.

"And if he calls on the phone, I wouldn't give him the time of day," Jacqui said.

Rose was troubled, though.

"But he's been so nice to me," Rose said.

"Of course he's been nice," Lois said. "He probably wants to get us to all invest in his orchids or whatever new scam he has

Animal rights protesters from CHIRP — Citizens Hoping to Irritate Ruthless People — gather to protest the killing of Muscovy ducks outside C Building.

going. And he's just using you to soften up the rest of us."

"I just can't believe ... " Rose started, and then she noticed the cluster of protesters outside the front gate of Shady Palms. "What's going on here?"

Lois slowed the Chrysler as it neared the entrance.

"Honk if you like ducks," read a big banner strung in front of the entrance. And the other signs, which included "Ducks are nicer than people" and "Fowl Play, Not Foul Play," were held over the heads of the protesters who eyed Lois' car as she slowed.

Then Herman Schmidlapp materialized in the middle of the cluster, jumping out in front of Lois' car and pointing an accusing finger at her.

"Zis is zee vooman!" Herman shouted to the duck protesters.

Lois, who had to stop her car to avoid running over Herman — an option she considered seriously — was surrounded by the members of CHIRP.

The Citizens Hoping to Irritate Ruthless People had been itching all morning to confront the actual duck-killer, and now they had Lois where they wanted her.

"Murder-er! Murder-er! Murder-er!" they chanted.

Lois smiled, lowered the driver's side window, turned off her car and pulled her key chain out of the ignition.

"No, Lois," said Rose from the back seat. "I know what you're thinking, but please, not here, Lois. Not to these people."

The crowd parted to allow CHIRP's leader, the ever-fashionable Lori Kirkland-Smythe, to do the interrogation of Lois.

"Are you the duck-killer?" the younger woman said, resting her hands on the door of Lois' car.

"Get your hands off my car," Lois said.

Beyond the circle of protesters, Lois could still hear Herman's voice shouting, "You must teach the schweinehund a lesson."

"This must be the death car," Kirkland-Smythe said.

"Stand in front of it and find out," Lois said.

"Lois!" Rose said. "Don't make a scene."

"I'm not making a scene," Lois said. "They're the ones making a scene."

"On behalf of all the animal lovers in the world, I command you to ... "

"I said get your hands off my car," Lois said, still smiling.

"And this is the last time I am going to say it."

"Please!" Rose shouted to the younger woman. "Listen to her, she's not fooling."

But Lori Kirkland-Smythe was foolish enough to think she was in control of the situation here. She had the crowd, the media and the moral conviction of her cause.

"I command you," she continued to Lois, "to make a public apology for ... "

For what? Lois didn't wait to find out.

She blasted Kirkland-Smythe with Mace, and while the rest of the protesters peeled away from their retreating leader, Lois calmly started the engine and drove past Hector, the gate guard, who saluted her and smiled as she drove by.

"One of you has to remind me to buy more of that stuff," she said to the rest of the Wonder Walkers, who were too stunned for words. "I'm running low."

Back outside the front gate, Lori Kirkland-Smythe's second-in-command was on her walkie-talkie giving a description of Lois' car to the commando unit of fake-blood splatterers who had managed to get through security.

"Now what?" Lois said, as she saw the cluster of police cruisers in the C Building parking lot.

She parked the car, and the four women walked to nearby D Building, where residents had gathered outside a police barricade to watch what would happen to Lou Margolick, who was still lashed to his beloved orange tree.

A police negotiator with a bullhorn was asking Margolick what it would take for him to put down his rifle and discuss the fate of the tree in a calm manner.

Lois turned to her friends, "Did it ever occur to you how many crazy people live here?"

"Look who's talking," Maddy said.

Just then, Lois heard someone breathing heavily behind

her. She calmly reached for her Mace again and turned around, preparing to squirt if provoked.

But she was surprised to see it was Ricardo, looking miserable with the bandages still wrapped around one of his shoulders and his mouth wired shut. In all the confusion, she must have missed seeing his car parked in the C Building lot.

"Ricardo, what's the matter?" she asked, seeing his wide-eyed look.

"Mmmm mm mmmmm m mmmmmm!" he said.

"What?"

"Mmmm mm mmmmm ... "

"Hold that thought," Lois said, reaching into her purse and pulling out a pen and a sales receipt. "Write on the back."

Ricardo frowned at the little space, and then drew a female stick figure and next to it "26C" with an "X" over it.

It took Lois a few guesses, but eventually she figured out what he was trying to say: Yolette was not in the condo.

"Maybe she's with that horrible guy, Demetrius?"

"Mmmm mm mmmmm mmmmm?"

"If you're asking me where Demetrius is, I have no idea. The only time I had the pleasure of his company, we terminated the conversation rather suddenly," she said, tapping on the Mace canister in her hand.

"Mm?"

"Yes."

"Mmmm!"

"You look terrible, Ricardo. You should be resting instead of worrying about that Haitian girl. I'm sure she's fine. Maybe she's with Bernie. Have you tried him?"

Ricardo shook his head.

"C'mon," she said. "Let's go find Bernie. I'll bet Yolette, Demetrius and Bernie are together somewhere."

The rest of the women wanted to wait and see what the

police were going to do about Lou Margolick, so it was just Lois
and Ricardo who walked toward C Building. By the time the two
of them had reached the C Building lot, the two-member CHIRP
commando unit had already made visual confirmation of her car.
They were about to pour the fake blood on the Chrysler when
they spotted Lois herself. And being that they'd heard on the
walkie-talkie that this woman had physically assaulted their
leader, Lori Kirkland-Smythe, they altered their plan.

"Let's splatter her with the blood," one of them said.

"What about the little guy she's with?"

"Guilt by association."

So the duck lovers crept car-by-car to the point where they
would be close enough to surprise Lois and douse her before
she knew what had happened. But soon, there was another person in the way. A young black man without a T-shirt was walking
into the lot from the other side.

"There's Demetrius," Lois said to Ricardo.

"Mmmm mm mmmmm," Ricardo was trying to shout across
the parking lot, motioning for Demetrius to walk over to them.

Demetrius, who was dripping sweat from a long run,
looked at Lois and put up his hands.

"You're a crazy woman," he said. "Stay away from me."

"Demetrius, please. I come in peace," she said. "It's about
Yolette."

Demetrius warily walked closer to them.

"She's not in the condo. Do you know where she is?"

"No, she was there when I left this morning."

They were standing next to each other now.

"And she didn't say where she was going?"

"I'm nobody's nanny," Demetrius said. "I got enough to
worry about without having to keep track of some little girl."

"Mmmm mm mmmmm mm mmmmm mmmm," Ricardo
said.

"What?"

"Don't mind him. This is Ricardo, he's the guy who found Yolette. And he came by this morning to ... "

"Oh, so this is the famous Ricardo. That's all she talks about, her father and Ricardo."

Ricardo smiled, at least he tried to in his present condition.

The CHIRP commandos were in position now, maneuvering so they would be behind the big black man, who would partially screen their assault and allow them to douse Lois in a head-on soaking.

The men stood up and began walking straight toward Demetrius.

"Mmm mmm mmmmm mmmm?" Ricardo said in a curious voice.

Lois saw the baggies of dark red liquid in their hands and quickly figured out their intentions. She took a step toward Demetrius, using his big body as a screen, then reached for her Mace, and shouted to him, "Duck!"

The commandos let fly with their fake blood, which might have hit Lois squarely in the face if Demetrius had ducked his head as Lois had commanded.

But when Lois said "Duck!" Demetrius didn't think she was telling him to crouch down. He thought she meant that one of those ugly Muscovy ducks had waddled up and was about to peck at his feet, like they did when he went jogging.

So instead of getting out of the line of fire, he simply glanced down at his feet. Not seeing any ducks, he turned around to look behind him — just in time to receive nearly all the contents of two bags of fake blood in his face.

Blinded and flabbergasted by the chain of events, he heard Lois again shout "Duck!" to him, and he turned around to look at her, still not realizing she was using the verb rather than the noun form of the word.

Lois, seeing an opportunity to Mace her two attackers, was counting on Demetrius to get his head out of the way. The adrenaline of the situation took over, making her squirt her canister for all it was worth in the direction of the two men.

But luckily for them, it was also still the direction of Demetrius' face, which caught the brunt of the spraying.

"Ahhhh!" Demetrius screamed.

"Mmmmm!" Ricardo shouted, wishing he were healthy enough to run after those two guys, who were now sprinting away in the parking lot.

"Nuts!" Lois said. "I missed them."

Demetrius stumbled back, horrified to see though his burning eyes what he thought was blood dripping down his body.

"I've been shot," he said, sitting down on the pavement.

Lois looked down at Demetrius.

"I wasn't trying to Mace you this time," she said. "I told you to duck. Twice."

"I've been shot," Demetrius said. "I don't believe it. I've been shot."

"No you haven't," Lois said. "Get off the ground, you big baby."

"Mmm mm mmm mmmm," Ricardo said.

"You could say that again," Lois said.

Demetrius vowed to call his agent and demand a ticket on the next flight to L.A.

22 Publix enemy No. 1

Bernie Hamstein missed most of the commotion at Shady Palms, because by 9 a.m., he was off on another clandestine mission, once again trying to slip under the protective radar of his wife.

"I really appreciate this, Softer," Bernie said, as he got into the waiting car driven by one of his poker buddies, Mickey Faraday.

"No problem, Bern. Like I was saying, I need something out there myself for the gig this afternoon."

Faraday, the drummer in the condo's big band, The Swinging Palms, even talked too loud. But Bernie didn't mind this morning. The heart attack had sidelined him from his friends too long — and from being part of the little rituals of life he had come to expect and love.

"How was the poker game last night?" he asked.

"Not the same without you, Bern," Softer said. "And Johnny, he brought that young fella along, your new renter."

"Demetrius?"

"Yeah," Softer said. "You shoulda seen the two of them, joking around. That is until your buddy gets $100 down in no time — most of it to Johnny."

"Where's Demetrius getting the money to play poker?" Bernie asked. "I'm the guy who's supposedly handling all his finances."

"I think Johnny fronted him the money," Softer said.

"And the medicine."

"What?"

"Nothing," Bernie said. "That damned Johnny Fox, he's getting his hooks into everybody. You know what he told me? He said he'd let me work off the $600 I owe him by acting in his next theatrical production. Some Shakespeare fiasco."

"Ah," Softer said. "To be or not to be the laughingstock of your community? That is the question."

"And the answer is no," Bernie said. "That's why I'm slipping out here with you to the shopping center. I'm going to apply for a bag-boy job at Publix."

"Since when do you want to bag groceries, Bern?"

"Since I owe Johnny $600. And since I don't have money of my own anymore, and I can't eat a Cheerio without Rose first reading the package and telling me about antioxidants, free radicals and triglycerides. I just need some space, Softer. So maybe I can get a salami sandwich once in a while, play the Lottery and make enough money to get back in the poker game."

"Bern, I'm not sure that schlepping groceries in the sun is a good idea for a guy recovering from a heart attack."

"How stressful could it be?" Bernie said. "And besides, I like being around supermarkets."

For much of his life, Bernie had been in and out of supermarkets as a driver for the Big Top bread company in New York, a job he held for four decades and once thought would be the last job of his life. It would feel strange, he thought, to fill out a job application again. The last time he did it was when he was still in his twenties.

Softer pulled into the United Villages of West Boynton, a

shopping center whose name invariably invoked visions of abo-
riginal tribal unity in Bernie, a concept about as far-fetched as
possible in suburban Boynton Beach.

"I'm going to drop you here," Softer said, pulling the car in
front of Publix. "I've got to go to the men's shop for a clip-on bow
tie. I'll come find you here when I'm done."

Bernie walked into the store, breathing deeply the familiar
morning-supermarket fragrance of brewed coffee, fresh bread
and industrial-strength floor cleaner. He headed for customer
service, waiting patiently while the woman in front of him continued her complaint about the uncanny ability of the deli help to
avoid eye contact with customers waiting for service.

"Bernie, is that you?"

The voice was familiar, but Bernie couldn't place it at first.
He turned around and his heart sank.

"Joey," Bernie said, nearly completing the rest of the man's
nickname, "Alpo."

Bernie wished he had never seen Joey Alpo again. A year
ago, Bernie had thought that the man who took his weekly football bets was just another retiree like him. But he turned out to
be a notorious mobster, a guy who had a long career in the body
disposal end of the business.

Joseph Abrizzio got the nickname Joey Alpo because a rel-
ative worked at a dog food plant in New Jersey, a place that
apparently functioned much better than shallow graves for tidy
disposal of inconvenient former business acquaintances.

Bernie knew none of this until after Joey Alpo's arrest,
which was made possible because of the undercover police work
of Margo, the woman who would become Bernie's daughter-in-
law.

The papers had been full of Joey Alpo stories and about
how the mobster had apparently retired from the crime business
in New York, only to come to Florida and begin a second career

as a bookie for senior citizens.

"Long time no see, Bernie. What are you up to these days?"

"Yeah, well ... I ... you know. I'm applying for a bag-boy's job."

"Hey, great. C'mon," Joey said. "Let's talk."

That's when Bernie first noticed Joey was wearing a Publix apron and a name tag.

"I'm taking 10," he told an assistant manager, who appeared ready to say something but quickly changed his mind. "But you just ... Good idea, Joey. OK."

Joey led Bernie outside the store. Bernie wondered if some federal task force operative was clandestinely snapping pictures somewhere in the parking lot.

"Tell me, Bernie, were you one of those people who accidentally voted for Pat Buchanan?"

The recount of the Florida votes after the November presidential election had brought news reporters from all over the world to Shady Palms. The condo had the highest concentration of Buchanan voters in the county, despite Shady Palms' reputation as a vote vault for Democrats.

"Maybe, Joey. I don't know for sure."

Joey bellowed with laughter, nudging Bernie in the ribs.

"You people," the mobster said, shaking his head. "How do you figure out which end of the bran cereal box to open in the morning?"

Bernie felt indignant enough to momentarily forget his fear. "Well, if you had voted, maybe you too would have ..." Bernie began, before his self-preservation instinct made him stop.

"I voted," the mobster said.

"You did? But ... "

Once again, Bernie stopped himself from wondering aloud

how a lifelong criminal like Joey Alpo could manage to keep his
voting rights intact.

"Usually, I vote more than once," Alpo said. "But I didn't
like Gore or Bush. Gore's a choirboy. And all that Bush had
going for him was a big tax cut — but that's only good if you
happen to pay taxes in the first place. So, I only voted once this
time. For Ralph Nader. As a protest."

Joey sat on one of the benches outside the store.

"Siddown, Bernie."

"Joey, I'm kind of in a hurry and ... "

"C'mon. Siddown. No hard feelings, Bernie," Joey said.
"Things didn't work out so bad, after all."

"No?"

Bernie thought Joey was still talking about the election.
But the mobster was talking about his football bookie days with
Shady Palms gamblers.

"After I beat the charges from those task force jamokes,
my lawyer, he says to just start acting like a model citizen until
they get bored of watching me. So my wife, you know, she'd
been nagging me to get a job, and so I finally came down here
and applied for a bag-boy job."

"You're a bag boy?"

"Imagine that!" Joey said. "First time I've ever gotten paid
on the books. At the age of 75. I thought maybe I'd turn it into a
no-show job. You know, pull the manager into the meat freezer
one day and explain to him that it might work better if he just
mailed me a check every week without ever putting me on the
work schedule. But then I thought that I would give it a try. I was
bored. Other than running the Crime Watch Committee where I
live, I ... "

"You do Crime Watch?" Bernie said, unable to help himself.

"You'd be surprised how much crime is down in my neighborhood now," Joey said.

A surfer-looking teenager pushed a train of empty shopping carts by them, looking at Joey and saying, "Taking another break, Joey? C'mon, back to work, Grandpa."

The boy was smiling in a wiseacre kind of way.

"That's Todd," Joey said to Bernie after the teenager was out of earshot. "He's what you might call the capo of the younger crew."

"The younger crew?"

"The kids," Joey explained. "In this line of work, you're either one of us or a kid. Todd thinks because he's been here longer than anybody else, he can tell all the other bag boys what to do. I look out for the older guys, and I told this Todd, 'You got a problem with any of the senior-citizen bag boys, you talk to me.' But Todd ... he just thinks he can make up his own rules."

Then Joey paused and smiled before saying, "He doesn't know how much danger he's in."

"Oh," Bernie said, suddenly getting the picture of a simple job being not so simple anymore.

"Tell you the truth, Bernie," Joey said. "This job is the most fun I've had in a long time, almost as good as those early days in collection."

"Yeah, well, I'm not sure I really want to ... "

"Some days, I just come in," Joey said, interrupting Bernie, "and decide that I'm going to have some fun. So the customers, they're waiting for me to look at them and ask, 'Paper or plastic?' But instead, I just tell them, 'Paper.' And they'll say, 'No, I'd prefer plastic.' And I shake my head and say, 'Paper.' "

"Don't people complain?"

"Sure they do," Joey said. "But the management learned to back me up ... eventually."

"Oh."

"But this is the best, Bernie," Joey said. "This is why I

wanted to come out here and sit on the bench for a while."

"Why's that?"

"To watch what happens," Joey said. "Here, look out in this parking lot and tell me what you see on some of these cars."

Bernie was at a loss.

"Look at the radio antennas," Joey said. "What do you see? Tennis balls. Butterflies. Pieces of yarn. Little flags. All sorts of things. I never noticed them until I was a bag boy."

Bernie saw them now.

"People put them there so they can find their cars when they come out of the supermarket. Imagine that, Bernie! Go in the store for a container of milk, come out and have no idea where you left the car. Needing to look for a plastic butterfly on an antenna. I already told my wife, if I get like that, I want her to shoot me. I even showed her the spot on the temple to aim for."

Bernie wanted to get out of there. Fast. He looked down the parking lot, searching in vain for the approach of Softer's Honda.

"So, I come out here and switch things around. You see that tennis ball on that white Ford? It used to be on the blue Chevy in the next aisle. But I'll guarantee you that when that old lady walks back out here, she'll go straight to the car with the tennis ball and try jamming that key in the door several times before she figures out that it's the wrong make and wrong color of car."

"Oh," Bernie said.

"It's a beautiful thing to watch," Joey said, pronouncing the word "beautiful" as "bee-you-tee-ful."

Then Bernie saw Softer's car, the sight of it making him stand up and sigh with relief.

"Gotta go, Joey. Here's my ride. It was nice seeing you again."

"Hey, Bernie, aren't you gonna wait and watch? That

woman will be out any minute."

Bernie hesitated, hoping he wasn't showing Joey Alpo a discernible amount of disrespect. But the impulse to flee was too strong.

"I'd love to," Bernie said. "But I really have to go. Another time."

He jumped in the car and closed the door as Joey was saying, "But you didn't fill out your job application."

"Drive," Bernie said to Softer.

"That was fast," Softer said. "I didn't expect you'd be done so soon."

Bernie didn't relax until the car was out of the parking lot.

"Can you make one more stop for me?" Bernie asked.

"Sure."

"It'll be fast," Bernie said. "I just need to pick up something at the library."

"Anything in particular?"

"Nah. Just something to read," Bernie said.

He was hoping that the Shakespeare books would have plain, nondescript bindings.

On the way to the library, Bernie settled back in the car seat and noticed for the first time that Softer's car had a bright orange piece of yarn fluttering from the top of the radio antenna.

23 Bone tired

Demetrius Bone, still dripping with fake blood and sweat, walked into C Building and up to his condo for what he hoped was the last time.

He walked directly into the shower, turned on the water and sat down on the tile, allowing the spray to wash away some of his rage and disappointment. And while he did, he rehearsed the speech he would deliver to his agent, Brad Cohen. About how he gave it a try, but it was just not working out. He imagined himself talking reasonably and calmly and his agent realizing the depth of Demetrius' resolve.

As Demetrius dried off, he imagined his agent arranging for an e-ticket to be waiting for him at the airport, maybe first class as a way to apologize. After all, Brad wasn't an unreasonable guy, Demetrius thought.

But his fantasy world began to unravel with the first phone call. For starters, when he dialed the Los Angeles-based sports agent, he got only as far as Cohen's secretary, who assured him that while Brad was in the office, he was too busy to take Mr. Bone's call at that time.

"It's urgent," Demetrius said. "I need to speak to him right away."

The secretary said she would write that on the message slip, and Demetrius should just stay by the phone and Cohen would call him as soon as he got the chance.

"But he's very busy this morning," the secretary said.

Obediently, Demetrius stretched out on the couch with the telephone within reach. It was nice, he thought, to finally be alone in the condo. That Haitian girl was always looking at him and talking. It made him uneasy.

He never knew what to say to her. She was always talking about her father and how good life would be if only she could find her father. And Demetrius always found himself biting his tongue and fighting the urge to tell this innocent little girl how complicated and treacherous the world of fathers could be.

Demetrius soured on the notion of fatherhood soon after finding out who his father was. Demetrius wasn't much older than Yolette on the day the pastor of his mother's church took him to a Los Angeles Dodgers game.

Pastor Hutchins had always hung around the house, sometimes staying for dinner and once or twice even bringing Demetrius a present on his birthday. But Demetrius didn't think much of it, not until the time the big man with the deep voice and the smiley eyes passed him a Dodger dog and put his hand on Demetrius' knee before saying, "It's time I tell you about a little secret."

At first Demetrius was thrilled. He had believed his mother's story, that his father was killed in a work accident when he was just a little boy. So to suddenly have a father was like getting an unexpected gift.

But it didn't take long for Demetrius to understand the bittersweet condition of their relationship, that Demetrius would have to be part of a public charade for a man who preached about heaven but made a little boy's life a kind of hell.

To be treated in public like a stranger, to be left sitting in the pews with the others, listening to words about sin, the devil and the power of prayer, was too much for Demetrius, whose own prayers were not being answered.

"It's just that I have to be very careful," his dad once told him. "Nobody likes a preacher with a bastard child."

So that's what he was, a bastard child. Demetrius never forgot those words, and he quickly grew to make himself have no use for the man who spoke them. Years later, Pastor Hutchins showed up at one of Demetrius' college football games.

He had driven all the way from California to East Texas to see Demetrius play. It was supposed to be a big surprise. But his mother couldn't hold it back, and told Demetrius on the night before the game to look for Pastor Hutchins.

Sure enough, Demetrius saw his father sitting alone in the stands and still wearing his cleric's collar. At the end of the game, a game that Demetrius dominated with five touchdown runs, Pastor Hutchins was standing next to the team bus.

"Son," the preacher said, hugging Demetrius, who quickly freed himself from the embrace and stepped back.

"We have to be careful," Demetrius said. "Nobody likes a star running back with a bastard father."

And with that, he got on the team bus and never saw his father again.

He nearly told Yolette that story, if for nothing else, just to inoculate her from the infection of hope that seemed to be inflicting her. The girl was irritating, but still he didn't want to see her get hurt the way he had.

In the end, though, he told Yolette very little about his thoughts on fathers and fatherhood and instead acted gruff to her, hoping it would eliminate any expectation of emotional coddling or confirmation from Demetrius.

And now she was gone — it wasn't his concern where — and he was alone in a condo that he hoped would be his address only for the next few hours.

Outside, the sounds of Lou Margolick's citrus standoff and the forcible removal of the fake-blood throwing animal-rights activists were creating quite a ruckus. But Demetrius tuned them out, allowing his ears to listen only for the ringing of the phone just a few inches from his head.

But after an hour, that ringing still hadn't happened. Bernie and that guy, Ricardo, with the wired jaw, knocked on his door looking for the girl, but Demetrius just sent them away without even getting off the couch.

"She's not here," he shouted. "Now leave me alone. I'm expecting a very important phone call."

Sometime during the late morning, he had fallen asleep on the couch, and hours later he was startled by the sound of the ringing phone.

"Demetrius, you sound groggy."

"I fell asleep waiting for your call. Where've you been, Brad?"

"Demetrius, you're not my only client. What's the matter?"

"I'm done here, Brad. Finished. I want you to put me on the next flight to L.A. This place is ... "

"Whoa, whoa, whoa. Slow down, Demetrius. You haven't been there that long. We knew right from the start there would have to be an adjustment period, and ... "

"I'm through adjusting, Brad. And I'm through living in this twilight zone. I'm ready for South-Central again. I was safer there."

"What are you talking about?"

"Brad, I've been Maced more than once already at Shady Palms. I've never been Maced in the hood. And when I go for a run here, the gate guard calls the cops, saying there's a burglar running through the complex. And they got these big mutant ducks here, and they chase you, biting at you when you try to run by them. The people here are ... "

"Demetrius, these all sound like adjustment issues. You just need to give it time."

"Time for what? Brad, it isn't safe here for me. These people are dangerous. And I haven't even told you about the way they drive. Half of them can't even see over the dashboard."

"Demetrius, I have a hard time believing that you ... "

"Have you ever been here, Brad?"

"Well, I ... no, not really, but I'm sure that ... "

"Then you have no idea. Maybe you've been getting all your information from reruns of *The Golden Girls*."

"All I know is that you need a little structure in your life, Demetrius. And being a solid citizen for a while in a place where law-abiding people live would only ... "

"Did you say law-abiding?" Demetrius said. "For starters, your Uncle Bernie's got me sharing a place with an illegal Haitian castaway. We're supposed to be hiding her out from immigration."

"Her?"

"Don't worry, Brad. She's 11 years old. And this morning, in the next building, there's a man who has strapped himself to an orange tree. He's armed to the teeth, and the last time I checked, he was holding off an entire S.W.A.T. team."

"Demetrius, I didn't ... "

"The man's ready to take some people out, just because they want to chop down his orange tree. This place is crazy, Brad. At least in the hood, people fight about important things like money and sex. Here, they fight about orange trees or parking spaces. Did you know they can't have soap in the showers at the clubhouse because two people complained it made the floor too slippery?"

"If you just give it a few more weeks, I'm sure ... "

"Wait, I'm not finished. You think this place is so wholesome. Well, I've already smoked plenty of pot here. And they get great stuff, too — by prescription."

"Demetrius, you're kidding me, now."

"No, that's word. My man, Johnny, has a serious stash. And did I tell you they gamble here big time?"

"Demetrius, you know the problems you've had with gambling and how you ... "

"That's just what I'm saying, Brad. What do you think these old guys do at night? Sit around dunking cookies in warm milk? I'm already in a poker game. I lost $100 on the first night. You should have seen me, Brad, smoking dope and playing cards."

"Demetrius, I can't believe that ... "

"Well, you better believe it, Brad. Get me back to South-Central L.A., where I'll be safe and happy. This place is ... "

There was loud knocking on Demetrius' door.

"Hang on," Demetrius said to his agent, then yelled to the door, "Go away. I'm on the phone."

It was Bernie at the door, and he didn't go away. He kept pounding and saying, "C'mon, Demetrius. Open up. It's an emergency."

"Somebody at your door?" the agent asked.

"It's your beloved Uncle Bernie."

"What's he want?"

"I don't know, and I don't care. Brad, you've got to put me on the next plane. I'll behave in L.A. I'll work out. I'll get a better job than that bouncer's job.

I'll ... "

"Put my Uncle Bernie on the phone," the agent said. "I want to talk to him."

"Are you listening to me?"

"Yes, I am, Demetrius. But please, let me speak to my uncle."

Demetrius put down the phone and walked to the door, opening it for Bernie, who started telling Demetrius something. But the younger man wasn't listening. He just handed the phone to Bernie.

"It's your nephew," Demetrius said. "He wants to say hello."

"Hello, Brad?"

"Uncle Bernie, what the hell's going on there? The S.W.A.T. team? Dope smoking? People getting Maced? Federal fugitives? High-stakes gambling? Violent ducks? Bernie, tell me what I've been hearing isn't true."

"Brad, I'd love to talk, but I can't right now. We have an emergency here, and I need to borrow Demetrius for a while."

"Uncle Bernie, before you hang up, I need to ask you if ... "

But Bernie hung up. Just like that.

"Hey, what did you do that for?" Demetrius asked.

"No time to talk on the phone right now," Bernie said. "C'mon, Demetrius, you need to come with me."

"I was on the telephone to my agent, and you just come in here and ... "

"Put your shoes on, c'mon. I'll explain when we're on our way."

"On our way where? I'm not going anywhere right now. I have to talk to my agent."

"You're coming with me, Demetrius," Bernie said, putting his hand on the younger man's arm. "Please."

"What's this about?" Demetrius said.

"Yolette," Bernie said.

"What about Yolette?"

"I'll explain in the car," Bernie said. "I just hope we're not too late."

24 Out on a limb

Yolette waited in the woods until she was sure no one was coming after her. Then she moved away from the sound of the helicopters and toward an opening in the trees on the far end of the lot.

When she got there, she saw that this piece of undeveloped land was nothing more than an island of nature in the middle of a sea of suburban sprawl. Beyond the edge of the trees, a black asphalt parking lot spread out before her like the surface of a hot grill, sending up shimmering heat vapors in the late-morning sun.

And then she saw it, rising up from the wavy air, its yellow sign as bright and reassuring as a kept promise: Denny's.

Yolette's heart leapt with joy. She had no idea her father would be so close to her. To think that all the days she had spent in that lonely condo, he had been right there, walking distance from her.

Yolette wiped the leaves and the dirt from her clothes, ran her hands through her hair and walked up to the sidewalk that ringed the restaurant. She looked through the big glass window and saw that the restaurant was crowded. Each table was full of people, who hovered over what looked like too many plates and glasses. The people were picking through piles of food while the workers moved from table to table, cleaning up after them, or filling their cups and glasses with coffee or water.

Yolette walked to the front door, through the foyer and up to the counter, where a selection of pies stared at her from a glass case, and a white woman who looked too young to live at Shady Palms eyed her from behind the cash register.

"What do you need, honey?" the woman asked, as she went back to adding up numbers on a calculator she kept next to the register.

Yolette reached into her precious plastic bag and pulled out the small photo of her father and waited for the woman to finish her computation and look up at her.

"Here," Yolette said, handing the woman the photo. "Tell him Yolette is here to see him."

"Who's this supposed to be?" the woman asked.

"My father."

"Looks a little young to be your father."

"His name is Jean Claude Germond."

"Don't look familiar to me."

"This is his restaurant," Yolette said.

"Really?" the woman said, letting a crooked smile come to her face. "He's the boss?"

"Yes," Yolette said, returning the smile.

Then the woman did something that shocked Yolette. She laughed, not a petite little hee-hee laugh but a big belly laugh, one loud enough to turn a few heads.

"That's a good one, sweetie!" the woman said, before looking up at a group of people who approached the counter. "I'll take that check," the woman said as the four people gathered around, forcing Yolette to step back.

But before she did, she took the photograph from the counter and walked deeper into the restaurant, still convinced

that the woman at the cash register was wrong. As Yolette
walked through the restaurant, she caught a glimpse of a black
man carrying a large plastic bucket and walking into the back of
the restaurant. His back was to Yolette, but she was sure he was
her father.

She ran toward him and found herself in the restaurant
kitchen, where a chorus of voices began shouting,

"Hey, get out of here!" and, "What are you doing here?"

The man she had been following turned around, and it was
not her father at all.

"Jean Claude Germond," she said.

"The bathroom is the other way," one man told her.

"But my father ... "

"You have to leave now."

She waited outside the restaurant for much of the afternoon, watching for her father's car to roll up. Maybe he would
have one of those big fancy cars like Ricardo. She imagined herself walking into the restaurant, holding her father's hand, while
all the workers there who had led her to believe she was mistak-
en would say, "Oh, of course! Mr. Germond's daughter! How
could we be so blind! He talks about you all the time!"

But instead, Yolette noticed that the woman behind the
counter kept looking out the window at her, and at one point
Yolette noticed the woman appeared to be talking about her to
another employee, both of whom would then look out at Yolette.

Minutes later, Yolette noticed the woman was speaking on
a telephone and looking out at Yolette at the same time. She did
not have a smile on her face. Yolette wondered if the woman was
trying to reach her father. But two minutes later, when she saw
the green and white Palm Beach County Sheriff's cruiser coming down the street, she correctly guessed that the woman had
called the police on her.

Yolette ran back to the woods, watching as the car parked

and the officer went inside, shortly to return to the parking lot and begin looking around. By that time, Yolette had climbed a tree, moving higher and higher, until she had managed to get to a point that both frightened her yet made her feel safe from the officer below. After about 10 minutes, the officer returned to the restaurant, and then five minutes later, he walked out to his car and drove away.

Yolette breathed a sigh of relief until she realized she could not figure out a way to get down from the tree. She nearly cried, but right at the point of despair, she saw a gleaming new Bentley pull into the restaurant parking lot.

Her father had arrived, she thought.

But it was Ricardo who stepped out of the car. One of his arms was in a sling, and he had a big wad of bandages over his left shoulder, but it was certainly him.

"Ricardo!" the girl shouted.

The man stopped walking toward the restaurant and turned toward the woods.

"Ricardo," the girl said. "It is Yolette. In the tree."

She was surprised to see that Ricardo could not speak and that the accident had left him too frail to get her out of the tree himself.

"Mmm m mmmmmm mm mmmm," he said, before holding up his finger and heading back to his car.

He drove away, and 10 minutes later, he returned with Bernie and Demetrius, and close behind them was a second car with Lois and Rose in it.

Bernie, Rose, Lois and Ricardo stood under the tree, looking up at her. Demetrius, after seeing Lois, decided to wait in the car.

"Can you get down?" Bernie asked.

Yolette shook her head.

"Stay put. Demetrius will come up and get you," Bernie

said, before walking over to the car to get the younger man.

"Like hell I will," Demetrius said. "She climbed up. She can climb down."

"She can't get down, Demetrius," Bernie said. "She's stranded. Like you were in Miami Beach."

"Don't remind me. I should have stayed there."

Demetrius could see the others looking at him, and when his eyes glanced up the tree, they met Yolette's eyes.

"Dag!" he said. "This is the very last thing I'm doing at Shady Palms. After this, you're taking me to the airport."

The 11-year-old Haitian castaway ran away from Shady Palms in search of her long-lost father. Yolette didn't get very far, ending up stuck in a tree.

He stepped out of the car and pointed at Lois.

"And I'm not coming any closer until that crazy woman clears the area," Demetrius said.

"Mmmm mm mmm mmmmm," Ricardo said.

"Get in the car, Lois," Bernie said.

"I will not be ... " Lois started to say indignantly.

"C'mon, we'll run the air conditioning," Rose told her friend, guiding her back to the car.

"That last time was an accident," Lois said to Demetrius as he took a wide circle around her.

Demetrius climbed up the tree easily, and when he reached Yolette, he could see she was terrified. Actually, he was a little frightened, too, after looking down and seeing how high they were. But he wasn't about to tell the girl that.

"OK, now," he said. "Let's just climb down together, one step at a time."

Yolette shook her head, and Demetrius could see her eyes were as wide as saucers.

"Then hang onto my back, and I'll climb down for the both of us," he said.

The girl draped herself over his back and wrapped her arms around his shoulders, pressing her cheek against the back of his head. Her legs quickly encircled his waist, turning herself into a human backpack.

"Am I hurting you?" Yolette asked.

"No, this is good," Demetrius said.

And it was. Having the girl hang onto him like that gave him a sense of her fear and vulnerability. Being a running back, he was used to people hanging on his back, but this was the first time he hadn't been trying to shake somebody off.

"We're doing fine now," he reassured the girl as he slowly descended.

He patted her forearm, and she squeezed him harder. Whether it was out of fear or appreciation, he couldn't say.

It took them about 20 minutes to get down from the tree, and during that time, Demetrius realized he had thought of nothing other than the task at hand. He didn't think about football. About Shady Palms. Or about returning to L.A. He just listened to the sound of the girl's breathing, felt the touch of her skin on his and the thudding of her heart on his back. His world was reduced to a patch of sky, a collection of tree branches and the employment of muscles that had been conditioned for far more demanding — yet curiously less satisfying — work than they were doing now.

While Demetrius made his way down the tree, he had no idea of the drama unfolding below him. The deputy who had been looking for the girl returned in his squad car, and seeing the scene under the tree, walked over to ask questions.

By the time Demetrius got to the bottom of the tree, he saw that Bernie, Rose, Ricardo and Lois had surrounded the cop and were all talking to him at once.

"So this is the father?" the deputy said, pointing to Demetrius.

Demetrius, smiling from his triumphant descent, thought he must have heard something wrong.

"The waitress in the restaurant said the girl was looking for her father in the kitchen."

"Yeah, well ... " Bernie said. "She's got an active imagination."

Yolette pressed herself harder against Demetrius' back, once she saw the uniformed officer.

"Hey, wait a second," Demetrius said. "Did somebody say that I ... "

Bernie cut him off.

"Hello, Demetrius. We were just telling this nice deputy how great it is to have a young man of color living with us at Shady Palms."

"You live at Shady Palms?" the young white cop asked Demetrius.

"Not for long," Demetrius said.

"I thought Shady Palms was an adults-only community," the cop said.

"It is," Rose said.

"But we're trying a pilot program ... " Bernie said. "To see if kids will work out."

" ... and black people," Lois said.

"Mmmm mm mmmm mm!" Ricardo said, nudging Lois with his knee.

"Did I mention my daughter-in-law works for the sheriff's office?" Bernie asked.

"Yes, about three times," the deputy said, frowning now.

"Wait a second here!" Demetrius said. "I think there's a big misunderstanding. Did somebody say ... "

"Demetrius is going to be trying out for the Miami Dolphins," Bernie said.

"You should see him run," Rose said.

"He's a natural," Lois said.

"Mmm mmm mmmmm mmm mmmm."

They were all trying to interrupt Demetrius at once, all of them looking at him, imploring him with their eyes to shut up, to let this cop think he was the girl's father. But he wasn't going to let them push him around like this.

"What misunderstanding?" the deputy said, looking right at Demetrius.

Yolette pressed harder on his back, and he felt her tremble slightly. And she whispered the word "please" in his ear so softly that he might have confused it with the breeze.

"Um ... " Demetrius said.

Yolette squeezed tighter. Bernie's lip began to tremble. Rose looked at her feet. Ricardo reached for Lois' hand.

"I'm not ... I'm no ... " Demetrius said. "I'm not an owner at Shady Palms. I'm just renting."

"Mmmmm," said Ricardo, purring softly like a contented cat.

25 A lullaby for Demetrius

"Now, don't get any ideas," Demetrius told the girl. Since he carried her down from that tree earlier in the day, he would notice her staring at him from time to time.

"I only said I was your father to keep you from getting in trouble."

They were back in unit 26C at Shady Palms. And after several unsuccessful attempts to get his agent, Brad Cohen, to call him back, Demetrius had decided to institute Plan B. If Cohen wasn't going to cooperate in getting him out of Shady Palms, he'd have to do it himself.

He began stuffing clothes in a gym bag, choosing what to take and what to leave behind. He'd have to travel light.

"Where are you going?" she asked.

"Los Angeles," he said.

"Where is that?"

"Far away."

"How will you get there?"

Demetrius had wondered the same thing himself. Having no money or credit cards complicated what could have been a simple exit. His first idea was to borrow the money from somebody at Shady Palms. He didn't even bother trying Bernie because he knew Bernie would try to talk him out of leaving.

So Demetrius asked Johnny Fox.

"What do you need $300 for?" Johnny had asked when Demetrius showed up at his door.

"A one-way ticket to Los Angeles."

"You're leaving us?"

"As soon as possible."

"But what about the $100 you already owe me?" Johnny had asked.

"Oh that ... " Demetrius had said, completely forgetting the poker debt. "I'll ... I'll mail it to you once I get settled there."

Not only did Johnny not give him any money, but he also phoned Bernie to alert him to Demetrius' plan to flee Shady Palms.

"Bernie," Johnny had said, "if your friend here disappears without repaying me, I'm putting you on notice that I'll tack the $100 he owes me onto your $600."

"Don't worry, Johnny," Bernie had said. "He's not going anywhere."

Bernie got to 26C in time to see Demetrius packing his gym bag.

"So where you off to, Demetrius?"

"None of your business."

"Los Angeles," Yolette said.

"None of your business, either," Demetrius said, glaring at her.

And then much to his surprise, the little girl's bottom lip quivered, and her eyes began to mist before she turned around, ran into the bathroom and closed the door.

"Dag! Now, why did she have to do that?"

"She likes you, Demetrius," Bernie said. "It's obvious."

It was obvious to Demetrius, too. After he had carried her down from that tree earlier in the day, she continued to cling to him. She had wrapped herself around him, resting her head on his shoulder. At first he thought she was just frightened from the tree and the cop, but then he heard her sigh when, subcon-

Demetrius, desperate to escape from his life at Shady Palms, tries his hand at hitchhiking on I-95.

sciously, his big hand patted her arm reassuringly.

This wasn't the plan. He had come to be a football player, not a surrogate father to some castaway who, like him, was probably just homesick.

He wanted to knock on the bathroom door and tell Yolette not to take it personally. But he didn't know where to begin, so he finished zipping his bag and stared at the bathroom door for a second before facing Bernie.

"Thanks for everything, Bernie," he said. "This isn't your fault."

"So you're leaving," Bernie said. "And how will you get there?"

"Hitchhike."

Bernie nodded. And then to Demetrius' surprise, the old man didn't try to talk him out of leaving.

"I'll drive you to I-95," he told Demetrius. "It'll be easier hitching a ride from there."

■ ■ ■

It was the height of the afternoon rush hour when Bernie pulled his Camry onto the shoulder of I-95, just north of the Boynton Beach Boulevard exit.

"This is as good a place as any," Bernie said.

"So this is goodbye," Demetrius said.

Bernie extended his hand.

"I'll be looking for you in the NFL."

Bernie sat for a moment and watched as Demetrius put the gym bag at his feet and stood near the shoulder of the road, holding his right thumb out toward traffic.

Then Bernie pulled the Camry back onto the highway and drove off, tooting his horn and waving as he passed Demetrius.

When Bernie got back to his condo, he was glad to find that Rose had already left for her book club meeting at the clubhouse. She left his dinner plate on the counter. Bernie ate all of the baked potato, picked a few bites out the salad and none of the meatless hamburger.

"It's like eating bread on a bun," he announced to Lucky before tossing it in the dog's dish, where it quickly disappeared.

Then Bernie sat in his TV chair and flipped on the weather channel, paying special attention to the local radar picture and the line of clouds moving across Lake Okeechobee. He channel-surfed for another 15 minutes, got his car keys and started out the door. The ringing telephone stopped him. Bernie expected it might be Demetrius, calling from a roadside pay phone, telling him that he had reconsidered his hitchhiking plan.

But Bernie frowned when he heard the voice of his nephew from Los Angeles.

"What's going on over there, Uncle Bernie?" the sports agent asked. "My secretary said Demetrius called several times this afternoon, demanding I wire him money or else something drastic would happen."

"Well, Brad, it's like I tell a lot of people here. Condo life isn't for everybody."

"And then I call his number a few minutes ago, and a child answers the phone," Cohen said.

"That would be Yolette."

"Who's Yolette?"

"It's a long story, Brad. And actually, I was just heading out the door to pick up Demetrius, so I can't talk right now."

"Pick him up? Where is he?"

"He's hitchhiking on I-95."

"Uncle Bernie!"

"Brad, everything is under control. Listen to me. I'm a condo building president. I know what it's like to deal with headstrong people. Sometimes you've just got to give them enough rope to hang themselves."

"Uncle Bernie, I've made quite an investment in Demetrius, and I hope that sending him to you wasn't a ... "

"Everything's under control, Brad. Don't you worry."

Bernie drove back to I-95, and his heart sank when he approached the shoulder where he had left Demetrius and saw no one there. Maybe he had miscalculated. Bernie, always the gambler, figured the odds were extremely long that anyone would pick up a large, young, muscular black man on the side of I-95 in Palm Beach County.

But Demetrius wasn't there. Bernie drove by the spot, slamming his hand against the steering wheel and considering the need for a heart pill, when he saw a lone figure walking on the shoulder of the road about a half-mile ahead of him.

Bernie eased the Camry onto the shoulder, and Demetrius, thinking that someone had finally offered him a ride, broke into a big smile as he scooped up his bag and ran toward the waiting car.

But the smile disappeared and his run slowed to a walk when he saw it was only Bernie.

"I thought we said goodbye."

"See those clouds?" Bernie said, pointing to the purple sky in the west.

"I don't care," Demetrius said, walking away from the car and holding out his hitchhiking finger.

Bernie turned off the engine and sat there watching Demetrius. After 15 minutes, Demetrius walked over to the car and said, "I can't get a ride with you sitting here like this. Leave."

"That storm is getting closer, Demetrius. C'mon, let's go get a big, fat cheeseburger at Checkers."

"You're not tricking me into staying," Demetrius said. "I'm gone."

To make his point, he turned away from the car and began walking away. Bernie just sat there and watched him getting smaller and smaller up the road.

Bernie drove to Checkers, got himself a double cheeseburger and ate in the car on the way back to Shady Palms. He disposed of the evidence in an outside dumpster and walked into his apartment, deciding he'd better wash his hands after Lucky kept smelling his fingers.

Bernie sat in his TV chair, flipped on the set with the remote control and heard the first big splats of rain. The patter turned to a downpour, and he sat there, waiting for it to end.

And that's when he fell asleep. The busy day, the double cheeseburger and the hypnotic rhythm of the raindrops put Bernie in a deep slumber.

The next sound he heard was his wife's key in their condo door. Startled, he popped up from the chair just as Rose walked in.

"What time is it?" he asked.

"Nine," Rose said. "Hey where are you going?"

Bernie was already out the door.

The rain was still falling lightly. It bothered him that he hadn't heard from Demetrius. Maybe some trucker had felt sorry enough for the hitchhiker in the rain. Maybe Bernie miscalculated the odds. It wouldn't have been the first time.

He drove up I-95 to the Lake Worth exits without seeing a trace of Demetrius. He turned around on 10th Avenue North and headed south to Boynton Beach Boulevard, craning his head to the northbound side, again not seeing the man. He made a second northbound trek on the interstate, and this time, he spotted a figure squatting on the grassy shoulder near the Hypoluxo Road exit. Bernie slowed and pulled over. The figure stood and walked toward the path of Bernie's headlights.

Demetrius was dripping wet and shivering, despite the

humid night. He didn't smile and didn't argue, either. He just got in the passenger seat of Bernie's car.

"You ready to go back to Shady Palms?" Bernie asked.

Demetrius just nodded and looked out the window.

They drove in silence, and when Demetrius walked into the condo, Yolette looked up from the television to regard his wet, haggard appearance.

"Demetrius," she said. "Did you try to swim to Los Angeles?"

He took a hot shower and got into bed. He stretched out, staring at the ceiling and feeling about as helpless as he had ever felt in his life.

The girl walked in, sat in a chair and looked at him. She had that picture of her father and the sealed envelope with the letter addressed to him.

"I know you are not my father," she said to Demetrius, and then she put the photo and the letter on the night stand. He remained on his back, staring at the ceiling.

Now it was time for the big man's lip to quiver.

"Do not worry, Demetrius," Yolette said. "I feel like this often. It goes away. You will see."

And then she sang a song, a haunting lullaby Demetrius had never heard, sung in a language he didn't understand.

"*Dodo, ti pitit maman-ni ... Maman-li ale nan rivye ... Papa-li ale peche krab ... Si li pa dod, krab-la va manje-ou ...* "

"What does it mean?" Demetrius asked when she was finished.

"Sleep, mother's little baby. Your mother has gone to the river. Your father has gone to catch crabs. If you do not sleep, the crabs will eat you."

Demetrius nodded.

"Baby's all alone," he said.

"My mother used to sing it to me," the girl said.

And then she sang it to him again.

26 More than just a friend

The Wonder Walkers cut short their morning laps outside the closed stores in the Boynton Beach Mall to allow themselves more time to chat over sticky buns in the food court.

The previous day's events had given them so much to talk about: Yolette up a tree. Demetrius on I-95. The animal-rights group's assault on Shady Palms. And the nine-hour S.W.A.T. standoff outside D Building that ended in the surrender of Lou Margolick in front of his beloved canker-stricken orange tree.

Any one of these topics could have been a full morning's discussion. So the women wasted no time in going from walk mode to talk mode.

Rose, Lois, Maddy and Jacqui were so absorbed in the discussion that they didn't notice the approach of a woman and two men.

"Margo!" Rose said, shocked to see her daughter-in-law standing there. "What are you doing here?"

"Hi, Rose. Ladies," Margo said. "I'd like to introduce you to detectives Licata and Washburn. They're with the economic crimes unit."

Maddy rolled her eyes and looked at Lois.

"Did your charge card overheat, girl?"

Lois scowled. But Rose went pale.

"Does this have anything to do with Bernie?" she said.

"No," Margo said, sitting down and patting her mother-in-law's hand reassuringly. "I'm sorry for surprising you like this, Rose, but I didn't want to tell you this in front of Bernie."

"Then it is about Bernie," Rose said. "I told him to lay off the gambling. I told him that after what happened last year he needed to ... "

"Ma'am," one of the detectives said. "This has to do with you, not your husband."

"Me?" Rose said. "What did I do? I know I claimed a lot of charitable deductions last year on our taxes, but I have the receipts from all the ... "

"Rose," Margo said. "Relax. You haven't done anything wrong. Detectives Licata and Washburn are here to ask you to help them."

"I don't understand."

The rest of the women leaned forward, intent on not missing a word. Jacqui, who had a wad of sticky bun in her mouth, stopped chewing.

"Remember when you asked me to check on that guy, Vince Campo?" Margo said. "Well, when I noticed some recent criminal activity in his record, I happened to mention it to detective Washburn here."

Washburn pulled up a chair on the other side of Rose.

"Ma'am, we've had our eye on Mr. Campo. Detective Licata and I were the ones who shut down his orchid scam a few years ago."

Rose was flustered again. She didn't like to hear these people saying bad things about Vince, not in front of her friends, who would be quick to chime in with their I-told-you-so remarks.

"He just seems like such a nice man, I can't believe ... "

"Ma'am, all con artists seem like nice people," Licata said.

"That's how they dupe others."

Rose didn't like being told she was a fool. And she didn't appreciate Lois' next observation, either.

"So now I know, Rose, where you got that beautiful bunch of orchids on your dining room table," Lois said.

Margo looked at her mother-in-law sympathetically.

"Rose, at first I told the detectives that I couldn't ask you to do this."

"Do what?" Rose said.

"But they assured me there was absolutely no danger in it, and they'd be monitoring the situation the whole time and would be right there if anything happened," Margo continued.

"What are you talking about?" Rose said. "If what happened?"

Washburn spoke next.

"Ma'am, we have reason to believe Campo has begun another scam. He may not have learned his lesson with the orchids."

Rose put her hands to her head and said, "Stop! Please. I know nothing of his business. We sit next to each other in a class. He took care of my dog. He made me a beautiful lunch. I don't know what you're talking about. You and these orchids of yours."

"It's like this, Mrs. Hamstein," Licata said. "Campo buys a small farm in Florida that actually does grow orchids. Then he finds gullible investors and tells them that they can get a 19 percent annual return on their investment. Nineteen percent sounds good to a lot of people. And Campo makes it sound credible. He takes them out to the farm. Shows them the actual rows of orchids they could call their own and explains that the market is so good for orchids that their investment is safer than it would be in the stock market."

"And people give him money?" Maddy asked.

"Millions of dollars, eventually," Washburn said. "And at first, they're very happy. Because they start getting the 19 percent return he promised them. Campo is their hero. The money comes in. They feel like financial geniuses. They tell their friends. Their friends tell other friends. Soon, a lot of people want to plunk down $15,000, $25,000, even $50,000 to get a piece of Mr. Campo's wildly successful orchid business."

Licata jumped in: "The problem is he's selling the same rows of orchids to more and more people. On paper, the farm looks enormous as new investors buy another piece of it. But they're just buying a piece that other people have already bought. And the money he's paying out in dividends isn't from the sale of orchids, it's the new investor money going to pay the old investor dividends."

"So eventually," Washburn said, "the scheme collapses from its own greed. There aren't enough new suckers to pay off the old suckers. And once he can't keep making payments to the old investors, they start getting suspicious and then start asking tougher questions and demanding to see accounting that doesn't exist. Before long, they're calling us after they realize that they own nothing. Most of their capital investment went into Campo's pocket, and the rest went to temporarily fool other marks like them."

The Wonder Walkers sat there mesmerized.

"That's awful," Jacqui said.

"I knew he was trouble," Lois said. "But I had no idea he was this much trouble."

"Why isn't he in jail over that orchid business?" Maddy said.

"He should be," Washburn said. "And the orchids weren't his first crooked enterprise, either. But regretfully, we made some procedural mistakes during the investigation and had to settle for a rather lenient plea bargain."

Rose's mind flashed to the lunch she had with Vince on his back patio, and his boat named "Plea Bargain."

"So he got off?" Jacqui said.

"Not exactly," Licata said. "He pleaded guilty to one felony count, but nearly all of his sentence was suspended."

"Which means," the other detective piped up, "he's a free man as long as he keeps his nose clean. But if we catch him running another investment scheme, he goes away for 20 years, no questions asked. The judge was very clear on that."

"Twenty years," Maddy said. "You're talking about a life sentence for people our age."

Rose felt so many emotions tugging at her. She was hurt to learn that a man she thought was sensitive and caring could be so cruel. She felt embarrassed to think of herself as a "mark" for a con artist. And she felt confused, too. Because a part of her still wanted to believe that there was another explanation for everything the detectives were saying here today. She wanted Vince Campo to show up at the table, right then and there, to say why the detectives had completely misrepresented his actions. Maybe this would end up just like Lois' jewelry, which Vince was accused of stealing but didn't.

Rose must have been lost in thought for a while, because the next thing she knew, detective Washburn was looking at her and saying, "Mrs. Hamstein? Mrs. Hamstein?"

"I'm sorry," Rose said. "I wasn't listening. What did you say?"

"They want you to wear a wire, Rose," Lois said.

"A wire?" Rose said, wondering how her choice of brassiere had anything to do with the current discussion.

"It's a hidden microphone, Rose," Margo said. "This way what he says to you will be recorded, and there won't be any doubt about whether or not certain words were spoken."

Rose frowned, and said, "I don't know if I can ... "

"Mrs. Hamstein," Washburn said. "If Campo's new scheme takes root, there's no telling how many more people will lose their nest eggs with this scam artist. It will literally ruin the lives of dozens of people, many of them senior citizens like yourself."

Margo patted Rose's hand.

"I wouldn't have agreed to let them talk to you, Rose, if I thought you'd be in danger, or if they were doing something that wasn't worthwhile," the younger woman said. "But the reason we came here is because I didn't want to spring this on Bernie, considering his heart attack."

"And he's already jealous of Campo, too," Lois said.

"Oh, I think he's just pretending to be jealous," Rose said.

"No," Lois said. "He's jealous."

"Well, that's nonsense," Rose said. "I mean, Vince and I, we're just ... "

And then she looked at the detectives and stopped talking.

"Mrs. Hamstein," Washburn said. "Vince Campo knows more about computers than most people. Why do you think he would drive from Boca to Lantana to enroll in a beginning computer class for adults?"

Rose had no answer for that. The detective answered his own question.

"To look for marks for his new scheme," Washburn said. "He picked you. Why? Who knows? You're friendly. You both have Italian-American backgrounds. You live in a big condo with a wide circle of friends. Once he suckers you in, you'll tell these ladies here. They'll invest. You'll all make a little money. Then you'll tell others. And boom, we're off to the races again."

Lois snorted.

"Maybe these girls would give Campo money," she said. "But not me. I smelled a rat right from the start."

"Oh, yeah?" Rose said. "Then why did you let him take Lucky when Bernie was in the hospital?"

"Let's not fight," Maddy said. "Let's just help our Rose."

"It's strictly your decision, Rose," Margo said. "Nobody's going to force you."

"We don't think it will take that long," Washburn said. "If he has already tried to impress you with his home, he's probably ready to let you in on a little investment opportunity."

"So what would I have to do?" Rose asked.

"Don't miss any opportunities to see him. Act natural. Wear the wire. He'll do the rest," the detective said.

Rose thought about the $50,000 she and Bernie had saved. How they saw their savings wiped out by their children's college years and then gradually built up by her husband, who could have retired three years before he did, but kept working so they could have a bigger nest egg in retirement.

Would she have blown it all, like a fool, just because of a smooth guy like Vince Campo? Would her and Bernie's sacrifices and hard work have disappeared over a man with a soft touch, a twinkle in his eye and the voice of a lark?

Rose was thinking again how Vince had sung her favorite song to her that night in Boca. *I'll Be Seeing You*, he sang. And now she was seeing him in a whole new way, a way that made her feel ashamed of herself.

Rose looked the detective in the eye.

"I'll help you," she said.

27 The melancholy Danish

Bernie Hamstein walked into the Shady Palms clubhouse auditorium and took a seat in the back row, hoping nobody had noticed his arrival.

About 50 people were clustered near the stage, many of them reading scripts or talking in small clusters. Bernie knew most of them. This was the core group of the Shady Palms Players, a gaggle of equally dedicated and obnoxious residents who, in Bernie's mind, lived for the sole pleasure of inflicting their meager theatrical talents on their neighbors for a nominal charge.

Their founder, inspiration and dictator was none other than Johnny Fox, the card-playing, stoned-by-prescription creditor to Bernie's poker debt. Fox was in the process of trying to corral his minions into the first few rows of seats when Bernie sat in the dark shadows of the auditorium's last row.

Bernie slumped lower in his seat, hoping to remain undetected for as long as possible. He still wasn't sure he could go through with this.

He had read in *The Shady Palms Gazette* that this was the first day of rehearsal for Johnny's original musical extravaganza, *Shakespeare Goes Catskills*. The brief story in the condo newspaper said this production, one of Johnny's most ambitious, would include musical accompaniment by The Swinging Palms, playing a completely original score.

"What I've done," Johnny was quoted as saying in the newspaper, "is combine two of the most entertaining forms of theater the world has ever known — the works of playwright William Shakespeare and the razzle-dazzle of Borscht Belt stage shows."

To Bernie, it seemed like putting mustard on ice cream. But his interest in the musical production had nothing to do with its merits, only with its ability to erase the $600 debt with Johnny.

"So if I agree to perform in your production, I won't owe you the money?" Bernie had asked Johnny during a furtive phone call Bernie made a day earlier while Rose was out food shopping.

"That's right," Johnny had said.

Bernie couldn't imagine why his role in the production was worth so much money to Johnny.

"It's like this, Bernie," Johnny had explained. "I wrote this part with you in mind. You'd be perfect for it. I have very few men to choose from, and between you and me, they don't have the spunk or the presence to pull off this role."

"And I do?" Bernie had asked.

"In more than one way. You're big. You're loud. And you're well known here. Having you in the show will bring in more ticket revenue. Bernie, you'll end up paying for yourself. Trust me."

So, that was it. Johnny was going to pay himself the $600 Bernie owed him out of ticket receipts, rationalizing that Bernie's addition to the show would bring in that much extra money. It was a projection Bernie doubted and seemed more like another clever way Johnny had figured to skim money off his beloved enterprise.

"Well, I'll have to think about it," Bernie had said.

And so there he was, sitting in the back of the auditorium, still thinking about it, still giving himself the option to bail out. But the truth was, whatever Johnny had in store for him couldn't be as bad as his alternative: bagging groceries with Joey Alpo, the mobster. It was safe to say that the indignities associated with *Shakespeare Goes Catskills*, no matter how considerable, would not rise to the level of felonies — something Bernie couldn't say about getting involved with Joey Alpo.

But then again, it wasn't wise to underestimate the indignities associated with a Johnny Fox production. He was capable of orchestrating an evening of theater that, in its level of discomfort, could rival a colonoscopy. So, Bernie thought it might be safe to remain undetected until he could determine if *Shakespeare Goes Catskills* was a show he could stomach, or if it was in the unpalatable league of some of Fox's other contrived gems, particularly that outer-space musical from a couple years ago, *Houston, We Have a Polka*.

But Bernie's cover didn't last long.

"Bernie, what are you doing here?"

Bernie turned to see his friend, Mickey "Softer" Faraday, drummer for The Swinging Palms, who had just come in the back door and was now plopping in the seat next to him. Softer spoke about as quietly as he played the drums.

"I didn't realize you were going to be in Johnny's production," Softer said, in a voice loud enough to blow Bernie's cover in the back of the theater.

Johnny Fox looked up from his script in the front of the auditorium, spotting the two men and smiling.

"Ah, I see a representative of The Swinging Palms has arrived," Fox said. "And Bernie Hamstein, you're here, too. Bravo! Take a seat up here, Bernie. I'll get to your part in a moment."

The rest of the cast swiveled in their seats to look as Bernie stood up and began walking forward with Softer. Some of the women were smiling at Bernie, but the few men who were there had scowls on their faces for this newcomer, this intruder who was taking a part in the show away from them.

"Great," Bernie whispered to Softer as they sat down in the front of the auditorium. "Now I get to be hated outside C Building, too."

Johnny was in the process of describing the show's opening number and answering questions from the confused cast.

"No, no, no," Johnny was saying. "It's just the women, the ones stage left who are singing the 'Avon calling' part."

Then Johnny got on stage to demonstrate.

"OK, I'm Shakespeare. And I'm here center stage, introducing myself to the audience, OK? And I'm singing, 'I'm the bard of,' and as I sing the word, 'Avon,' the kick line of women stage left lean forward, press their imaginary doorbells and say, 'Avon calling.' "

There are murmurs of comprehension from the actors.

"And that's when I answer the make-believe door and say to the Avon Ladies that, while I'm not interested in buying any of their products, I'd like to show them some of mine," Johnny said. "And then we're off on our musical tour."

More murmurs of approval from the cast.

"And who's playing Shakespeare?" someone asked.

Bernie held his breath.

"I am," Johnny said.

Bernie exhaled.

"Johnny should be committed," he muttered to Softer.

"Bernie, did you have a question?" Johnny asked.

"Um," Bernie said. "No, I was just wondering when we were getting fitted. For costumes."

Johnny continued with his quick run-through of the show,

a show that in Bernie's mind had the potential of being even worse than the outer-space musical.

"And that brings us to our big curtain closer for Act I, which is Hamlet," Johnny said. "And for that, we'll feature the debut of our newest member, Bernie Hamstein."

There was more muttering from the Players, who apparently took the announcement of Bernie's Hamlet as a bit of big, unsettling news.

Johnny hushed his group.

"I know a few of the men here had their hearts set on this role, but as artistic director and the author of *Shakespeare Goes Catskills*, you'll have to trust my intuition that Bernie will be right for the part."

Bernie didn't know *Hamlet* from an omelet. When he checked out books on Shakespeare at the library, he tried reading a couple of his plays, but the flowery and antiquated English kept putting him off.

"You are familiar with the story of Hamlet, aren't you, Bernie?" Johnny asked.

Bernie shrugged. The rest of the cast began chattering about their fondness for *Hamlet*, and somebody asked Johnny a question.

Bernie was lost.

"Who are Rosencrantz and Gildenstern?" Bernie asked Softer.

The drummer said he wasn't sure, but he thought they might have lived in F Building.

"You'd think there would have been an item in *The Gazette*," Bernie said. "Mort's usually pretty good about getting all the obituaries in."

Johnny was talking again, explaining his vision of Bernie's role.

"Forget what you know of *Hamlet*, Bernie," Johnny said.

"That won't be hard," Bernie whispered to Softer.

"Because we're playing *Hamlet* for laughs," Johnny continued. "Imagine Henny Youngman playing Hamlet. In fact, when you come out, your first line will be, 'Take my life — please.' "

This brought laughter and applause from Johnny Fox's sycophants.

Bernie turned to Softer and said, "He probably wrote this when he was high."

"What did you say, Bernie?" Johnny asked.

"I said ... um, 'I'll give it a try.' "

"Excellent," Johnny said. "In my production, we're going to be putting the role of Hamlet on its ear. I don't want Melancholy Dane, I want Melancholy Danish. Richard Burton may have been a memorable Hamlet, but I'm looking more for Judge Chuck Burton than Sir Richard Burton. I want nobody to leave this theater without remembering Bernie Hamstein's Hamlet."

Bernie said to Softer, "That's what I'm afraid of."

"What's that, Bernie?" Johnny said.

"I said, 'I'll show them what I'm made of.' "

"That's the spirit," Johnny said. "OK, so Hamlet's on stage, doing his shtick. By the way, we're going to need a skull. If anyone knows where we can find a human skull, please let me know. OK, so there we are, Hamlet's on stage and he's got Yorick's skull — now get this — in a doggie bag."

More murmurs of approval from the cast.

"And that brings us to our big Hamlet number, *You Call That a Question?*" Johnny said. "Bernie will be singing, 'To be or not to be?' and the chorus will be answering, 'You call that a question?' and Bernie sings again, 'To be or not to be,' and the chorus answers, 'Maybe he's got indigestion?' "

Bernie cleared his throat and spoke up.

"Excuse me, Johnny. But ... I'm not much of a singer."

"Which will make it all the more funny," Johnny said.

Softer patted Bernie on the back.

"Congratulations, Bernie," he said. "You're going to get some laughs."

Bernie wasn't so sure. More laughingstock than laughs was his prediction.

Johnny Fox continued his run-through, and Bernie became more convinced that he had gotten himself mixed up in a production that would take years to live down.

As he headed up the aisle, to slink away and figure out how he could possibly explain to Rose what he was doing without disclosing the $600 debt, he was stopped by Johnny's voice.

"Wait a second, Bernie, you've got to get measured for your costume," Johnny said.

A minute later, Bernie was standing with his arms extended as Estelle Fishman from D Building lassoed him with her tape measure.

"You don't have to worry about the pants," Bernie said. "I've got a pair of black slacks I can wear."

Estelle shook her head.

"Nice try, Bernie," she said. "But we're going authentic on the costumes."

"What does that mean?" he asked.

"Have you ever worn tights before, Bernie?"

"Very funny," Bernie said.

Estelle raised her eyebrows and looked at Bernie with a face that made him realize she wasn't joking.

"Tights and pumpkin pants," she said.

"Pumpkin pants?"

She showed him a drawing. Elf shoes, tights and blousy, bulbous shorts that looked kind of like ... a pumpkin.

Bernie swallowed and tried to smile.

28 The father-daughter dance

Demetrius Bone woke up to the sound of pounding at his condo door.

For a second or two, he forgot about the previous night: the hitchhiking escape that never materialized and the ignominious return to the condo, softened by the little girl's lullaby.

The pounding on the door continued.

"Who do you think that is?" Demetrius whispered to Yolette.

Yolette shrugged, smiled and patted his hand. A day ago, this might have unnerved him. But something in Demetrius snapped out there on the highway. Some measure of confidence left him as he spent hours on the side of the road, growing ever more convinced of a world that didn't care for him. By the time he had returned to the condo, he was feeling more lost and alone than he'd ever felt and more in need of somebody willing to console him.

And it figured that the girl would be the one to understand that. After all, she was so needy herself and undoubtedly no stranger to those same emotions.

"Thanks for the lullaby last night," he told her.

"I could sing it again," she said.

Since leaving Haiti, Yolette Germond, 11, has carried a snapshot of her father, Jean Claude, a man she has never known, but hopes to find.

"Don't you think we'd better see who's at the door first?"

When he opened the door, he was nearly trampled by an excited and impatient Ricardo, who waved a piece of paper in his hand and started talking nonstop.

But Demetrius had no idea what Ricardo was saying, because all that came out of his wired jaw was "Mmmm mm mmmm mm mmmmmmm, mm mmmm! Mmmm mm ... "

"Hey, slow down, man," Demetrius said, as Ricardo thrust the paper under Demetrius' nose, excitedly pointing at a few lines of it.

Had Ricardo been able to talk, he might have explained that a couple of days ago, he had managed to convey to the law firm that represents his family's sugar mill that he was in search of a local man named Jean Claude Germond. And that the law firm used one of its investigators to do a public records search, which had turned up a man by that name who had received a citation for an expired motor vehicle tag last year.

The Jean Claude Germond in question was 35 years old
and had a Delray Beach address, which was written on the piece
of paper Ricardo was waving frantically.

When Ricardo saw Yolette, he rushed to her and showed
her the street address, which meant nothing to the girl.

"Mmmmmm m mmm mmmmmmm m mmmmmm," he
started saying.

Then he saw the snapshot of her father clutched with the
sealed letter in one of the girl's hands. Ricardo took the photo
and held it up next to the paper. And suddenly, she and
Demetrius knew exactly what Ricardo meant.

Fifteen minutes later, they were in Ricardo's Bentley, heading for the Atlantic Avenue exit on I-95. Demetrius, who was sitting in the back seat, leaned forward and patted the girl's
shoulders, which were trembling slightly from the anticipation.

"I am going to see my father," she kept saying.

Ricardo drove east on Atlantic for a short way, then south,
making a few more turns, until the car slowed in front of a small
house with a dirt front lawn and three small children playing out
front.

A squat Haitian woman holding an infant was standing
inside the front doorway, waiting for Demetrius, Ricardo and
Yolette as they walked toward the house. Behind them, neighborhood boys started circling their bikes around Ricardo's
gleaming red Bentley.

"We're looking for Jean Claude Germond," Demetrius said.
"Is he here now?"

The woman said, "No speak English."

Yolette, unable to contain herself, burst out with a torrent
of Creole, speaking for a couple of minutes and holding the snapshot of her father out to the woman, who glanced at it momentarily, then shook her head. Demetrius didn't know what Yolette
was saying, but he could see from the hardening transformation

of the woman's face that this was not going to end up as a friendly exchange.

As Yolette talked, the woman kept shaking her head. And
when Yolette finished, the woman spoke briefly in Creole, then
shut the wooden door in their faces.

"She said that a man named Jean Claude once lived here,"
Yolette said. "But he has gone back to Haiti."

"Dag!" Demetrius said.

Dejected now, the three of them made their way back to
the Bentley, which was now ringed by kids. Demetrius shooed
away a girl who looked to be about 6 years old and was standing
next to the passenger side window looking in.

"Excuse me," Demetrius said, as he climbed in the car, and
then looked out the window at the girl, who remained frozen,
staring at him while she held the hand of a slightly younger boy.

Demetrius could hear Yolette trying to stop her sniffles
from the back seat. Ricardo started the car and was about to pull
away, when something clicked with Demetrius.

"Wait," he said, putting a hand on the steering wheel.
"Don't go yet."

"Mmmm?"

"Look at those kids," Demetrius said, motioning to the pair
outside his window. "The girl, she looks just like the woman we
spoke to in the house. Right? You can see the strong resem-
blance. Same eyes. Same cheekbones. Obviously that woman's
daughter."

Yolette stopped sniffling and looked out her window.

"Now, look at the boy she's with, the one she's protecting
like a little brother," Demetrius said. "Who does he look like?"

Ricardo shrugged his shoulders.

"He looks like Yolette," Demetrius said.

"Me?"

"Sure. Look again."

"Me."

"Mmmmm!"

"Yolette," Demetrius said. "That woman in there wasn't telling us the truth."

"What do you mean?" Yolette said.

"Your father isn't in Haiti."

Demetrius didn't know how to explain this to Yolette without breaking her heart. But he was sure of it, now, as sure as he was of anything these days. Yolette's father had his own family in America. The woman at the door holding the infant was his wife, and these were his children. The family life Jean Claude Germond had with Yolette's mother was, most likely, ancient history to him — a history he may very well have chosen to forget. And the arrival of Yolette at his Delray Beach home was probably a disappointing surprise, and certainly unwelcome news to the current woman in his life, who already had more than enough children of her own with him.

"Where is he?" Yolette asked from the back seat.

"I don't know," Demetrius said. "But I'd sure like to talk to him someplace other than this house."

Ricardo must have followed Demetrius' line of thinking, because he turned off the car, pointed to his head as if indicating he had a plan, and then motioned for Demetrius and Yolette to follow him back to the front door of the house.

The woman, who was watching them from behind the curtains, was standing with her baby at the threshold again as they approached the door.

Ricardo held out a piece of paper, pointing emphatically to the name of Jean Claude Germond and saying, "Mmmm mm mmm mm mmmmmmm m m mmmmmmm!"

Demetrius said, "Dag, Ricardo. You dragged us out of the car for this? This isn't going to work with this woman."

The woman just stared at them, saying "No speak

English."

"Mmmmm isn't English, lady," Demetrius said.

Yolette was confused. Why was Ricardo trying to talk to this woman again? She had already said she did not know her father.

Ricardo stopped pointing to the name, then put his finger in the air, as if to say, "Now, watch this."

He reached into one of his pants pockets and pulled out a money clip that was fat with cash. The woman's eyes widened and then widened even more when Ricardo peeled off a $100 bill, waving it in front of her eyes and then putting it on the front step and placing his shoe over half the bill.

He motioned again to the name of Jean Claude Germond. The woman hesitated momentarily.

Ricardo peeled off another $100 bill from his clip, put it alongside the first one and placed his shoe over both of them.

Again, Ricardo pointed to the name.

"What are you doing, Ricardo?" Yolette asked.

Demetrius concentrated on the woman's face, seeing her face cloud over with thought.

Ricardo placed a third bill under his shoe.

"We do not need any more children here," the woman said.

"Hey, hey, hey," Demetrius said. "Look who speaks English, after all."

Yolette looked confused.

Ricardo now had five $100 bills fanned out under his shoe.

"The girl just wants a chance to talk to her father," Demetrius said. "That's all."

The woman bent down and touched the bills. But Ricardo did not move his shoe.

"Where's Jean Claude?" Demetrius asked.

"She knows where my father is?" Yolette said.

The woman, coming to some decision, stood up, leaving

the bills where they were under Ricardo's shoe.

"Your father is dead!" the woman said to Yolette.

"Dead?" the girl said. "No, that cannot be true."

"Yes," the woman said. "To you, he is dead. He will always be dead to you!"

"No, no, no!" Yolette wailed.

The woman's infant, jarred awake by her mother's outburst, began to bleat. Ricardo scooped up the five bills from under his shoe, stuck them back in his pocket and hung his head. He was unaccustomed to money not being the ultimate problem solver.

Demetrius hugged Yolette and stared venomously at the woman.

"There's no reason to be so cruel," he said. "I know where you're coming from. But I don't like your style."

The woman was shaking with her own emotions and still yelling at Yolette.

"That is your father!" she said, pointing to Demetrius. "You leave us alone! We do not need you! You have your father!"

Yolette was crying, holding out the old photo of her father.

"No," she said. "This is my father. He is just ... Demetrius."

Demetrius picked up Yolette and walked to the car.

"C'mon, Ricardo," he said. "Let's get out of here."

29 Lois drives 'em crazy

The following morning, Demetrius got out of bed and tip-toed around the apartment so as not to wake Yolette. He didn't want the child to know where he was going.

This was a mission, he decided, best handled without her.

He dressed quietly, occasionally stopping to watch the child asleep on the hide-a-bed.

The night before, she had asked him to read her to sleep. He read the only material he could find, a thick booklet entitled, *Rules We Can Live By — The Unabridged Regulations of Shady Palms*, which turned out to be more interesting than either of them had imagined.

They made it through the vagaries of permitted and out-lawed flags, the surprising "what constitutes a truck" discussion in the parking lot regulations, and the procedures to follow for out-of-town guests staying beyond their second weekend. It was some time during the reading of the swimming pool rules that Yolette began to snore. Demetrius pressed on, reading deep into the bathing cap rule.

"Regardless of gender, if the hair of the tenant, or guest, is longer than four inches at any point on the head, he or she must wear an approved bathing cap (see approved bathing caps, page 47) while using the pool or spa. The bathing cap must be placed on the head so that ... "

And then he had become drowsy himself.

So, this is what it must be like to have children, Demetrius thought. Reading bedtime stories. Watching them as they sleep. Worrying about what will happen to them. Wondering if they're happy from moment to moment.

A lot of responsibility. Too much, Demetrius thought, for a yet-to-emerge football star. Still, carrying Yolette away from that house in Delray Beach, feeling her small helplessness in his arms, tapped something in Demetrius he didn't know was there.

No, he couldn't be her father. But he couldn't walk away from her, either.

And so that morning, he waited quietly in the living room until he heard Ricardo's soft tap on the condo door. Demetrius had come up with this plan last night and had told Ricardo about it over the phone.

"If you can help me," Demetrius had said, "tap on the phone four times."

"Mmmm," Ricardo said, before tapping four times.

And sure enough, there he was at Demetrius' door the following morning, right on time.

"You did remember to bring another car, right?" Demetrius whispered as he opened the door to Ricardo.

Ricardo gave Demetrius the thumbs up.

Demetrius double-checked his pocket to make sure he didn't forget the sealed letter to Jean Claude Germond that Yolette had brought with her from Haiti.

The two men walked quietly out of the condo and into the parking lot. The sunrise was still nearly twenty minutes away, but already the sky was beginning to brighten in the east.

"Where's the car we're using?" Demetrius asked, a moment before he heard it approach them as they stood in the parking lot.

Demetrius groaned at the sight of the car.

"Don't tell me you're coming, too," he said, as he got in the back seat of the Chrysler.

Lois Rodgers looked in her rear-view mirror and scowled.

When Demetrius had told Ricardo his plan and the need to be in a car other than the Bentley, which would be recognized, Ricardo instantly thought of Lois and her car.

It gave him a reason to stop by and see her and take another step in patching up their latest split. Not talking made communication tricky, but Ricardo was able to convey the request for her car. But exactly why he needed it wasn't something he could represent in the crude pencil drawings he made.

So Lois, playing it safe, opted to drive Ricardo wherever he wanted to go. It meant missing Wonder Walkers, but it also meant having some control over what might be one of Ricardo's crazy plans. If she had known it involved Demetrius, a man she had Maced on multiple occasions, she would have hidden her car keys.

Ricardo sat in the passenger seat trying to calm both of them down by making orchestral hand gestures and saying, "Mmmm mm mmmm mmm mmmm."

"Don't try to smooth-talk me," Lois said, and then she looked back at Demetrius. "What sort of mission are you two on anyway?"

Demetrius told her. They were going to Delray Beach to stake out the house where Yolette's father lived. Demetrius told her about the man's wife, and how hostile she had been about the prospect of her man having a child with another woman.

"So, I figure, we wait and watch for old Jean Claude to pull out of the driveway and go to work, and then we follow him," Demetrius said.

"And do what?" Lois asked.

"Get his feelings on the subject," Demetrius said. "That's why we gotta do this without Yolette. I don't want to put her through another experience like yesterday."

"And if the father doesn't want her?" Lois asked.

Demetrius shook his head. There was a silence in the car.

"Mmmm mm mmmmm," Ricardo finally said.

Lois and Demetrius looked at Ricardo, who nodded, as if to put an exclamation point on his last observation.

"Do us a favor, Ricardo," Lois said. "If we ever get to see this guy, let somebody else do the talking."

By the time they got to Jean Claude Germond's neighborhood, Lois was antsy.

"You didn't tell me this guy lives in a ghetto," she said, pressing the electric door locks on her car. "Are you sure we're safe here?"

Demetrius enjoyed her discomfort.

"As a precaution, I would start blasting a hip-hop station on your radio," he said.

"I've got a better idea," Lois said, fishing in her purse for the Mace.

That took the smirk off the young man's face.

The three of them sat in the parked car, watching as the sun came up. Demetrius had directed Lois to park down the block from Germond's house, far enough away so as not to draw suspicion, but close enough to see the white car in the driveway.

"C'mon," Demetrius kept muttering. "Get up and go to work."

"Suppose he doesn't work," Lois said. "I'm not prejudiced, but it's a fact that a lot of you people don't even have alarm clocks."

"Is that so?" Demetrius said. "Where did you learn that? On the KKK channel? And what do you mean by 'you people?' I'm African-American and he's ... "

"I used to like it better when we didn't need the hyphens," Lois said.

"Yeah, I'll bet you're just pining for the good old days when you could just say the 'N' word, and nobody would blink an eye."

"Listen to me, young man," Lois snapped. "One of my best friends just so happens to be black, and she's ... "

The two of them would have probably continued arguing if

Ricardo didn't silence them with a "Mmmmm!" as he pointed his finger at the white Nissan Stanza, which had just backed out of the driveway and motored past them with a black man at the wheel.

"There he goes!" Demetrius said. "Follow him! Faster!"

Lois didn't like being ordered around. So she took her time. By the time she backed her Chrysler and headed up the street, Jean Claude Germond and his car had already made the left turn on Atlantic Avenue, heading west.

"He's probably going to the highway," Demetrius said. "Can't you get any closer?"

"I'll have you know I have a safe driver discount on my insurance," Lois was saying, intentionally slowing down to prove her unwillingness to be bullied into driving faster.

Demetrius watched as the Stanza went under the highway overpass and veered into the right turning lane.

"He's going south on I-95," Demetrius said. "If you drive a little faster, we might make this next light."

Again, she refused to speed up, and sure enough, the light turned red just before she reached it. Calmly, Lois tooted her horn three times and drove through the red light.

"Mmmmmm!" Ricardo shouted, as a truck nearly side-swiped them.

"Everybody's in such a hurry these days," Lois said.

It wasn't hard tailing the Nissan on I-95, because it trailed a plume of sepia smoke and stayed in the right lane, cruising five miles under the speed limit.

At the Palmetto Park Road exit in Boca Raton, the car left the highway and, just as the light was turning to yellow, made a left turn at the end of the exit ramp. Lois' Chrysler was about five lengths behind, clearly close enough to gun the engine and follow the car onto Palmetto Park Road. But as soon as she saw the yellow light, she hit the brakes.

"No!" shouted Demetrius. "Go! Go!"

"Mmmmm!" Ricardo also urged, pointing forward.

Lois made a point of coming to a complete stop. Then she calmly tapped her horn three times and drove through the intersection.

Or at least partly through the intersection.

A champagne-colored Lexus driven by Mitzie LaBoosh, one of Boca's many hard-charging real estate agents, clipped the back of Lois' Chrysler, bringing both cars to a screeching halt under the light.

Fortunately, both cars were just accelerating after being stopped, so the crash was not a destructive one. But it created enough damage to dent the hood of the Lexus and smash the left rear light of Lois' car.

LaBoosh was talking furiously on her cell phone and heading to west Boca to close a deal when the crash happened.

"Those cell phones should be outlawed," Lois said, looking malevolently at the real estate agent who emerged from her car to survey the damage without interrupting her phone call.

"He's getting away," Demetrius said, pointing to the white Nissan.

"This is all your fault," Lois said to him. "If my insurance premium ... "

Demetrius knew he didn't have time to waste. At least he was wearing his running shoes. He threw open the back door, climbed out of the car and, without another word, began running away from the crash scene, heading east on Palmetto Park Road in the direction of the disappearing Nissan.

Mitzie LaBoosh was startled by the sight of Demetrius. She had never seen a man so big run that fast. And he ran right by her.

With hands slightly trembling, she walked up to the car and got a look at Lois and Ricardo sitting in the front seat. They were just a nice old white couple. Poor woman, the real estate agent thought. And the guy, he looked kind of beaten up. His shoulder was bandaged, and his jaw was all swollen.

"You just hang on, deary," the real estate agent said to

Lois. Then out of habit, LaBoosh handed Lois one of her business cards, while saying, "If you ever want to sell your home."

Lois had been preparing to accuse the real estate agent of
causing the crash — a preposterous claim under the circumstances, but one Lois would make with all the righteous indigna-
tion she could muster.

But the woman, much to Lois' surprise, wasn't angry and
confrontational. She even patted Lois' shoulder and said, "You
did the right thing."

LaBoosh stood next to Lois' car and dialed 911.

Lois looked at Ricardo and shrugged her shoulders.

"Yes," LaBoosh reported into her cell phone. "I'd like to
report an attempted abduction."

Ricardo leaned over, saying, "Mmmmm mmmm mmmm!"

The younger woman stopped talking on the phone and
said to him, "Just try to relax, sir. The police are on their way.
They'll catch him, don't you worry."

Ricardo got out of the car and said, "Mmmmm mmmm!" to
her, motioning frantically.

LaBoosh was still on the phone: "All I know is that he's big
and black. He came jumping out of the car after the crash, trying
to run away. No, I didn't see a weapon."

Then she looked at Ricardo.

"Sir, did the big black man have a weapon?"

"Mmmmm!" Ricardo said, stomping his foot.

Lois got out of the car, and the real estate agent asked her
for a description of the suspect.

"I don't know," Lois said. "He's just one of those ... you
know ... African-Americans, or whatever you call them these
days."

Ricardo put his hand to his head.

"Mmmmmm!"

"You'd better hurry," LaBoosh said into her phone. "I think
the old guy's going into shock."

30 Rich man, poor man

Demetrius Bone ran along the sidewalk, straining to see the little white car somewhere in the line of traffic ahead of him.

"Dag!" he said, convinced he was about to lose sight of the car as the light on the other side of the highway overpass turned green.

He could see the little puff of brown smoke trailing behind the car as it accelerated beyond the traffic light. There would be no way to catch up now, Demetrius thought. In another minute, the car would be traveling at 30 miles an hour, and then surely it would disappear.

Demetrius slowed down, about to give up the chase, when he saw the car switch lanes and indicate with a signal light that it was about to turn left into the nearby shopping plaza.

Then he saw the Denny's restaurant up ahead on the left. So, here it was. The girl had been right. Her father did work at a Denny's.

Demetrius picked up his pace, running into the road and crossing traffic as he angled toward the Denny's. Cars beeped at him, jammed on brakes and swerved to avoid hitting him. He could hear the first distant wail of a siren.

He ran as hard as he could to stop the man in the white car

before he had a chance to walk inside the restaurant to begin
work for the day.

Jean Claude Germond was locking his car door when
Demetrius, too winded to speak more than a couple of words at a
time, ran up and blocked the Haitian man's walking path
between the parked cars.

"Back ... in ... the car ... Now!" Demetrius said.

The startled Jean Claude held out his hands and pleaded
for his life.

"Three dollar, three dollar," he said, turning his pocket
inside out, allowing three crumpled bills to flutter to the pavement. "You take them."

Demetrius didn't bother looking at the bills. But he did
notice the two police cars that sped by them on Palmetto Park
Road heading toward the scene of the crash.

"In ... the ... car," Demetrius said, putting a grip on the
man's shoulder and motioning him to get back behind the
wheel.

"Please," Jean Claude said, his lips beginning to tremble,
as he held out his car keys to Demetrius. "Take the car, but
leave me alone. I have three children who need me."

"Four," Demetrius said. "In the ... car ... Now!"

Jean Claude was confused. He was no stranger to street
crime. He had been mugged in two countries. He knew the drill
by now. Complete passivity. Allow the thief to get what he wants
and then get away.

But why wasn't this man taking the money, or his car, and
then running? Why was he trying to get Jean Claude back inside
his car? And why did he think he knew how many kids Jean
Claude had?

Something was terribly wrong here, Jean Claude thought.

But the man's grip on his shoulder grew stronger and left
Jean Claude no choice but to unlock his door and get back inside

the car. In a flash, the big man had circled around the car and jumped into the passenger seat.

"Drive," Demetrius said.

"But my job," Jean Claude said.

"You're going to be late."

Jean Claude backed his car out of the spot and over the three crumpled dollars still on the pavement. He was sure the big man was going to kill him. They'd end up driving to a dirt road near the Everglades, and then the big man would tell him to step outside the car, before shooting him in the head and throwing him to the alligators.

As they drove west on Palmetto Park Road, Jean Claude saw the police cars up ahead, their lights flashing. The road was blocked.

"Turn here," Demetrius said, motioning Jean Claude to head northbound on I-95.

"I have a baby," Jean Claude said, barely above a whisper. "What will my little baby do?"

"Yes, I saw your baby," Demetrius said.

"You did?"

"Your wife didn't tell you?"

"Tell me what?"

"I came to see you at your house yesterday."

"You did?"

Then it dawned on Jean Claude. This must be a case of mistaken identity. Someone in his neighborhood probably had an unpaid debt with a loan shark or a drug dealer, and this was the muscle man that was going to beat the money out of him. Or worse.

"Now, I understand," Jean Claude said.

"You do?"

"Yes. I am not who you think I am. I am Jean Claude Germond. You must want someone else who ... "

"No," Demetrius said. "You're the guy."

"No, I am not," Jean Claude said. "It is a big mistake. I know you have the wrong man. You said I have four kids. I have three. See? You are looking for someone else."

Demetrius shook his head.

"Let's go someplace quiet where we can talk," he said. "Is there a park around here?"

Jean Claude exited the highway and drove aimlessly, hoping to cross paths with a police car.

"This is good," Demetrius said, motioning him to turn into a parking lot of a golf course.

Men were already warming up on the putting green, and clusters of golfers were zipping around in carts, making their way to the first tee.

This was a strange place for an execution, Jean Claude thought. He turned off the ignition and looked at Demetrius, who dug in his pants pocket for something. Brass knuckles? A switchblade? Piano wire?

Demetrius handed Jean Claude the letter.

"Read it," he said. "It's for you."

The Haitian man opened the letter. Demetrius studied Jean Claude's face while he read, seeing surprise become recognition and finally something that looked like sorrow or regret.

"Where did you get this?"

"Your daughter. She's in Boynton Beach."

Jean Claude nodded, put the letter back in the envelope and gave it back to Demetrius. The Haitian man's hands were shaking, and his eyes looked more frightened than before.

"I cannot," Jean Claude said.

"You can't what?" Demetrius said. "What does it say?"

The Haitian man looked out of the car window at the golfers. He looked like he was about to say something, then stopped. Demetrius opened the envelope and looked at the letter himself, unable to make any sense of the Creole.

"Read it to me," he told Jean Claude, handing him the letter. "In English."

Jean Claude cleared his throat before he spoke.

> *"Dear Jean Claude, I apologize for writing this letter. I know when we said our goodbyes to each other 12 years ago that I told you I would not do this. That the child I was pregnant with would always be my child. And my child only. I understood why you left and why you could not take me. And Yolette. That is what I named her. Yolette. She is a wonderful girl and has been the best part of my life. But it is a life that will soon be over. By the time you read this, I will be one day closer to death with a terrible disease I have kept secret from Yolette. I did not have the courage to tell her, or the heart to see her stay here in Haiti, where there will only be poverty and sadness as she watches her mother waste away a little more every day. I have seen others die from this disease, and it is painful and slow. I hear from people in the village that you have a big house and a restaurant in America. They say you have a car and are a rich man. And so I have decided to break my promise to you. I hope you will understand. I saved whatever I could, and tomorrow I will put Yolette on a boat, never to see her again. It makes me crazy with loss, yet comforted to think that if you are reading this, she must have made it safely to America, where she will have a better life, with you — her father. Please, do not tell Yolette about my condition. Not until I am dead. If you let her know I am dying, she will want to come back to Haiti, which will do nothing except ruin the only opportunity she may have in this life. That is all that matters to me now. Love, Marie."*

Jean Claude folded the letter, put it back in the envelope and handed it back to Demetrius.

"I cannot take her," Jean Claude said matter-of-factly. "I am not a rich man. You have seen my house. I have three children and a wife. I do not own a restaurant. I wash dishes. I do not make enough money to feed the family I have."

"Maybe you can get some help from the government," Demetrius said.

Jean Claude laughed.

"Help getting deported."

"But you're her father," Demetrius said. "And she's your own flesh and blood."

"Marie and I were young and very foolish," Jean Claude said.

"And that young foolishness has created a beautiful girl," Demetrius said.

"How do you know her?" Jean Claude asked.

"Yolette and I, we ... um ... we're just roommates. Temporary roommates. She's like a little sister to me."

"Then you can be her father."

"No. She already has a father."

"It takes more than biology to be a father," Jean Claude said.

Demetrius thought of his own father then and wondered if the old pastor ever had any regrets, any second thoughts about his decision to toss away a child in order to keep his clerical collar.

"What will I tell Yolette?" Demetrius said. "Should I tell her I finally found her father, but unfortunately, he's not interested?"

Jean Claude stepped out of the car and sat down on the hood, staring at the line of golfers teeing off. Demetrius waited in the car, expecting him to return, but he did not. So Demetrius got out and sat on the hood next to him.

For a couple of minutes, they did nothing but stare ahead. Then Jean Claude, his eyes beginning to brim, turned to

Demetrius.

"You know what I liked about that girl, Marie?" he said. "Her laugh. I fell in love with her laugh."

"You should hear Yolette laugh," Demetrius said, realizing he never heard the girl laugh since he met her.

"No! I do not want to hear about it," Jean Claude said. "I do not want to know anything about her."

A golf cart pulled up next to the car.

"Excuse me, fellas," the guy driving the cart said. "But employee parking is in the rear."

Demetrius clenched his jaw. But Jean Claude smiled and spoke.

"Thank you, sir."

Jean Claude and Demetrius got in the car and headed out of the parking lot.

"I can drop you off somewhere," Jean Claude said. "Then I have to get to work. I am late."

Demetrius looked at him.

"Better late than never," Demetrius said, hoping the man would take the remark more as a commentary on parenting than on getting to work.

But Jean Claude's mind was elsewhere. He was thinking about those three crumpled dollar bills and hoping they were still in the Denny's parking lot. If not, he would not have enough gasoline to drive to work for the rest of the week.

31 Dialing for dollars

Rose Hamstein jumped every time the telephone rang.

"What are you so nervous about?" Bernie had asked his wife. "You're not drinking caffeinated coffee again, are you?"

"Who's nervous?" Rose would say, breathing a sigh of relief every time the caller was somebody other than Vince Campo.

She wondered how undercover agents could stand all the tension of their kept secrets. Twenty times a day she wanted to blurt out to Bernie about the conversation she had in the food court with the detectives.

It would be such a relief to confide in her husband and not have this secret mission hanging over her head. But she knew it wasn't a good idea. Bernie's heart was already being taxed by the Muscovy duck problem and the travails of the Haitian girl and the football player in 26C. He didn't need something else to worry about.

And then there was something else going on with him, something secret of his own, she was sure. There was no other explanation for his sudden arrival home with a script for Johnny Fox's new musical, *Shakespeare Goes Catskills*.

"Since when are you a thespian?" she asked.

"Rose, not everybody in theater is homosexual," he said. "I

just thought I'd try my hand at acting."

"Did you lose a bet, Bernie?"

"Rose, is it a crime if a man wants to be a part of his community's theater group?"

"But you said a million times how you can't stand Johnny Fox's productions, and how the people in them are ... "

"So now I'm going to make them better."

"Hah! Since when did you become an actor?"

Bernie was about to make a snappy reply, something about being a condo board member giving him plenty of opportunity to sharpen his theatrical skills, but he was stopped by the ringing telephone on the end table next to his chair.

Rose jumped. Bernie reached for the phone.

"No! I'll get it," Rose said, nearly running across the room.

But Bernie picked up the phone before his wife could reach it.

"Hello?" he said.

"Bernie?"

"Yes."

"Hi, Bernie. This is Vince Campo."

"Oh, hello, Vince," Bernie said, frowning at his wife, who seemed to go pale.

"The heart's just fine, Vince ... Uh-huh. Yes, well ... Rose? She's here, somewhere."

Then Bernie took the phone away from his ear, and yelled, "Rose," as if she weren't standing right next to him.

Rose tried to grab the phone, but Bernie wouldn't let her.

"She must be in the bathroom, Vince," Bernie said. "I think she's taking care of her rash."

Rose tried to grab the phone again, but Bernie wouldn't let her.

"She didn't tell you about her rash? ... Yeah, it's a mystery, the way it blisters up and oozes. And to have it on the inside of the thighs is no picnic."

Rose lunged, this time yanking the phone from her husband's hand.

Bernie smiled triumphantly and sat back in his chair.

"Vince," she said. "Don't listen to my husband, he's such a joker."

"Rose," Vince said. "I just called because I'd like to talk to you about something."

"Oh," Rose said.

So this was it. The detectives had said that Campo was probably ready to move to the next phase of his scam.

"And it's something that I don't want to talk about on the phone," Vince said.

"Is everything all right, Vince?"

"Oh, everything is fine," he said. "But I don't want to miss this ... opportunity to tell you about something."

The sales pitch. Here it was. Just like they had said. They'd said he'd talk about a golden opportunity that would only be available to a few people. This is what they wanted her to record on tape.

"This isn't a good time," Rose said, remembering her instructions to not let him talk until she was wired.

"No, you're right," Vince said. "It's something I want to talk to you about in person."

"Yes, sure," Rose said.

She could see Bernie pretending to read his Shakespeare, but she knew he was listening to every word.

"When could we meet?" Vince said.

"Oh, I don't know. Let me call you back, Vince. I'm in the middle of cooking."

"I'm sorry, Rose."

"No, that's all right. Got to go now, though."

"OK. But you'll call?"

"Yes. Bye."

Bernie was looking up at her.

"What are you looking at?"

"You're not in the middle of cooking."

"I didn't want to talk to him."

"Why? Because I'm here?"

"Bernie, you have an active imagination."

"Is it because you'd like to say things to Vince that I might find a little too flirty?"

"Bernie Hamstein, I haven't cheated on you in 47 years of marriage. Isn't that worth a little bit of trust?"

"Seventy-two is no age to be looking for a boyfriend, Rose," he said, getting up out of his chair and heading for the door. "I'm going to the clubhouse."

But he simply closed the condo door, then stood in the hallway with his ear pressed to the outside of the door, listening to see if his wife picked up the phone again.

Rose waited 30 seconds, then walked to the door and said, "Bernie, you can come back in now."

Then she opened it, nearly causing her husband to stumble back into the apartment.

■ ■ ■

Demetrius Bone walked most of the way back to Shady Palms. He was in no hurry to get to the condo, where the girl would certainly want to know what had become of the letter to her father.

What would he say? What could he say? He rehearsed a few phony explanations, but none of them sounded very credible to him. Maybe, he'd just have to tell her the truth — he had found her father, but the man didn't want to make room in his life for her.

Demetrius wasn't sure he could watch Yolette read that letter and learn in the course of a few seconds that she had neither a father nor a mother who wanted to see her again.

Demetrius wondered how he had let this happen to himself? How had he gotten drawn into a child's life, a life that was destined for heartbreak? He was never a good blocker. He was better when somebody else was looking out for him. He was a runner, a man with an instinct for flight, not protection.

It hadn't dawned on Demetrius what he was about to do until he had sat there in that car with Yolette's father and watched the pain and uncertainty in the man's face.

"I wish there was something I could do?" were the last words the man told Demetrius before dropping him off.

Of course, there was. But Jean Claude Germond would have to learn that himself, just as Demetrius had come to learn on this morning.

The answers, sometimes, come to you in strange ways.

And so, Demetrius, drenched in sweat from the morning sun and light-headed from a lack of water and an epiphany, walked until he found a pay phone in the shopping center near Shady Palms.

It would only be about 8 o'clock, California time.

He called collect, surprised that he had remembered the number so effortlessly.

He had spent the morning looking for Yolette's father, only to find his own.

"Pastor Hutchins," the voice said.

He could tell he had woken the man. The operator asked if he would accept a collect call from Demetrius Bone. There was a long pause.

Then the man cleared his throat, and said, "Yes."

"Demetrius?"

"Yeah, it's me."

"You sound far away."

"Florida."

"Your mom told me that you ... you were hoping to get back to the NFL."

"Yeah," Demetrius said. "I've suddenly become a big fan of second chances."

There was a silence.

"Is that what this call is? A second chance?"

"I don't know."

"What can I do for you?" the man said, and then, after a

beat, added the word "son" in a voice that was almost too soft to hear.

"I need $1,000," Demetrius said.

"That's a lot of money. I live a simple life here, relying on the blessings of my congregation, who as you can imagine, don't ... "

"I need you to wire it to me today."

"I ... I don't have that kind of money, Demetrius."

"Take it from your church bank account."

"But Demetrius, I can't just ... "

"Yes you can. In fact, it would mean more to me if I knew you had to steal the money."

"I'm not a ... crook, son."

"The question isn't whether you're a crook. It's whether you're a father."

"Oh, Demetrius, there have been so many times that I ... " and his voice stopped.

"I don't want to hear it, not now. Not until I'm back in Los Angeles."

"You're coming back to Los Angeles?"

"That's what I need the money for. There's a Delta flight out of West Palm Beach tomorrow morning."

"But son, if it's just a plane fare you're needing, it surely won't cost that much."

"Yes it will," Demetrius said. "I'll be flying with one other person."

■ ■ ■

It wasn't until later that afternoon that Bernie finally left the apartment. Rose made sure he was really gone this time before she dialed up Vince Campo and arranged their meeting.

She made it for tomorrow morning. This way Bernie wouldn't be suspicious. He'd think she was at Wonder Walkers.

"Just come to my place," Vince said.

"I've got a better idea," Rose said. "Let's just meet for breakfast someplace."

When Vince arranges to meet Rose in person to discuss something important, he has no idea that she knows his criminal past and is prepared to secretly tape record their conversation.

The detectives had told her to make the meeting at a public place so they could be there to protect her and make the arrest.

"But I could make breakfast for us at home," Vince said.

"No. This will be my treat," she said.

The detectives had suggested a particular restaurant that would be both close to him and easy to monitor.

"OK," Vince finally said, a little reluctantly. "But you don't have to ... "

"No, I insist," she said. "I owe you, Vince."

There was a part of Rose that made her want to reconsider what she was about to do. She had to keep telling herself that he was really a bad man who had financially ruined a lot of innocent people.

"You don't owe me anything, Rose," he said.

He sounded tense, as if maybe a part of him regretted what he was about to do.

Rose felt the same way as she hung up and dialed the detectives.

32 Secret plans

Demetrius Bone felt guilty as he watched the girl search the condo over and over for the letter to her father, the one he had hidden in his suitcase.

"I told you," he said. "It must have gotten thrown away by mistake in the trash. It's not here. We've searched the whole place."

"But I must find that letter," she said.

Eventually, he'd give it to her, he reasoned. But not now. The truth would be too hard to take for the 11-year-old girl, Demetrius told himself.

"The important thing is that we get everything packed before we go to bed tonight," he told her. "Because tomorrow we get off to an early start."

He still wasn't sure why he just couldn't run from Shady Palms alone.

Maybe it's because for the first time in his life, he had stopped thinking of himself as a football player. It was over. He was never going to play in the NFL, he had reasoned. He had come to see himself as a person lost in a dream world, a world of nipping ducks, nosy neighbors and suspicious glances. He had come to feel like an inmate in an institution, and the more he told people he was really just a football player making an unorthodox comeback, the less he believed it himself.

So if he wasn't a football player, what was he? The only real thing he experienced during his time here had been this little girl, who had gone from a nuisance to a kind of needy, but wise, younger sister. She had sung him to sleep, and she had looked at him with eyes that seemed to register a goodness in him that he hadn't known was there.

Yolette knew of a pain he could only imagine. And as he began to cope with his own loss, he found himself drawn to the little girl whose losses were so much greater, so much more lasting and profound. Demetrius began to wonder if he was drawn to this untethered girl as a way of tying up his own lost connections.

And he also knew that she deserved more than being treated like an unwanted stray. He knew enough of the feeling to want to protect her from it.

"Why do I have to take everything, Demetrius?" she asked.

"Because we're not coming back."

"But we must say goodbye to everybody."

"No, we'll call them when we get there," he said. "We want to make it a big surprise."

"Where are we going again?"

"California."

"How did you find my father in ... Calidonia?" she asked.

"It's called California."

"Where is California?"

"You'll see. And as for your father, it's a long story," he said. "I'll explain once we're on the way."

He would have to do some explaining to others, too. What would he say to his agent, Brad Cohen? He rehearsed his lines: "Brad, I don't think I've got a good shot at playing football again, but if I don't blow it, I've got a good shot at making a little girl happy."

Even the people at the condo wouldn't buy it. They'd tell him he was nuts. That he needed a baby sitter himself. They didn't see the goodness in him that Yolette saw.

So he was doing what any enterprising inmate would do: He was breaking out.

He'd provide for her somehow in Los Angeles, maybe with the help of his absentee father who came through by wiring him the money hours after Demetrius had called.

Maybe this would be the time for the pastor to make up for his significant lapses as a shepherd. Demetrius wondered if taking the girl with him wasn't, at some level, driven by his desire to either distance himself or force a new closeness with his own father.

It was still too confusing for him to sort out. But he knew through experience that it was time to act.

The key was movement. Just like in running the ball. You improvise. You get your legs moving and start looking for holes. When one isn't where you thought it would be, you spin, weave, slide to the side — even run backwards a few yards — just keep moving until an opportunity opens up. Just don't stand still.

Soon after getting the money from his father, Demetrius stopped by Johnny Fox's condo and handed him the $100 he owed him.

"What a pleasant surprise," Johnny said, counting the money. "Will you be at the next game?"

Yolette, who was standing next to him, blurted out, "No. We are going to California."

"I'll be at the next card night," Demetrius said, easing Yolette away from Johnny.

After they walked back to their condo, Demetrius told Yolette that it was important that nobody knew about their plan.

"They'll just ruin the surprise," he had told her.

By the time he was telling Yolette to keep quiet, Johnny was already on the phone to Bernie.

"I just thought you'd like to know, Bern," Johnny said. "Your football player got some money somehow, and I think he's planning to leave tomorrow."

Bernie called Lois, who was still peeved about the traffic accident and blamed Demetrius for running away from the car so fast that she had to cast herself as a crime victim for police.

"It took hours before Ricardo and I could get out of there," she said.

Lois did say that she and Ricardo had talked to Demetrius that afternoon, and he had told them about his conversation with Yolette's father. But Demetrius didn't say anything about planning to leave with the girl.

"Do you think that's really his plan?" Bernie asked.

"There's only one way to find out," Lois said.

Later that evening in her apartment, Bernie and Ricardo watched as Lois called the airlines, claiming to be "a friend of Mr. Bone" who had changed her plans and was now able to be on the next day's flight with him.

"And I'm just wondering if there's any way you can put me in the seat next to him," she said.

There weren't many flights going from West Palm Beach to Los Angeles, so it took her less than a half hour to determine what flight Demetrius had booked. She also found out that the best she could do was sit across the aisle from him, because "his daughter" had the seat next to his, the reservation agent said.

With that information, Bernie hatched his plan. He called up Hector the gate guard and told him what to do if a taxi showed up the next morning to take Mr. Bone to the airport. Hector said he would personally take care of it.

"All set," Bernie told Lois and Ricardo. "We'll meet in the morning, down in the parking lot."

"Mmmm," Ricardo said, making steering wheel gestures with his hands.

"Yes, Ricardo," Lois said. "You'll drive."

"Where's this restaurant we're going to?" Bernie asked.

"It's the Denny's near I-95, on Palmetto Park Road in Boca Raton," Lois said.

■ ■ ■

Rose Hamstein had no idea what Bernie was up to, because she had her own secret plan in motion. While Bernie, Lois and Ricardo were in Lois' condo figuring out a way to stop Demetrius from taking Yolette to California, Rose was at the West Palm Beach apartment of her son, Sam, and daughter-in-law, Margo.

Bernie thought his wife was just making a social visit. But Rose was mainly there to get reassurance from Margo that she was about to do the right thing.

"It's just that Vince has always been so ... good to me," Rose said. "He took care of Lucky when Bernie was in the hospital. He ... "

"Rose," Margo interrupted. "That's how con men work. They're the most upstanding citizens in the world, right up until the time they take your money."

"I don't know, Margo. You really think he's no good?"

"Yes, based on what detectives Washburn and Licata have told me, I think he's just out for your money and eventually the money of all your friends."

Rose sighed. It was as if she were in a kind of mourning, grieving over the loss of a friend. Sam, who had been playing on the floor with her grandson, spoke up.

"Mom, what does Dad think?"

"Your silly father calls Vince 'my boyfriend.' He's completely hopeless on the subject. So I haven't told him anything about what's going to happen. I didn't want to stress his heart. He doesn't need any excitement in his life right now. He thinks I'm going to Wonder Walkers in the morning."

Rose tried talking about other things that night, but she couldn't get her mind off what she was about to do. Her daughter-in-law sensed her discomfort.

"Don't worry, Rose," she said. "Along with Licata and Washburn, there will be two other plainclothes detectives right there."

"It's not that I'm worried for my safety," Rose said.

"You need to go home and get a good night's sleep," Margo said.

When Rose got back to her condo, Bernie wasn't there. Good, she thought. She wasn't sure she could hide her agitation from him. She changed into her nightgown, poured herself a tumbler of white wine and rummaged through the medicine cabinet until she found the sleeping pills.

By the time Bernie got back, he found his wife asleep in their bed, with the lights on and Lucky curled up on Bernie's pillow.

"Rose?" he said, debating whether to shake her, but instead, he roused Lucky, who gave him a low growl before slipping under the covers.

Bernie really wanted to tell Rose about Demetrius, Yolette and the plan to take the girl to meet her father the following morning at the Denny's restaurant.

But Rose looked so peacefully asleep that Bernie decided not to wake her.

He would tell her in the morning, he figured. But he didn't get the chance, because before the sun came up, Rose quietly slipped out of bed, got dressed and walked out the door.

Before driving away from the condo, she reached into her purse, looking for the piece of paper that had the directions she had written down.

The detectives told her she wouldn't be able to miss it. And Vince knew right away where the restaurant was when she had told him. But just in case, she double-checked the directions.

She unfolded the piece of paper and read again how to get to the Denny's on Palmetto Park Road in Boca Raton.

33 Unhinged

Demetrius phoned for a taxi, then waited 15 minutes before he picked up the suitcases and headed out the door.

"Remember," he told the girl. "We need to be quiet, and if anybody says anything, let me do the talking."

It was about 8 a.m. when he and Yolette got to the lobby with the suitcases and waited at the curb for the cab. Moments later, he heard a toot-toot of a horn and saw a car pull up sharply to the curb in front of them.

But it wasn't the cab. It was a familiar Bentley. Ricardo was driving, Lois sat in the passenger seat and Bernie was in the back.

Ricardo popped the trunk, and Bernie got out to help Demetrius with his luggage.

"Hey," Demetrius said. "I called a cab. I don't need ... "

"The cab's waiting outside the wrong building," Bernie said. "We're your cab."

Yolette had already climbed into the back seat, happy for a chance to see Ricardo again.

"I'm tired of you people getting in the way of my plans," Demetrius said to Bernie as they stood outside the trunk. "That's why I didn't tell you anything."

"I wish you would have talked to somebody about this,"

Bernie said.

"I know what I'm doing," Demetrius said.

He got in the back of the car, leaving Yolette in the middle, between him and Bernie.

"I presume you know where to go," Demetrius said.

Ricardo nodded and began driving.

Ten minutes later, Demetrius realized Ricardo was heading the wrong direction on the interstate.

"Hey!" Demetrius said, leaning forward in his seat. "We're supposed to be going to the airport."

"The airport?" Yolette asked. "We need to go on an airplane to see my father?"

"Yes," Demetrius said, at the same time that Bernie said, "No."

"Mmmm!" Ricardo said, waving his finger in the air. "Mmmm!"

"Dag! You guys are messing me up," Demetrius said. "I don't need your help. I know what has to be done."

"Mmmm!" Ricardo said again.

"Ricardo, just drive," Lois said. "Let us do the talking."

But Ricardo, beyond frustration with his wired jaw, pulled over to the shoulder of I-95, popped the trunk and stepped out of the car.

"Ricardo, what's the meaning of this?" Lois said.

A minute later, Ricardo closed the trunk and sat back in the car. He had a pair of pliers and wire cutter in his hand. He tilted the rear view mirror his way, and for the next 30 seconds, he twisted, mashed and clipped at his mouth until he had managed to free up his jaw.

"Ricardo has something to say," he said, in a calm voice.

Everyone was transfixed by the sight of the blood streaming down his face.

"Lois, please take Yolette for a walk."

"Out here?" Lois said, looking out at the trash-strewn shoulder.

"Just do it," Ricardo said, wires dangling from his mouth, which was already getting puffy with his clumsy tool work. He did not look like a man to argue with.

"C'mon," Lois said to Yolette as she got out of the car.

"Ricardo will be brief," Ricardo said as he spun around to face Demetrius. "What you are planning to do is noble. But it is not wise. We must give this man a chance to see his daughter."

Demetrius shook his head.

"You weren't there, Ricardo. I saw the dude yesterday. He isn't going to take her. The girl's been put through too much to face something like this."

"No," Ricardo said. "There is no complete substitute for the love of a parent. She will always wonder. You must give the man another chance, or the girl will grow up looking back instead of looking forward."

Bernie's mind went to his own father, back in the tailor shop in Brooklyn, crying as he told Bernie he couldn't be the father to a boy who would marry an Italian girl. And Bernie, just 18 then, stood there defiantly, saying that he didn't care. He would get married to Rose, and he didn't care if it meant never having a father again. But he did care, eventually, and even now, decades after his father's death, he regretted how both of them stubbornly held to their course of mutual nonexistence.

"Fathers sometimes need another chance," Bernie said. "One day when you're a father, you'll ... "

"When I'm a father, I won't blow it," Demetrius interrupted. "Not like this guy ... or my father. I know more about fatherhood than I care to know."

"Then think of it this way, my friend," Ricardo said. "You ruined your chance to play football, and yet, here you are, still trying. That is what Ricardo is talking about, giving a person another chance."

"Well, I'm through with football."

"Since when?" Bernie asked.

"Since now," Demetrius said, looking at his watch. "You're

going to make us miss our plane, Ricardo."

"You give the father of this girl another chance," Ricardo said, "and if he does not want her after meeting her, Ricardo will pay for both of you to fly to Los Angeles. First class."

"So that's the deal? You're planning to just show up at the Denny's with her and think he's going to change his mind?" Demetrius said.

"Yes," Ricardo said. "That is what Ricardo thinks."

Demetrius sat back and shook his head and said, "It's your dime."

Yolette and Lois got back into the car, and they continued driving to the Denny's on Palmetto Park Road in Boca Raton. Nobody spoke.

Lois glanced over at Ricardo.

"So what magic words did you use?" she asked softly.

"Ricardo just talked about the sanctity of fatherhood."

Lois snorted.

"You mean like how Elian belonged with his father?" she asked, mockingly.

"That man is not a father," Ricardo said. "He is a communist."

"Ricardo," she said. "I'm already beginning to miss your wired jaw."

■ ■ ■

Rose Hamstein walked into the restaurant and spotted Vince Campo, sitting in a booth and twisting a paper napkin in his hands. He gave her a little wave and a tight smile.

Rose walked toward him, trying her best not to look as nervous as he did.

"Rose," Vince said, standing up and taking her hand as she sat across the table from him. "You look great today."

"You do too, Vince," she said.

She scanned the restaurant, hoping to spot the undercover detectives her daughter-in-law promised would be here.

But she didn't see any likely candidates. She noted a loud

Vince Campo explains why he has taken an interest in Rose Hamstein.

table of workers from a furniture truck parked in the lot. Next to them was what looked to be a family on vacation, the dad reading a road map while his wife refereed a food fight between the kids. Across the aisle, she spotted two tables of retirees. A pair of uniformed police officers sat at the counter, reading the newspaper and trying to flirt with the waitress. But nobody who looked like Joe Friday or James Bond was in the crowd.

She and Vince exchanged some small talk, then the waitress took their orders. Rose excused herself, saying she needed to use the restroom. But what she needed was some assurance that she was in the right place.

On her way to the restroom, she looked out the big windows and spotted detectives Washburn and Licata sitting in an unmarked car with a good view inside the restaurant. Rose was so relieved she nearly waved to them.

Inside the restroom, she opened her blouse and made sure the tape recorder was working and the tiny microphone hidden on her jacket was in place. All she had to do now was go back to the table, sit and listen and wait for Vince to make his move. Oh, and there was one other thing.

The detectives wouldn't be able to hear her conversation at

the table. So if Campo proposed a scheme to her, the detectives had told her to signal them so they could move in and make the arrest. The signal was for Rose to blow her nose with a yellow tissue.

Rose looked in her purse, checking that the travel-sized container of yellow facial tissues was there, then she walked back to the table, arriving at the same moment as the food.

It didn't take long for Vince to put down his fork and start talking.

"I guess you're probably wondering why I wanted to talk to you," he said. "Forgive me for sounding so urgent on the phone yesterday. But I couldn't hold this from you any longer. It's time I let you know about a little secret."

He reached across the table and held both her hands.

Showtime, Rose thought. The detectives in the car outside sat up straight. Vince cleared his throat. A couple of the guys who appeared to be furniture movers nodded subtly to each other.

■ ■ ■

Ricardo drove his Bentley into the Denny's lot and began searching for a parking spot.

■ ■ ■

"Sometimes, opportunities come along in life, and if we don't grab them, we end up living with regret," Vince said.

Rose felt the warmth of his hands and tried to ignore what looked like sincerity in his eyes.

"Are you giving me a sales pitch, Vince?" Rose asked.

"Yeah," he said. "I guess I am."

"What are you selling?"

"Rose, it was no accident that I ended up sitting next to you in that computer class," he said.

"It wasn't?"

Rose wasn't expecting this.

"No, I planned it that way."

"Vince, I don't understand."

"I only wish I would have gotten to know you years ago," he said.

"Vince," Rose said, pulling her hands away from him. "I'm married. I've been married for 47 years. If you're trying to meet women, there are plenty of available women out there. You're good looking, talented and sweet. You should have no problem getting practically any available woman you desire. But you ... "

"Rose, you don't understand. I'm not interested in any woman. I'm interested in you."

"Vince, I already told you, that I'm happily married for ... "

"Rose," he said, "I'm not interested in you that way. In fact, I'm not interested in any woman that way. I'm gay."

"You're gay?"

"Yes, but that's not what I'm here to tell you about."

"You're gay?"

"Yes, but please, can we just get beyond that for a moment?"

"You're gay?"

"Please, just listen," Vince said, reaching for Rose's hands again.

■ ■ ■

Ricardo parked the Bentley. As he did, Bernie Hamstein looked out the back window and blinked twice.

There was his wife, who he thought was speed-walking in the Boynton Beach Mall, sitting in a booth, holding hands with a silver fox of a guy with an open-collared shirt and a thick gold chain around his neck. Vince Campo! No wonder she had acted so strange when Campo had called the condo the previous day.

Bernie felt his face flush and his heart begin to gallop.

"Hey Bernie!" Demetrius said, "What's the rush?"

But by then, Bernie had already slammed the car door and started walking purposefully — as quickly as his somersaulting heart would allow — toward the restaurant.

34 Breakfast scramble

"Remember the day you had lunch at my house?" Vince said, still holding Rose's hands. "You told me the story about how your dad walked out on your family when you were just a girl."

"Yes, I remember," Rose said. "But what does that have to do with ... "

"And you told me that one day, soon after your father left, you bumped into him on the street. You were just 10 years old. And you asked him, 'Daddy, why won't you come home?' "

"Yes," she said.

Vince seemed to be getting choked up.

"That nearly broke my heart," Vince said. "I only wish that ... "

"Vince, that was more than 60 years ago," Rose said. "I don't see why you have to ... "

"And you never saw your father again," Vince said.

"Vince, I don't understand why you're bringing this up."

"Rose, I saw your father after that. I saw him for years."

"Vince, what are you saying?"

"The reason your father left was because of me," Vince said.

"What?"

"Rose," Vince said. "Your father is my father, too. When he left your family, my mother was pregnant with me. When he left your life, he entered mine."

"But your name isn't Cangelosi," Rose said.

Vince pulled a copy of a birth certificate out of his pocket. It showed his birth name as Vincent Cangelosi, the son of Anthony Joseph Cangelosi.

"Oh, my God," Rose said.

"I changed my name to Campo when I was 18. I thought Vince Campo sounded more like a singer's name. Vincent Cangelosi sounds like a boxer."

"He sang," Rose said, as if making the connection. "He sang. Just like you. When he was with us, I'd wake up, and the first thing I'd hear was him singing while he made breakfast. I loved his voice. He had a voice ... like yours. Oh, Vince, I never realized it until now. Maybe that's why ... "

"He taught me how to sing, Rose," Vince said. "But like him, I never made it to the top. And like him, I did some bad things along the way ... although I hurt strangers. He hurt the ones he loved. Like you, Rose."

Now Rose was getting choked up.

"I didn't even know about you and the others," Vince said. "It wasn't until Dad was dying. He had pancreatic cancer when he was only 59. It was swift and merciless. I still thought I was an only child. I remember sitting by his bedside those final days. I slept in a chair next to his bed, and one morning — the last one — I woke up with him staring at me.

"Vincent," he said. "You're not alone."

"That's when he told me about his other family," Vince said. "At first I was happy, but then I felt ashamed and confused. I couldn't imagine how it must feel for you and your brothers and sisters. So, I did nothing for a long time. And then five years ago, I buried my mom. And that's when I became determined to find the rest of my family."

"You waited a long time, Vince. There's only three of us left now."

"I know. But I had to do it. And when I found out you lived so close, it just ate away at me. I've imagined this conversation for years, Rose. I've imagined ... you."

"How did you ... "

"I hired a private investigator," Vince said. "He told me about the computer class, and I joined the next week."

"Why didn't you just tell me this from the start?"

"Rose, I was afraid you'd slam the door in my face. I was afraid you'd be bitter still, that you'd think of me as some bastard child, not really connected to you."

"Oh, Vince, why would you ... "

"You remember him, Rose, what a charmer he could be. Put him in a room with a bunch of people, and it was as if a bright light followed him around. Right? Well, a little of that rubbed off on me, enough to make me think that if I could first get you to know me, then maybe my chances would be better."

"My friends all thought you were flirting with me," Rose said.

"I was, in a way."

"Oh, Vince. This is such a wonderful surprise."

"So, does that mean I have a family again?"

Rose nodded, and her eyes got misty. She absent-mindedly reached into her purse, feeling for the package of tissues. She pulled one out and blew her nose on the bright yellow tissue.

By that time, Rose's husband was breathing heavily and trying to put off having another heart attack. Bernie made his slow, purposeful walk into the restaurant and up the aisle to the table, where his wife and Campo were still leaning intently toward each other. Because Bernie approached from behind,

Bernie Hamstein makes quite a first impression with his wife's new acquaintance, Vince Campo, after unexpectedly interrupting their breakfast conversation at Denny's.

Rose didn't see him coming, and Vince, having never seen Bernie before, thought he was just part of the table of retirees.

Bernie got to the table, just as Vince told Rose, "I feel like the luckiest man in the world right now."

Bernie surprised them both by stepping next to Campo and saying, "Your luck just ran out, Romeo," just before punching Campo squarely in a key component of his vocal instrument: his big Italian nose.

What happened next was nothing short of chaos.

By blowing her nose on the yellow tissue, Rose accidentally had signaled the awaiting detectives to arrest Campo. Within moments after her signal, the men who appeared to be furniture movers jumped up from their table, flashed guns in the air and handcuffed an already stunned and bloodied Campo.

"You have the right to remain silent ... " one of them started shouting.

In the process, Bernie was knocked onto Rose's table, where he sent breakfast plates full of food clattering to the floor and all over his wife.

"No! No! No!" Rose was shouting, trying to get around her sprawled husband to tell the detectives they were making a mistake.

Bernie had no idea why Campo was being arrested but agreed wholeheartedly with the action, thinking perhaps it was a matter of divine intervention. It bothered him, though, that his wife was trying to prevent the arrest.

"Still trying to save your boyfriend, Rose," Bernie said, panting and holding onto his throbbing punching hand, while pancake syrup dripped from his hair.

"Bernie, you fool!" she said. "He's not my boyfriend."

And then Rose shouted louder than she ever had in her life.

"HE'S MY BROTHER!"

Everybody froze. Well, almost everybody.

By that time, Demetrius Bone was 6-feet-3-inches and 235 pounds of lightning-quick muscle and determination. From the instant he saw the shabbily dressed men pop up from the table and attack Vince, Rose and Bernie, he knew what it was.

An armed robbery.

Demetrius, still in the parking lot, started sprinting inside.

The two uniformed cops sitting at the counter had been eyeing him before he started running. Just a day ago, they had been called to a nearby crash scene, in which an old white couple had been nearly abducted by a man who seemed to fit the description of the man approaching the restaurant.

When Demetrius started running for the door, the police officers jumped off their stools and headed for him, shouting, "You! Stop right there!"

Demetrius couldn't believe how stupid these cops were. An armed robbery was going on in the back of the restaurant, and they were pulling the typical let's-harass-the-big-black-dude routine.

He'd have to explain later. So, rather than stopping and putting his hands over his head, Demetrius deftly sidestepped the first cop. He evaded the second cop with a twirl move, squeezing his body into what looked to be a perilous path between the cop's grasp and a hot pot of coffee sitting on the counter.

Once by the cops, Demetrius barely broke his stride as he leapt over a stroller, avoided plowing down an old man blocking the aisle and changed directions at the last second to miss a waitress emerging from around the corner with a serving tray full of Grand Slam breakfasts.

Seeing him approach, the biggest of the detectives posing as furniture movers stepped into the aisle. The detective, a competition weight-lifter who was used to having suspects quake in his presence, stuck out his arm and said, "Hold it right there, junior."

Instead, Demetrius ran over him as if he weren't even there.

Then he barreled into the detective who was handcuffing Campo, and they fell into a pile on the floor. But before Demetrius could get up, three gun barrels were pointed at his head, and for the first time he saw the badges on the men he thought were thugs.

Lois and Ricardo had been arguing in the car with each other, which had caused them to miss seeing Bernie's performance and most of Demetrius' run. When they finally looked up to see what they were missing, Demetrius was being handcuffed.

They got out of the car, hoping to unscramble events. As

they walked into the restaurant, the two uniformed cops saw them, taking particular note of Ricardo's bloody jaw.

"Look, it's those people who were nearly abducted yesterday," one of the cops said. "It looks like that black guy tried to get them again today."

They radioed for an ambulance, and despite Ricardo's protestations, told him to sit down and relax.

"We got the bad man, sir, you don't have to worry."

"He is not a bad man," Ricardo said. "Ricardo knows the bad man."

"Who's Ricardo?" one of the cops asked.

The other rolled his eyes and whispered, "I think the old guy's getting delirious on us, again."

In all the confusion, Yolette sat in the back seat of the car, alone and confused. No one had told her anything.

Where was she? She looked outside the car window, looking for something familiar. But she was far away from Shady Palms. This must be California.

Then she saw the sign, the big yellow one out front. Denny's, it said.

Could this be her father's restaurant? She got out of the car and walked across the asphalt and into the restaurant.

In the confusion, no one paid much attention to her. An ambulance arrived. Police cars zoomed up with their sirens blaring. Yolette did not care. She knew no one would hurt her now. This was her father's restaurant. She would be safe here.

She walked in the door and through the restaurant, looking table to table. She did not see her father anywhere.

She walked toward a back corner of the restaurant, where there was a big cluster of people, many of them talking loudly. She wedged herself between them, moving through them until she had worked herself clear.

She stepped beyond the forest of people, and there,

crouched in front of her, was a little man wearing an apron. He was kneeling on the carpet and putting pieces of broken plates into a rectangular black bucket.

The man was much older than the face in the photograph, the one she had memorized. But it was the same face.

Yolette knelt in front of him and without saying a word, she began picking up pieces of the broken plates and putting them in the man's bucket.

Jean Claude Germond did not look up. But he saw the girl's fingers. And each time the girl's hand moved into his field of vision, he studied the hand a little more. It was the thumb that fascinated him. The shape of it was peculiar. His mother had a thumb like that, and so did he. And now so did she, this girl. This one who wanted to be a father's daughter.

He finally dared himself to look up.

And when he did, she was looking straight at him, with eyes as infinite and dark as time itself.

"*Alo, papa,*" the girl said. "*Se mwen-mem Yolette.*"

35 The big man in the back seat

Six law enforcement officers paraded Demetrius Bone in handcuffs out of the Denny's.

"This is all a big misunderstanding," he said.

The uniformed Boca cops said they wanted him in connection with an attempted abduction of a couple of seniors.

"You got this backwards," Demetrius told them. "Ricardo and Lois are the ones who abducted me! I would have been on a plane to Los Angeles this morning if they hadn't ... "

But they just got glassy-eyed and started reading him his rights.

Meanwhile, the undercover Palm Beach County Sheriff's deputies told him he was being charged with resisting arrest and two counts of battery on a law enforcement officer.

"How did I know you guys were cops?" Demetrius said. "You were dressed like furniture movers and acting like dudes pulling an armed robbery. I was just ... "

They also got glassy-eyed.

They walked him out to the parking lot and left him alone in the back seat of a city squad car, while the officers hashed out the details of their reports. It hurt to sit on his handcuffed hands, and it hurt to think how a day that started out with great

Demetrius Bone is led in handcuffs to a squad car in Boca Raton after his scuffle with undercover police officers inside Denny's.

promise had so quickly gone wrong.

Then he became aware of voices coming from just outside the door of the car. He looked out the window, hoping to see Bernie there explaining everything to the cops. They'd listen to Bernie, Demetrius knew. Bernie could get him out of this jam.

But it wasn't Bernie.

"Dag!" Demetrius said.

The guy standing with the cops was an older guy. He was big and had a deep voice that seemed to be filtered through gravel. As he spoke, he took a few notes on a clipboard he was holding. The cops all seemed to know him, and Demetrius could see from their body language that this was some authority figure to them.

A minute later, the back door on the other side of the squad car opened, and the big man sat down in the seat.

"Demetrius," the man said. "We need to talk."

"I'm through talking to cops. You people just twist every-thing I say. I'm talking to a lawyer, that's who I'm talking to."

"Demetrius, I think you may have the wrong impression ..."

"Wrong impression? No, you're the ones with the wrong impression. Go talk to Bernie, he'll tell you."

The man looked down at his clipboard.

"Bernie Hamstein," he said. "Yes, we just had a long chat inside the restaurant about you."

"So, if Bernie already told you," Demetrius said, "when are you planning to let me go?"

"Let you go?" the man said and then laughed. "Letting you go is the last thing on my mind. If I have my way, you won't be going anywhere for the next two years."

"Two years!" Demetrius said. "I didn't do anything in there. I was just ... "

"No, Demetrius," the man interrupted. "I'm afraid I have to disagree with you. You did quite a lot. I was watching you as you walked in the door. I saw you, the way you got by the first two officers who tried to stop you. I saw it all. The way you jumped over that stroller, which could have injured that young child, and the way you nearly knocked down that waitress and that old man."

"I didn't touch any of them," Demetrius said.

"I know, and you didn't slow down, either," the man said. "I thought for sure you wouldn't have enough room to get around them the way you did."

"You can't charge me for almost knocking somebody down."

"And the way you knocked over that big undercover detective," the man said, shaking his head. "Ouch! He's going to feel that for a few days."

"I was just trying to save Bernie and his wife from what I

thought was a robbery," Demetrius said.

"Didn't Bernie explain any of this to you?"

"Bernie told me you're a football player."

"Not any more."

"No? Then what are you, Demetrius?"

It made Demetrius think. The last thing he had seen as they were leading him out of the restaurant was Yolette crouching on the floor with her father.

"At the moment," Demetrius said, "I don't know what I am."

"By the way, my name is Howard," the man said, extending his big hand for a shake, then realizing that both of Demetrius' hands were cuffed behind his back.

"Oh, sorry," the man said, withdrawing his hand.

And that's when Demetrius first noticed the man's hands, not for their size, but for the two enormous rings. The Super Bowl ring was on his right hand, and the NCAA championship ring was on his left.

"Howard what?" Demetrius said.

"Howard Schnellenberger," the man said. "You might have heard of me. I've done a little footballing myself."

"Those rings," Demetrius said.

"The one on the right is the Dolphins' perfect season. I was an assistant under Coach Shula. And the one on the other hand is when I coached the University of Miami, the year we beat Nebraska for the national championship in the Orange Bowl."

Demetrius nodded.

"I've done some other coaching. I started out with Bear Bryant at Alabama, did a stint with George Allen for the Los Angeles Rams, and at the University of Okla. . ."

Schnellenberger stopped and looked at Demetrius. "Not much of a student of the game, are you?"

"I'd rather play than watch," Demetrius said.

"But not a player anymore, eh?" Schnellenberger said. "That's too bad. Bernie told me you played ball for a couple of years in college and then dropped out. And then you went to camp with the Raiders and almost made the team."

"Yeah, well, almost doesn't count," Demetrius said.

"No, you're right about that." Schnellenberger said. "Especially if you're kicking field goals."

When Demetrius didn't laugh, Schnellenberger frowned and cleared his throat.

"Demetrius, don't you want to know why I'm sitting here talking to you?"

"I expect you'll get around to telling me," Demetrius said.

"I'm working for a university about a mile from here. It's called Florida Atlantic University."

"Never heard of it," Demetrius said.

"Hardly anybody has," Schnellenberger said. "That's because FAU has been a school without a football team. Now, you say FSU, and everybody knows what you're talking about, because Florida State has a nationally ranked football program. But you say FAU, and people around America give you blank stares."

One of the cops tapped gently on the window.

"Just give me five more minutes, officer," Schnellenberger said, then he turned his attention back to Demetrius. "Guess what mascot FAU has had?"

"I don't know," Demetrius said.

"C'mon, guess."

"A tiger."

"A tiger! Oh, what I would have given for a tiger! Or a panther, or some ornery reptile. But no, we've got a bird — and we're not talking about a hawk or an eagle or some kind of other respectably manly bird. FAU has a burrowing owl. A frail, practically endangered little bird that hides underground and grows up to the fearsome height of 9 inches."

"Might as well dress the fellas in pink jerseys," Demetrius said.

"Exactly! So, FAU wants a football team, and they bring me in, and the first thing I do is get rid of that wimpy little bird. We're stuck with owls. But I get them to change it to a big nasty-looking owl, at least."

The officer knocked again on the window. Schnellenberger held up two fingers.

"Two-minute drill, Demetrius," he said. "I'm telling you about the owl because, well, that's the easy part. The hard part is that in September I'm going to run out onto the field at Pro Player Stadium with a bunch of young men who will be playing the first-ever collegiate football game in this school's history. And Demetrius, I don't want to lose. I've never enjoyed losing."

"Howard," Demetrius said. "I already played college ball. I'm ready for the pros, not some little school nobody's heard of. I've been there, done that, already."

"The pros? Oh, you're ready for the pros. You didn't tell me that. I thought you told me you were through with football. My mistake. What pro team has invited you to camp this year?"

"Nobody's invited me anywhere."

"Here's the deal, Demetrius. If FAU's brand new football team puts an average of 16,000 fans in the seats for the first two years, we will go from Division 1-AA status to Division 1-A status. By then our lease at Pro Player Stadium will be expired and — if we figure out a way to relocate some of those little wimpy owls on campus — we'll have our own $100 million home stadium right here in Boca Raton."

"I don't know what I have to do with any of this," Demetrius said.

"So this morning, as I'm sopping up my eggs, I'm thinking about the couple dozen players I get to give scholarships to, and the rest of the team, a group of walk-ons. And I'm thinking, which one of these kids is going to fill those seats? Who is going to make people want to watch FAU football? It's beginning to make me nervous, Demetrius. I'm thinking that what I really need is a running back, a guy who won't make it necessary to have a great passing game. A guy who can make enough first downs to keep an inexperienced defense off the field for as long as possible. And then I see you go through here like a young Mercury Morris, and I think, 'Howard, if there's a God, this young man will have a couple of years of college eligibility left.' "

Demetrius shook his head.

"What's wrong?"

"What's the name of this school of yours, again?"

"Florida Atlantic University. FAU."

"I'm 23 years old," Demetrius said. "That's too old to be running over those college boys."

"You won't get much blocking," Schnellenberger said, "but I suspect you prefer it that way. Make your own holes, like you did in the restaurant this morning."

"Howard, I know if I got the chance, I could run for more than 1,000 yards in the NFL next season. What would I prove with a bunch of 1-AA ball players?"

"You'd get noticed," Schnellenberger said. "I'd make sure of it. Come to my office one day, and I'll show you my phone book."

The officer opened the door of the car.

"Coach," he said. "We really have to transport the prisoner now."

Schnellenberger took out one of his business cards and stuck it in Demetrius' shirt pocket.

"Demetrius," he said, before getting out of the car. "You told me before that nobody invited you to football camp. As of this moment, you're wrong."

36 A day of firsts and lasts

Demetrius Bone never did take up Ricardo's offer for a first-class ticket back to California.

It took a couple of weeks to clear up his legal mess. And then a few days later, he appeared unannounced in Howard Schnellenberger's office at Florida Atlantic University. The coach acted as if he were expecting Demetrius.

But he wasn't expecting Demetrius' demands.

"Let me get this straight," Schnellenberger said, writing it down. "A full-time job on campus that pays at least $15 an hour, and a slot for a fifth-grader at the Henderson School."

"That's it," Demetrius said.

"Demetrius, that school is already full, and I don't know of any jobs that ... "

Demetrius started standing up, as if to leave.

Schnellenberger motioned him down with his hand.

"I'll see what I can do."

After that was settled, Demetrius called his agent, Brad Cohen.

"You're what?" Cohen said.

"I'm a college student again," Demetrius said.

"Let me talk to Uncle Bernie."

"He's not here. I'm calling from the dorm."

Brad Cohen hadn't heard of the FAU Fighting Owls, either. But he did know who Howard Schnellenberger was. And once Demetrius told him the full story, Brad's tone softened considerably.

"So, I guess that means you don't need an agent, at least for the next year or two," Brad said. "Will you at least call me when you play?"

"I will."

And he did. The Fighting Owls played their first college game with a packed stadium and a seasoned head coach who was promising great things from his unseasoned team — in particular, his starting halfback.

Before the game, sportswriters asked the coach what they could expect from the Fighting Owls offense, and Schnellenberger was quick to provide a much-quoted line:

"Let's put it this way," he said. "The wishbone is an offensive formation, but we're going to make the defenses on other teams play the wishbone."

Schnellenberger waited for their puzzled stares and questions.

"You see," he finally continued, "once they get a look at Bone running the ball for us, they're going to wish he was on their team."

Demetrius dressed for the game in the Dolphins locker room at Pro Player Stadium. He had imagined himself here so many times, but certainly not under these circumstances.

"Towel, Mr. Bone?"

Demetrius shook his head at the little man who was standing next to him holding out a towel.

"How many times have I got to tell you to just call me Demetrius," he said, taking the towel from the older man.

"Yes, sir."

Demetrius shook his head again.

"Is she here today?" Demetrius asked the man.

"She woke me up at 6 this morning, afraid we would be late," the man said.

Demetrius smiled, and Jean Claude Germond stepped back as a few sportswriters found Demetrius and began asking questions.

"Demetrius," one of them asked. "Why did you decide to play for FAU?"

"I think it was the school's national reputation as a football powerhouse," he deadpanned, then winked at Jean Claude.

"Either that, or they had the highest paid equipment manager in college football," he said.

The reporters looked at each other, noting silently that Demetrius Bone appeared to be a first-class flake. They moved on to the next player, hoping for a quote they could use for their stories.

Minutes later, when Demetrius walked onto the field, he had no idea that the stadium would be so crowded. The thundering sound of more than 30,000 people assaulted his ears. His heart quickened. His eyes scanned the stands, searching halfway up Section 114, unable at this distance to pick out the people he knew were there.

Lois Rodgers scanned the FAU players with her binoculars.

"What number is he again, Rose?"

Rose turned to her right, "What number is he, Vince?"

"Twenty-one," Vince Campo said.

Vince had been spending a lot of time with his half-sister, Rose. Especially now that Bernie was busy with his theater production and Vince was officially out of the investment business for good.

Vince was also singing less these days. His voice was different now, affected by the broken nose Bernie gave him. He sounded like somebody else now, somebody he didn't quite like to listen to as much.

Bernie and Rose had apologized a hundred times, but Vince had told them he wouldn't change a thing. And he really believed it. Life, he had come to believe, must be a zero-sum game of happiness. You can't have it all. For every happiness, there's a sorrow waiting to counterbalance it. And so, he had gained a family and lost a voice at a breakfast table at Denny's. A fair trade.

"I see him now," Lois said before lowering her binoculars. "He looks scared."

"My dear," Ricardo said. "It is impossible to tell at this height whether a man on that field is frightened."

Lois glared at Ricardo.

"Shush," she said. "I thought you were getting me a mai tai."

"My dear," Ricardo said. "This is not a cruise ship. This is a football stadium. They do not have umbrella drinks here."

Lois and Ricardo seemed to be itching for the opportunity to create another relationship-chilling argument. It was just a matter of time. Ricardo had been spending nights at the condo, and they had shared two solid months of companionable bliss, a clear sign that trouble was about to erupt.

"I think you misheard, Ricardo," Lois said. "The announcer said that umbrellas weren't allowed in the stadium. He didn't say anything about umbrella drinks."

"Uh, oh," said Brad Cohen, pointing down to the field.

Cohen was sitting between Ricardo and Pastor Hutchins, who flew cross-country with the sports agent as a surprise for his son.

"That's trouble," Cohen said, as he watched FAU's new mascot scamper onto the field with unbridled antic energy.

Cohen, the only person there who knew Demetrius' aversion to mascots, gave everybody a brief history. Then they watched in horror as the college kid in the owl suit tried to interject some humor in FAU's pre-game drills.

The owl lined up in the offensive backfield, tapping Demetrius on the shoulder and motioning to let him play. Demetrius ignored the owl, who then, in mock frustration, kicked Demetrius with a theatrically delivered foot to the rear end.

"Let us pray," Pastor Hutchins said, holding the hands of Brad Cohen and Yolette, the two people sitting next to him.

"Demetrius will not hurt the owl," Yolette said.

Demetrius turned around, while the owl stood there, taloned hands on hips. Demetrius made a fist with his right hand and drew it back.

"Oh, Lord, we beseech you," Pastor Hutchins continued.

"Demetrius will not hurt the owl," Yolette said again.

Demetrius brought his fist forward like a baseball pitcher making an overhead fastball delivery. But his hand stopped a few inches from the owl's beak, and then he opened the palm of his hand.

The guy in the owl costume gave him a "high-five." And then Demetrius stepped aside, allowing the owl to take his place in the drill.

"Young lady," Pastor Hutchins said, "how do you know so much about Demetrius?"

"Because we both were once alone together," the girl said.

Pastor Hutchins nodded and patted the girl on her knee.

"By the way, Lois, wonderful job on the hors d'oeuvres," Vince was saying down the row, as he reached into the Tupperware container to select another toothpicked treat.

"Yes, I wanted to make something that would go along with the theme of the day," Lois said.

"I didn't know there was a theme of the day," Rose said, as the Tupperware container kept working its way down the row.

"Well, I mean, the owls," Lois said. "So I thought something in the fowl family would be appropriate."

Vince, a gourmet cook himself, knew exactly what he was eating. He just didn't know where Lois got her meat.

"So where do you get your duck?" Vince asked.

"Duck!" Rose said, spitting it out in her napkin.

"Um," said Lois, "really close to where I live."

Ricardo also stopped chewing and was looking suspiciously at Lois. Vince, unaware of the reactions around him, kept on.

"Really? I didn't know there was a place by Shady Palms where you could buy duck. Is it walking distance from the condo?"

"Well," Lois said. "Yes and no. I mean, it's close, but I definitely need the car to get them."

Ricardo carefully spit the contents of his mouth into a paper napkin and then tried to steer the conversation to a different topic.

"The game is beginning," he said.

The drums pounded. The crowd stood and cheered. And the Florida Atlantic University football team began its first game by receiving the opening kickoff inside its own end zone.

Demetrius stood there alone in that end zone, watching the ball tumbling toward him from a cloudless blue sky.

In the press box, an announcer was saying, "Let's see if Bone chooses to run it out."

There was never a question in Demetrius' mind what he was about to do. His leg muscles contracted. His toes dug into the turf, and his eyes widened. He opened his arms, extended his fingers and took a deep breath.

The ball came to him like a present from the heavens, another long lost child landing in his sheltering arms. He cradled the ball against his chest, squeezed it for an instant and looked up field, where everything appeared green and inviting.

Demetrius ran.

■ ■ ■

Bernie ate. Oh boy, did he eat. The nicest surprise about being a cast member in a production by the Shady Palms Players was that Johnny Fox knew the meaning of the words "fully catered." Corned beef. Pastrami. Roast beef. A deli tray before every performance.

At home, Bernie Hamstein was eating tofu and broccoli, acting like a responsible heart attack survivor. But at the club-house, away from his wife's care, he was a ravisher of briskets, eating with audible moans and a gusto that made each meal seem like his last. And frankly, there were times when it felt like he was eating his last meal.

Like on this day, the final day of the long and undistin-guished run of *Shakespeare Goes Catskills*. Rose was off with the others at Pro Player Stadium to see Demetrius' first football game at FAU. Bernie would have loved to be there, too. But the theater group was putting on a matinee during game time and then an evening show to end the monthlong run.

"Slow down, Bern," Softer said, during the catered meal between shows. "It's not healthy to eat so fast."

"I'll make you a deal," Bernie said. "If you don't tell me how to eat, I won't tell you how to play the drums."

Softer seemed hurt. He always did when people criticized his drum playing. Bernie quickly tried to change the subject.

"So how many tickets are sold for tonight's show?" Bernie asked.

"I heard Johnny say it was only going to be half-filled," Softer said, "which means we're lucky if one out of four seats will be taken."

"We should just cancel the show and give people their

Bernie Hamstein, a reluctant star in the Shady Palms Players, performs his last memorable performance as the Melancholy Dane.

money back," Bernie said. "We'd be doing them a favor."

Bernie never really warmed up to his acting debut. After months of rehearsals, the show became an increasingly heavy penance to pay.

"I think I'm working off that $600 debt at a rate of 6 cents an hour," he said.

And then there was wearing pumpkin pants and tights.

Of course, he was the butt of a lot of jokes around the condo, and Mort Granger's review in *The Shady Palms Gazette* said that Bernie's Hamlet "took Shakespearean theater to unimagined new depths of tragedy."

Bernie had read that to his wife when the review first appeared.

"Rose, does that mean he liked me, or not?"

"Ask him," Rose said.

"Why should I?" Bernie said. "Who cares what Mort thinks?"

Johnny Fox did. He had predicted the show would be his greatest production, so he was bruised by the harsh review. But Johnny was right about Bernie Hamstein's box office appeal.

Lots of people showed up to see Bernie make a fool of himself. Condo board president Herb Troutman came twice. The louse.

"He's just looking for a new reason to get rid of me," Bernie had explained to his wife. "He can't use Demetrius any more. And even the ducks, for some reason, don't seem to be hanging around C Building too much these days."

And so on this, the last night of *Shakespeare Goes Catskills*, Bernie sat backstage holding Yorick's skull in a schlepper bag and waiting for his final entrance. He thought he should be feeling better about this, about finally getting out of these silly clothes and out from under that $600 poker debt. But he felt strangely adrift, alive with the sensation that time was slipping away and there was something yet to be done.

Softer was right. He shouldn't have eaten so much corned beef. He reached into his pocket and took one of his heart pills. He wondered whether Rose would be back from the football game to see his final performance.

It wasn't until he got out on stage during the show that he

saw the auditorium was practically empty. Hardly anybody.
Troutman, the louse, was here for a third time. And there was
Bernie's wife, Rose, sitting in the back by herself. But all in all,
the cast and the orchestra outnumbered the audience.

And so as Bernie asked, "To be or not to be?" — and the
chorus piped back, "You call that a question?" for the millionth
time — something washed over him.

It started in his gut, and before he knew it, he had dropped
Yorick's skull on the stage, and much to everyone's surprise,
including his own, he fell to his knees.

Members of the chorus stopped singing. The orchestra
stopped playing. And Rose, poor Rose, screamed his name as
she ran up the aisle.

By the time she got to him, he was on his back in the middle of a small cluster of people who were debating what to do.

"Get away! Give him air!" Rose shouted as she knelt at his
side.

He felt her hand on his face and her familiar perfume in his
nose. Ah, Rose. He'd punch a thousand guys in the nose for her.
He enjoyed her presence there for a moment, the view of her
face hovering over his, the raspy urgency in her words. He wanted to reach up and kiss her right there.

But he couldn't. Not now. Then he heard Johnny Fox's
voice. Johnny had dashed out from backstage. He was in the
middle of a costume change when word trickled back that
Bernie Hamstein had a heart attack on stage.

Johnny was so unnerved by hearing the entire production
come to a halt that he burst out of his dressing room without
realizing that he wasn't wearing his trousers.

And so here he was again, standing over Bernie. The last
time Bernie was in this position, Johnny had looked down on his
fallen body and proclaimed to their poker buddies that Bernie
was faking it.

But Johnny wasn't saying that now.

"Oh, God," he said. "Hang in there, Bernie. Please, hang in there."

Then he stood up and shouted to an audience that was mostly empty chairs, "Somebody call an ambulance."

Bernie stopped breathing, and Rose, seeing this, quickly placed her mouth over his.

And that's when he slipped his wife the tongue.

Rose drew back sharply, but not before she noticed that her allegedly dying husband had given her a sly wink when their faces were inches apart.

"Bernie!"

"Don't blame him, Rose," Johnny said, putting his arms around Rose. "I should have kept him away from all that deli food."

"Bernie!" Rose said, looking down at her husband.

Rose, wanting to laugh and cry at the same time, laid her head back on her husband's chest, and in a combination of mortification and relief, she whispered to him, "You big idiot."

"Get off me, Rose," Bernie whispered. "You're killing my big moment."

Bernie took her head in his hands and kissed her. Then he sat up and smiled. The chorus gasped, as if seeing a dead man spring back to life.

Bernie looked over at Johnny, who was as stunned as the rest.

"Now, that's acting," Bernie said. "We're even, Johnny. Oh, and by the way, you're not wearing any pants."

Johnny raced off stage, and Bernie stood up, taking his Yorick skull out of the schlepper bag and walking center stage with it, by himself now.

Bernie never did have a good handle on what all the fuss was about Shakespeare. Especially the soliloquies, which remained overwrought and impenetrable to him. And being a condo building president, he was of the disposition that few things were so sacred that they couldn't be altered, modified or tinkered with at whim.

Shakespeare, at least to Bernie's reckoning, paid too much attention to death. Pondering what death would be like was a waste of time, Bernie thought. And so he was doing his own *Hamlet* now. And why not? There was hardly anyone in the audience. He had already fulfilled his obligation to Johnny, and this was the end of his show biz career, his final moment on stage.

So why not do it his way? What did Shakespeare know about life at Shady Palms, anyway?

How many grandchildren did Shakespeare have? How many Great Depressions did Shakespeare survive? How many loaves of bread did Shakespeare deliver in the snow?

"To be," Bernie said. "Always. To be. Remember that."

Then he motioned to the skull in his hands.

"One day, we're all going to look like this," he said. "In fact, this looks better than a few people who live here."

Softer gave him a rim shot on the drums.

"But what's the rush?" Bernie continued. "And even if our best days seem done, there's still so much life to live, so many opportunities to make the most out of our retirements. Fixed income doesn't have to mean fixed expectations. Live. Every day, live. Pinch yourself — or better yet, get somebody else to pinch you — to remind you how lucky you are. Make your own rules. And then break them."

Bernie carried on for another five minutes. At least, that's what Rose told him. He didn't remember much.

Later that night, when Bernie and Rose got back to their condo, the phone was ringing. It was Mort.

"Why didn't you tell me you were going to steal the show tonight?" the publisher of *The Shady Palms Gazette* said. "I would have shown up and written about it."

Bernie watched as his wife went to their bedroom and lit the candles on their dresser.

"Listen Mort, I'd love to talk, but something just came up," Bernie said.

He hung up and started to take off his pumpkin pants and tights. But Rose stopped him.

"Leave them on for a minute," she said, smiling as she went into her walk-in closet.

"Really?" Bernie said.

"Really," Rose said.

New tricks? After 47 years.

"How about that!" Bernie said to Lucky the dog, who was staring up at him in wonder and adoration.

Dogs had the right idea, Bernie thought. Keep it simple. He could hear Rose changing in the closet. Bernie knew that meant she was putting on that lacy thing he liked.

The phone rang again. It was Herb Troutman this time.

The condo board president hadn't stayed for the end of the show.

"Bernie," Troutman said. "I'm a bit concerned about your erratic behavior tonight."

"Erotic?" Bernie said, watching as Rose emerged from the closet.

"Erratic," Troutman said. "And that business about people making up their own rules. That's just the sort of behavior we try to discourage here at Shady Palms. And then to have a building president spout it off on stage is just not the kind of thing ... Bernie? Bernie? ... Are you still there, Bernie? ... Hello?"

Frond memories
from 'Palms 2' readers

"Frank, Frank, Frank, you have done it again ... I have been diagnosed with Shady Palms *withdrawal. The doctor won't give me any good drugs for it."* — **Peggy Stumer**

"Reading the news had become so depressing that my day starts in a funk. So I save the best for last. I read Shady Palms. *And I actually laugh out loud. I wish it would never end. I realize that it is unreasonable, but can't you keep it up until at least the end of the season?"* — **Marie Gottfried**

"Just wanted to let you know how much my mother enjoys your writing. She is 90 years old and has never asked us to buy a book for her until your book Shady Palms *came out."* — **Dorie Meyerson**

"Yesterday I was shopping at the Target store on Lake Worth Road. As I was walking toward the front door, there were Rose and Bernie standing at the entrance. I wish I had a camera." — **Sandra Stearns**

"I had to write to tell you how much I enjoy your Shady Palms *stories. I'm only 45, but I lived in a condo for exactly one year and all these characters lived there, too."* — **Joe Gorman**

"Once again I am wiping a tear from my eye and a grin off my face after finishing the last chapter of Shady Palms 2. *I laughed, I cried — it was better than* Cats!*"* — **Sara Bernardin**

"I am still staying tuned for the publication of Shady Palms 2. *Where can I get it? I am waiting with bated breath, but I am running out of breath."* — **Ruth E. Campbell**

"I was so afraid that the sequel wouldn't be as good as the first book, but my fears were for naught." — **Marjorie Nelson**

"Next time, and there WILL be a next time, mention 'early bird' dining. And be sure to give us an update on Yolette and Demetrius. And don't forget Ricardo, my favorite character. OK. Enough chitchat. Get off your duff and start writing!" — **Paula Schatten**